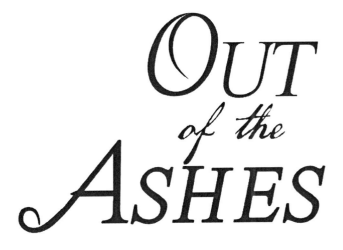

Out of the
Ashes

The Chicago Fire Series
Book One

Sandi Rog

Tulpen Publishing

Sandi Rog

Out of the Ashes
Tulpen Publishing
www.tulpenpublishing.com

© 2015 Sandi Rog
Cover Design by Roseanna White
http://www.roseannawhitedesigns.com

Printed in the United States of America.

ISBN: 978-0-9962746-1-6

60961876
9/16

Dear Readers

Had it not been for the Lord and the many thousands of people who prayed me through cancer, this book never would have been written. If you're one of the people who prayed for me, thank you. Mere words aren't enough to express my gratitude.

Having emerged back onto the writing scene after the two-year battle, and feeling rather beat up after the long fight, I needed something with a happy ending. Like a fairytale. Think *Cinderella*. That's what this book is, something bright and cheerful. So, *Out of the Ashes* is a lighter read than my other books: *The Master's Wall*, *Yahshua's Bridge*, and even *Walks Alone*.

What a blessing it has been for me to have the strength to write Nathaniel and Amelia's story. Thank you, precious readers, for walking with me as I dig my way out of the aftermath of this battle one step at a time. Or shall I say, one page at a time.

Blessings,
Sandi Rog

Sandi Rog

1 John 4:18

"Perfect love casts out fear."

Sandi Rog

Chapter One

Green Pines, Colorado, 1882

Gun smoke burned Amelia's eyes and her ears still rang. She blinked the tears from her lashes.

"Do you, Nathaniel Ward," the preacher scowled, "take Amelia Taylor to be your lawfully wedded wife?"

Amelia's father cocked his rifle and aimed it at the reluctant groom.

"I do," Nathaniel said, his voice firm and unwavering. Despite her father's threats, Nathaniel's very presence exuded power, his raised chin, broad shoulders and wide chest unflinching against the barrel of the rifle.

Amelia didn't dare look up at him. What must he

be thinking? How many women had hoped to get him this far, and now, here she stood where most women dreamed of standing—shotgun wedding, or not. If only she could melt into the parlor's wooden floor like the candle burning in the nearby lamp. Or disappear like the smoke. Disappear into nothingness, with no remnant left of her existence.

"Do you, Amelia Taylor, take Nathaniel Ward to be your lawfully wedded husband?" The preacher's words rushed over Amelia like a gush of foul air.

She stood paralyzed, unable to speak. She'd vowed never to marry. How would she bear this cross? She'd seen enough loveless marriages in her life to know it wasn't worth the heartache, despite the shame of spinsterhood. And now, to be forced on a man? What miseries awaited her? Abuse? Neglect? Slavery? Any man in his right mind would despise her for the rest of his days. It would be impossible—unthinkable—to procure his affection ... his love.

The minister, still in his nightclothes, cleared his throat. His wife, holding up the lantern, glowered from behind him.

Amelia swallowed, darting a glance at her terrifying father. With a snarl, he narrowed his eyes at Nathaniel and pressed closer with his rifle. Would he put another hole in the preacher's wall? Or Nathaniel's chest?

"Amelia, girl." Her father's voice sent a shudder down her spine as it echoed through the quiet house. "You know, I always keep my word." He'd threatened to kill Nathaniel if she refused to be his wife.

"I do," she said, her voice small and trembling, quite the opposite of the man next to her. The horror, the shame. How did her life come to this?

"I now pronounce you man and wife." The minister slammed his Bible shut and pointed it at her father. "Now get out!"

Shadows clouded Amelia's vision, and her legs wobbled like those of a newborn calf. Her knees buckled, but rather than landing on the hard floor, she found herself caught in Nathaniel's strong arms.

Now her husband.

Chicago, Illinois
Nine weeks earlier.

"You're the most stubborn man I know," William Goldman said to Nathaniel as they made their way through the ballroom.

The music and thick perfume nauseated Nathaniel. He never cared for tobacco, but in comparison to the party, he wished he had an excuse to leave and join the men in the smoking room. He could join the other men for cards, but William insisted that Nathaniel walk with him.

So now, he walked amidst the preening women and their mothers. He kept his hands behind his back, trying to forget the fact that he wore coattails and should be dancing. He'd already shared a number of dances, but the women were all the same: pretentious with money-hungry claws. He may now be wealthy, but if they knew he was once a street rat, they'd scurry in the opposite direction. They just assumed he was William's apprentice, now assistant. Which he was, but they didn't know the whole story. Only William knew, and he didn't belittle Nathaniel for it.

Charlotte fluttered her dark, long lashes in his direction and flashed him a demure smile. He'd already danced with her twice, the second time he'd been bamboozled into an extra dance by the mother. He nodded toward her, trying not to be rude, but kept on walking.

"You see?" William motioned with his bearded chin to the high-society woman. "There's a fine catch, right under your nose, but your stubborn pride keeps you from hooking it."

Nathaniel blew out air between his teeth. "Why the urgency to marry me off?"

They stepped onto a terrace, and William with his paunch belly faced him. "I'm not getting any younger. I want grandchildren."

Nathaniel studied his old friend. His green eyes reflected remorse. Nathaniel knew he missed his own children.

"When I first offered to let you live with me, you refused, saying you didn't take 'handouts.' I call that stubborn pride." William straightened and harrumphed. "Thank the good Lord you had enough sense to take the job I offered you." Leaning on his cane, he reached out and patted Nathaniel's arm, his gold ring catching the moonlight. "But the truth is you've always been like a son to me. You're the only family I have, and until you locate your brother and sister, I'm all you have."

It always pained Nathaniel to think of Michael and Rachel. With William's help, he'd sent detectives all over the country in pursuit of his siblings, only to discover they were nowhere to be found.

"I'll marry," Nathaniel said, resigned. "But not any of these women." He pointed with his thumb to the ballroom.

William straightened. "What's wrong with these women? They're of good breeding. And if not these, then who else is there?"

"There's someone I met while on the streets." What was he saying? How would he find her? What if she was already married? And what if she'd turned out like all these other rich snobs? Certainly her father and mother would have prepped and preened her the same way.

"A woman you met on the streets?" William raised a white brow. "Surely, you have better taste, better sense!" He puffed up his chest, clearly insulted by Nathaniel's rejection of the delicacies he set before him in the other room.

"I was twelve, and she was eight or nine."

"What? You're holding out for a little girl?"

"She's a lady." Nathaniel chuckled. "My hope is, more of a lady than anyone we can find here."

He prayed he was right. After all, how many of these women as girls would have dared chase down a street rat to give him their money?

"Does this woman have a name?" William eyed him beneath his bushy brows.

"Amelia E. Taylor." An uncontrollable grin tugged on Nathaniel's lips. He'd never spoken her name out loud. But he'd never forget her name. Never forget her kindness and … the kiss.

Green Pines, Colorado

Nathaniel didn't realize he'd have to become his own private investigator. After the hazards in finding his siblings, when he discovered Amelia was no longer in Denver, he thought he'd never locate her. But while he retraced his steps along Holliday Street from ten years ago, he had come upon a town clerk, spoken to a census taker and discovered that she'd moved to Green Pines, Colorado. And even better, she was unmarried.

So, here he stood, in Green Pines, only a day's ride by stagecoach from Denver. Apparently, her father had lost everything and whisked Amelia away in shame.

After finding a room at a hotel, he stood on Main Street in the late afternoon, leaning against the wall just outside a dry goods store that was about to close. Maybe Amelia would decide to buy something at the last minute. It was a small town, with one major street running through its center and a few outer streets with houses and businesses, so he expected he should find her—eventually. Tomorrow morning he'd go to the town clerk's office to learn what he could there.

With the brim of his hat pulled down low, he watched the people: those in carriages, women with children, men strolling by in cowboy hats and spurs, and especially any woman of about eighteen who might resemble Amelia. What would he do if he found her?

If Amelia was the kind of woman he suspected, one thing was certain, after losing so much—his brother and his sister—he was determined not to lose her.

Two men on the other side of the street lifted their hats to get a better view not far from where he stood. Nathaniel slid his gaze beneath his hat. Women. A young blonde walked with another woman carrying a basket. The woman with the basket laughed, her golden-brown hair falling in waves over her shoulder and down her back. Could she be his Amelia? The hair color was close to what he remembered. But could her hair color have changed as she grew older?

He kept his chin down, seeing the women coming his way. Their giggles carried to him from up the street.

"Oh, read it to me again," the blonde said, grabbing the other girl's arm.

The women stopped, and the one with the basket pulled out a dime novel from beneath a cloth. Not noticing him, the woman who could be Amelia flipped through the pages. She cleared her throat and with dramatic flair read the words, "'When the innocent maiden looked up from her curtsy, she wasn't looking at just the prince, but at the man who had rescued her from the pirate. The man who risked life and death to protect her virtue.'" She used the book as a fan. "Isn't that romantic? He was the prince that entire time and she never knew it!"

"He was her protector," the blonde said, casting a

dreamy look to the men watching them across the street.

The ladies giggled with delight.

Clearly, they had no idea Nathaniel was within earshot, and he wasn't about to stop them. While on the streets he had the privilege of overhearing numerous conversations, but none this amusing.

The woman with the golden-brown locks hastily stuffed the novel back into her basket, and they both turned to walk. But upon seeing Nathaniel, the blonde stopped. She reached to stop her friend, but the woman already gained too much momentum, stumbled into her, and a heap of dime novels fell out of the basket at Nathaniel's feet.

Nathaniel bent to retrieve the books and the woman with Amelia's hair did the same. Without warning, he found himself within a breath's distance.

Lilacs.

The scent poured over him like a revelation, and every fiber in his being yearned to cry out her name. "Amelia?" he whispered, so low that the sound barely made it past his lips, barely made it out of his airless lungs.

"Yes?" she whispered. Her emerald eyes flickered up to his, barely connecting with his own, then back as her trembling hands frantically grabbed and fumbled to collect her old, worn books.

Her friend knelt to help.

"Forgive me," Amelia said, shoving the books into her basket, her cheeks as red as cherries.

Once the novels were well-hidden in the confines of the basket and the cloth stuffed over them, the women stood, brushing off their skirts, their hands and fingers fluttering.

Nathaniel held out the last book, *The Pirate and the Prince*, to Amelia. "Your fan, my lady," he said, unable to keep from grinning, but glad he finally found his voice.

Gasping, Amelia snatched it from him, but this time when she looked at him, she saw him.

Nathaniel tipped the brim of his hat in greeting, for that was all he could do since words and air had again deserted him. Did she recognize him? Was it really her? Could finding her have been this easy? Providence perhaps?

Lips parted, Amelia looked up into the man's face as he bent over her, his blue eyes holding hers. Flustered, she looked down to his cleft chin and square jaw, shadowed by a thin layer of dark whiskers. He straightened and his broad shoulders towered over her.

"Oh my." Her hand flew to her chest. "Forgive me." With that, she grabbed Violet and dragged her away.

Amelia hugged her friend's arm as she hurried down the street, racing away from the man whose stare burned right to her bones. She ducked into an alley between the shops, pulling Violet with her.

Breathless, Amelia flattened her back against the side of the store, her bonnet hanging over her shoulder. "Who was that man?"

"No idea." Violet's eyes were wide, and she dared peek around the corner.

"Don't look!" Amelia snatched her back by her skirt. "I think he said my name. How would he know my name?"

"I didn't hear him say anything other than, 'Your fan, my lady.'" She spoke in a deep, lush voice. Violet sagged against the wall next to her and grimaced. "How humiliating."

"You didn't hear him say my name?"

Violet shook her head.

"I feel like I should know him, but I've never seen him before in my life." Amelia pushed away from the wall and looked onto the open street they avoided, fearful he might appear around the corner.

"Well, he was one of the most handsome men I've ever seen." Violet fanned herself with her hand.

Amelia held out the book. "Here, use this."

Violet looked down at the novel and raised a brow.

They burst out laughing.

"Let's take the back way home." Amelia pivoted and marched down the alley to the rear of the shops. "I can't bear to face him again."

"Since when do you care what anyone thinks?" Violet stuffed the book into Amelia's basket as they walked.

Amelia shrugged, unable to shake the image of the man standing over her with that teasing grin. "Perhaps he was just breathing?" She took Violet's arm again. "Besides, if he did say my name, how could he address me in such a familiar manner when I don't even know him?"

"Well, I never heard your name pass those

handsome lips." She leaned in closer. "He was attractive, wasn't he?"

Amelia giggled. "Yes, I have a fondness for cleft chins, dark hair and blue eyes." Really, she did, but she couldn't say why.

They turned and walked along the back of the shops. Why did she hear him say her name? Why would she imagine such a thing? As they came to the end of the shops, she remembered she had promised to deliver a number of the dime novels to Mrs. Samson and her daughters.

"We forgot to bring the books." Amelia stopped.

Violet studied her, clearly not comprehending. Then, understanding reflected from her face. "Oh, that's right."

They both looked in the direction of the street.

"We'll have to go by that man again," Violet whispered as if contemplating a daring adventure.

"Maybe he's gone." Amelia took a deep breath.

Together, they inched toward the street. When they reached the sidewalk, they looked in the direction of the dry goods store.

"He's not there." Amelia sighed in relief, her shoulders relaxing.

"Let's hurry. Mother is waiting."

Violet was expected home as soon as she finished work to help with the youngsters. Amelia usually met Violet when she was done sewing for Mrs. Nebel, since she had nothing better to do.

They walked along the sidewalk, watching for the stranger. A shame he wasn't there, despite her humiliation. Amelia would have enjoyed looking at the attractive man again—as long as he didn't see her.

"Oh, my." Violet took Amelia's arm. "It's Jeb and Sam. They witnessed the entire incident."

"Yes, but they couldn't hear what was said." Amelia lifted her chin and kept walking. Besides, she really didn't care what they thought, not nearly as much as she cared what a respectable stranger thought. "I'm sure there's nothing to worry about."

From the corner of her eye, she saw Violet cast a demure smile at Jeb. It was a wonder that Violet had taken such a fancy to the man when Amelia always felt uneasy around him.

"Good afternoon, ladies." Jeb and Sam removed their hats.

Head bowed, Jeb looked up at Amelia. His gaze raked over her as he placed his hat back on his head. No one ever noticed his roving eyes.

"Is your father still out of town?" he asked.

Amelia, knowing Violet would be disappointed that he wasn't addressing her, moved closer to her friend. "He's been back for two weeks now."

He raised a brow. "He's back, is he?"

"We better be going." Amelia tugged on Violet's arm. "Mrs. Samson is waiting for us."

"Good day, gentlemen." Violet waved at the two men as Amelia dragged her away.

"I don't trust that man," Amelia said under her breath as soon as they were out of earshot.

"Who?"

"Both of them."

"Why ever not?" Violet looked over her shoulder at the men. "That Jeb is quite good-looking. Don't you think?"

Amelia sighed. "Not so handsome with roving eyes."

Violet gasped indignantly. "I've never seen such behavior."

"Well, I have. All too often." It seemed all Violet could see was a handsome face. Amelia knew good looks only lay skin deep. What about the heart of a man? Why not search that? Her father was once handsome, but Amelia would never want to marry a man like him.

They turned off Main Street and neared Mrs. Samson's house. "You'd do well to stay away from him," Amelia said.

Violet remained silent, which caused Amelia alarm, but before she could question her friend, two of Mrs. Samson's youngsters ran up to greet them.

"Are you leaving again so soon?"

"So soon?" Amelia's father grunted as he packed his clothing into a small trunk. His frock coats and vests were brand new so as to make a good impression for clients, while she had yet to receive a new dress in two years. Good thing she hadn't gotten much taller. Besides, his work was far more important than anything she had to do.

"Where will you go this time?" It always made Amelia nervous when he left. Staying alone in the cabin at night brought on its own terrors, with coyotes and wolves, not to mention mountain lions, roaming the area. One dreadful evening coyotes had been scratching on the door, and Amelia didn't sleep a wink. Instead, she sat in the rocker with a steady fire burning in the hearth, her father's rifle on her lap, and a constant prayer on her lips.

"Father?" He still hadn't said where he planned to go on this business trip.

He waved at her in frustration. "Oh, the usual nearby towns. Possibly even as far as the Springs."

The Springs? So far? Amelia twisted her hands. "Since I'm no longer in school, may I come with you this time?"

"No, no!" He pursed his lips as if he wanted to spit at the idea. "This is business, not for women." He motioned to her dress. "Besides, you'd need the proper attire." Turning to look at his armoire, he rubbed his dark beard and mustache and grabbed more things to put into his trunk.

Since her father brought up her poor attire, which in essence was his way of not mentioning their lack of funds, she felt it would be safe to again bring up her desire to work. "Father, may I find work in town? Mrs. Jennings has an opening in the library, and there's—"

"Absolutely not!" He faced her, his teeth showing. "You will not shame me by taking a position in town!"

She looked down at the rug near the rocker. That chair seemed to be her only friend in this cabin. "But father, I'm eighteen. I can't stay here forever."

He grabbed her chin, his fingers digging painfully to the bone. "I said, *no.*"

Meeting his gaze, but not daring to show her true emotions, she looked down at his chin. But oh, how she wanted to glare, to shoot daggers with her eyes. But that would be disrespectful. She wanted to stomp, to scream and cry. Instead, she swallowed and kept her eyes on his short, dark whiskers with their specks of gray.

"No daughter of mine will work." He released her chin and patted her cheek. "Just be patient, Amelia. I'm almost ready to give you the future you deserve."

It had happened once that he forgot to leave her enough funds to buy food. They weren't even allowed to have a garden or a chicken coop. How did he expect her to take care of herself while he was gone? Thankfully, she had the church who helped out when he left, but so many churchgoers had their own needs. Didn't he realize the shameful burden he placed on them when he left and failed to leave her necessities for survival? She would think that would be enough to shame him, but he never took notice.

"How long will you be gone?" How long would she have to spend so many sleepless nights in the rocker?

"A number of months, maybe four or five this time."

"So long?" Air escaped her lungs and her chin still throbbed. How could he disappear for so long?

"Don't worry, child." He patted her on the cheek again, and she tried not to flinch. Last time she ducked from his touch, she got much worse than she anticipated. "I have big plans, and when I return, we can say goodbye to this life." He motioned to the cabin around them, a disgusted frown pulling on his features.

It wasn't the first time he'd said that to her before he left.

The following morning, her father didn't wake her to say goodbye, but all his thumping and scraping around the house made her realize it was time for him to go. He was in a mad rush to leave, so she stood in her nightclothes at the door in the chilly dark air with its fresh pine scents. She held a wrapper tight over her shoulders as she saw him off.

"Let's go. We're late," her father said, urging the driver to get on.

The man clicked the reins, and the wagon started forward. Dirt kicked up behind them as the driver urged the horses into a trot.

The sun's rays lanced through the dark trees as she waved goodbye, lighting up the forest with the first glimpses of morning.

Her father, wearing his top hat and fur coat, didn't look at her as the wagon sped off.

After he disappeared between the trees, Amelia stood in the silence, soaking up the feeble breeze as it whispered between the pines and through her hair. Alone again. The morning sun lit up dew on the leaves from bushes stretching over the small porch. It had rained last night. The fresh scent washed over her, and she breathed in the clean air.

Now what? She could take a hot bath. Then later, she'd go to her favorite spot near the stream to dry her hair in the sun. With Father gone, she did have more freedom to escape the confines of the cabin. The sun penetrating through the trees, and the clear sky above promised the weather would be warm. Yes.

She'd spend her day on her favorite boulder away from everybody. She wasn't looking forward to the town learning her father had left her again. What must they think of her if her own father didn't want to stay home, let alone take her with him? Violet didn't think Amelia cared what people thought, and for the most part she didn't, but when it came to being loved, she at least wanted them to believe her father loved her. How could she convince them when he never wanted to be around? How could she convince herself?

Taking a deep breath, she turned back into the cabin. How much money did Father leave her this time? She'd have to be frugal, especially if he was going to be gone for so long.

She reached for the clay jar marked "tea," the hiding place her father used to keep their money for when he left town. It felt light as she lifted it from the shelf. She pulled off the fabric cover.

Empty.

Sandi Rog

Chapter Two

Amelia flew to the door and swung it open. "Father!" she shouted, but she was met with silence. "Father!" she shouted again, desperate to reach him, but the trees swallowed her cries.

She had to get to him before he caught the stage in town.

Amelia slipped on her boots, her fingers fumbling with the laces. One boot wouldn't cooperate, and she knotted it the best she could. No time to change, she left on her nightgown and slipped her cloak on over it. She buttoned up the front to hide the fact that she was still in her nightdress.

She burst out of the door and raced for town.

"Father!" she shouted, hoping he'd hear her call.

No sign of him or the wagon as she followed the

small road cutting between the trees. How far could they have gotten? How long had she stood on the porch? Obviously, too long. She ran, leaping over fallen branches, and crunching over pinecones and sloshing through mud. She had to catch him. She had to.

After taking a shortcut through the woods, she jogged onto Main Street, her hem covered in mire. Loose hair escaped her braid, clinging to her cheeks. Breathless, she trudged toward the post office where the stagecoach usually waited to pick up passengers. To her dismay, it was gone. Perhaps it hadn't come yet. Perhaps her father waited inside. But the closed sign in the window revealed no one would be inside this early in the day.

Angry tears brimmed forth. How could he? How could he forget? He was so busy trying to get rich, that he always forgot what was right under his nose. What could she do? How would she get by with him gone? Hugging herself, she looked around at the empty town as it slowly began to come to life with men and women heading to their jobs either on foot or in wagons. She'd have to find work. Go against her father's wishes and find work to support herself. He'd be furious. But he didn't leave her any choice now, did he?

She turned to head back home, the hem of her nightdress sagging beneath her cloak, sagging like her heart. She was alone. Completely and utterly alone. Who really cared for her? Her true Father. Her heavenly Father. She replaced her earthly father with God a long time ago. "Lord, help me out of this," she whispered. "Take me away from here. You're the only one who really cares." That's when the church came to mind. They would likely help if she told them of her plight. Then she thought of the three widows who had far greater need. She didn't want to be a burden on the church and take away from those who truly weren't able to fend for themselves. She was strong and healthy, perfectly capable of working. She would simply go against her father's wishes and find a job.

At least one positive thing came from this. She'd been wanting to work for three years. Finally, she'd get her chance.

From his second story hotel room window, Nathaniel watched Amelia on the street below. She had been standing in front of the post office hugging herself for quite some time. She looked lost, perhaps afraid as she trudged away. He fumbled as he threw on his suspenders and looked out the window again. Her long frazzled braid hung in defeat down her back to her waist. Mud covered the hem of her long, white dress, and the laces on one of her shoes dragged in the dirt. He'd been on the streets long enough to know when someone was in trouble.

He grabbed his jacket and hat and rushed down the stairs of the hotel. He stopped when he nearly stumbled into a maid sweeping the wooden steps.

"Pardon me, sir." The woman pushed aside the runner, clearing Nathaniel's path. "The evening maid was sick last night, so she didn't come in." The maid wiped sweat from her brow. "I'm trying to catch up."

"No worries," Nathaniel said, tipping his hat and easing his way on the stairs.

By the time he reached the street, Amelia was gone. He looked from side to side. No sign of her. He walked in the direction he saw her go, glancing down each side street, only to find unopened businesses: a mill, a library, a church house. He continued to the end. Still no Amelia. The street curved away from town, taking him by more shops and houses, until he came to the woods.

Pines towered over him and a gentle breeze rustled through the high branches.

Like a ghost, she'd completely vanished.

Spotting a small road, he decided to follow it, keeping his hat down low. Why was Amelia so distraught? What had happened? It was so early in the morning, too early in the day for something to have gone wrong. One thing he learned on the streets was that trouble almost always occurred at night. Late night revelers were usually too drunk and tired to get up before sunrise to cause more trouble. Was her father a drunk? Surely not. But after having lost all his wealth, how would that affect the old man? How had it affected Amelia? What about her mother?

The other day when he saw her, she looked happy. Content. Even playful. What could have occurred since then to cause such distress? He was determined to find out. Before Amelia was to become his wife, he wanted to know everything about her.

A female sigh of frustration echoed through the woods. He swiveled toward the sound. A smaller road led farther into the forest. He followed it, jogging through the mud.

That's when he spotted her. A ghostlike figure stumbling between the trees.

He stopped.

She panted and huffed with each stomp of her feet, her cloak swinging behind her, revealing a white dress beneath its folds. Her long, frazzled braid swished along her back and shoulders.

"Oh, no!" She stopped and turned, looking at the ground. She fisted her small white hands and growled. A sob escaped her lips as she bent to pick up her boot. As she held it up, thick mud oozed from its heel and toe. Releasing a sigh, she turned and limped through the trees.

"May I help?" Nathaniel rushed toward her.

Amelia covered her mouth and faced him, eyes wide.

So as not to frighten her more, he removed his hat. "The name's Nathaniel Ward, miss. It looks like you could use some help."

Amelia's gaze darted about, perhaps to see whether or not he was alone. After all, a lone woman in the woods could be a mighty temptation.

Dirt on her chin, she wiped the tears from her cheeks, smearing a streak of mud over her nose. "And how would you do that?" Her voice choked.

Good question. He looked around. Nothing but trees surrounded them. "Where are you headed?"

"Home," she said, sniffing.

"How far is it?" He motioned around them, wondering where in the world a house could be in this dense forest.

She hugged her cloak tight around her front, looking away.

He gathered by her expression, she feared telling him where she lived.

"Miss, with the good Lord as my witness, you have my word, I mean you no harm. Allow me to see you safely home." He bent into a half bow and watched her, hoping she'd see the sincerity in his eyes.

With a trembling finger and still holding her muddy boot, she pointed.

He nodded and walked up to her, realizing the dirt on her chin was actually a bruise. How'd that happen? My, she was small next to him. No wonder she was fearful. He held out his arm for her to take hold. She gripped it and they moved forward.

As they walked, her shoeless foot sinking deeper into the mud with each step, he asked, "So ... may I ask your name?"

"Amelia Taylor. Thank you for helping me, sir."

"Not a problem." He cleared his throat. It was her. After all these years, he had her hanging on his arm. Something inside him knew, from the moment of their first meeting, that it was her this whole time.

The mire clung to her dress as she struggled to keep it from hugging each leg. She stumbled and he caught her.

"Oh ..." She released a frustrated growl. "This will never do."

Nathaniel chuckled.

She froze, her green eyes snapping up at his, loose strands of hair clinging to rosy cheeks.

"Forgive me, Miss Amelia Taylor." Oh, to say her name after all these years, made his mouth go dry. He pressed his lips together to keep from smiling.

She straightened, holding her dress away from her legs. Loosening her grip on his arm, she tightened her cloak. Again, she lost her balance, and again, he caught her by the elbow.

"Miss Taylor, please don't think me too forward, but ..." He looked in the direction they were heading. Still no sign of a house. He looked back down into her round eyes. "I can carry you. I think we'd make better progress that way." He cocked a smile. "A mite more pleasant than my dragging you through the mud." This time an uncontrollable grin tugged on his lips. "You have my word, I'll be a gentleman."

Amelia's eyes flashed in the direction they were heading, then back at him. "I'm half buried in mud already, Mr. Ward. I'm sure I'll weigh more than five-hundred barrels of lard."

The unbelievable comparison sent Nathaniel over the edge and he laughed. His voice echoed through the pines surrounding them. "I believe I can bear the load." Unable to control his widening grin, he marveled at how beautiful she was, despite her muddied, disheveled state.

He bent to lift her. "May I?"

She nodded, still holding her cloak so tight her knuckles turned white.

He scooped her into his arms and lifted her off the ground.

That was a mistake.

Having her soft form, her thin white dress—

despite her efforts to keep her cloak shut — and her lilac scent pressed against his chest, nearly did him in. Really, she could have been buried beneath a buffalo cloak and he still would have suffered.

"Are we going?" she asked, her voice unsure and laced with a thread of panic.

He nodded, having lost his ability to speak. He clenched his jaw, cursing himself for having initiated such intimate contact. No wonder the Lord said it wasn't good for a man to touch a woman. Now he would have to marry her. With the places his thoughts took him … he'd force her to become his wife.

After trudging through the muck, his boots heavy with mud, they came to a cozy cabin nestled in the woods next to a small drive. He brought her to the porch and set her on her feet.

"I told you I was heavy," she said, her entire face red this time.

"Not heavy at all." He cleared his throat. If she knew what he truly struggled with, she'd likely run and hide in her house, barring the door against him. Let her think he was weary from carrying her. In a manner of speaking, that was most certainly the case. After all the women he'd had the pleasure — what he now knew wasn't pleasure at all — of dancing with, that intimate contact never brought on such a powerful reaction as this trudge through the muddy woods.

"Thank you for your help, Mr. Ward." She gave him a quick bob and turned to go. "You've been very kind," she said, scurrying inside. As she closed the door, she peered out at him, then banged it shut, and the bolt slid into place.

Perhaps she'd read his thoughts after all.

Amelia peeked through a small opening in the curtain. Nathaniel Ward stood at the foot of her porch. The dark stubble on his face shadowed the dimple on his strong chin. He lowered the brim of his hat, shading those dazzling blue eyes, and turned to leave. He walked toward the road, his stride sure and confident. He was the same man she'd run into with Violet when all their dime novels spilled at his feet. How dreadful! Now he had to witness this spectacle. What must he think of her? She shook her head, and when she couldn't see him anymore, she let the curtain fall. No matter. She had more important issues at hand. Today, she had to find work. Maybe she could get that job at the library as she'd hoped. A thrill of excitement sailed through her.

She looked down at her muddied self. First, she'd need a bath. She hurried around the house to collect her buckets and kettles. After that, she slipped on her shoe, making sure the laces were nice and tight this time. She didn't want to find herself stranded in the woods again. She'd likely not be rescued by a handsome prince. She giggled at the thought. So romantic.

However, she knew not to entertain the notion that a handsome man like her "prince" would ever be interested in her. Father made it clear on numerous occasions that she wasn't very pretty without her upper-class attire. If that's what she needed to be beautiful, then she was doomed. And by the way she looked now, she certainly didn't have a chance of winning Mr. Ward. She could tell by the stern look on his face he suffered great agony having to carry her. Surprising that a man as large as himself would struggle under her weight, especially when he seemed to lift her with such ease. Embarrassing, really. Poor man.

She didn't want to marry anyway. She'd much rather be a spinster than be wed, despite it being the most shameful status a woman could assume. All she'd ever witnessed of marriage was misery. Her own mother's and the women she'd come in contact with. All of them warned her to be prepared. While marriage had its small joys, it was a yoke, a burden, with endless days of mending, cleaning, cooking and sewing—and abuse if the husband was violent. She'd seen more than her share of married women struck by their husbands. Violet's mother ended up with bruises and a bloodied lip on occasion. Amelia recalled her own father striking her mother, and he'd often done the same to her.

Marriage.

The very thought sent a shudder down her spine. She wanted nothing of it. But if she didn't plan on marrying, she needed a way to survive on her own. She didn't want to be dependent on a man, especially one as untrustworthy as her father.

The fact that her father forgot to leave her money turned out to be a blessing, actually. Yes. It was a good thing. A blessing from God. She'd finally be able to learn a trade so she could take care of herself.

Father wouldn't be around for months, giving her time to become an independent woman. Maybe she could even find her own place to live? He wouldn't always be around to take care of her, and most likely, he would marry her off to the first willing rich man if he got the chance, so learning to fend for herself would make her stronger. Perhaps it would give her the courage to finally stand up to her father? She was eighteen after all, officially an adult. Several of her friends were already married. And Violet would likely marry soon as well. Hopefully not to Sam or Jeb.

Refastening her cloak, she glanced back out the window. The man was gone. All was safe. She gathered her bucket and kettles and made her way to the nearby creek, avoiding muddy patches as she went. It would be a thrill to work in a library. How she loved books, all the marvelous stories hidden in their pages, the smell of paper, and the feel of the leather spines.

After the buckets and kettles were filled with water, they were too heavy to carry all at once. She lifted the largest kettle and lugged it back to the house, splashing water on her legs and the hem of her cloak and nightdress as she passed under pine boughs. Yes. Working in the library would be a perfect job for her. Perhaps God made this position available at this time because He knew she'd need to find a means to survive.

Once in the house, she hung the heavy kettle over the hearth and started the fire. This would give the water time to heat up while she got everything ready.

She went back for the other kettles and bucket, and one by one, carried them to the cabin. By this time, she was covered in water, and she'd trailed mud into the house.

Leaving her nightdress on, she scrubbed the floor, not wishing to dirty any of her other garments. What would a librarian do anyway? Certainly she wouldn't spend all her time reading. She'd have to organize books by their genre or by their subjects. She'd probably have to label and number them. Maybe she could take a certain time in the day to read to little ones? Mrs. Samson's children could come and listen to her read. She could encourage them to read aloud as well, just as she did when they read the dime novels together.

Once the floor was clean and she'd dirtied the water in the bucket, she carried it down to the creek to clean out and refill. She'd have to talk to Mrs. Jennings about the possibility of reading to the children. Maybe she could also help with acquiring more books for the library? The library here never carried dime novels. Maybe she could encourage them to do so. Hmm? Perhaps not. Too many people frowned on Yellow Backs, thinking them lurid and sensational. Sensational, maybe. Lurid, no. Clearly those who had no appreciation for dime novels had never read them.

After returning to the house, she pulled out the large barrel used for bathing and set out her lilac soap. It was her favorite scent, and one of the ladies in town taught her how to make it. One of the few things she was capable of doing. She laid out a towel for the floor and draped one over a chair.

She checked the water in the kettle over the hearth. It was boiling. Using a towel, she lifted the kettle and poured it into the tub, taking care not to spill and burn herself. She then added the colder bucket and kettles of water. Lukewarm, but warm enough to do the job. After removing her garments, she stepped in.

Today, she had a great deal to accomplish. Get clean and find work.

Hair pulled back into a tight knot, Amelia stood before Mrs. Jennings the librarian, her chin held high. While her body felt as rigid as a plank, her heart fluttered like a bird's wings.

Mrs. Jennings looked down her nose through her spectacles, her eyes stern, but kind. "I'm afraid the position has already been filled."

"So soon?" Amelia's heart dove to the pit of her stomach.

Mrs. Jennings placed a book on one of the high shelves and sighed. "Of course, he's a man, and Mr. Jennings would prefer hiring a man over a woman." She faced Amelia and raised a brow. "I thought your father didn't approve of your working."

Amelia looked down at the wooden floor all scratched from sliding tables and chairs. Used and battered, and now faced with reality, all Amelia could think was how her father would do the same to her once he found out about her working. "He doesn't approve." She took a deep breath. "But he left me with nothing, so I have no choice." Shame swept over her. Dare she be so open with Mrs. Jennings about her father's neglect? Perhaps the woman would tell her she deserved it.

"What do you mean?" Mrs. Jennings placed another book on the shelf and pushed up her spectacles so she could focus on Amelia.

Amelia's lungs emptied of air, and she couldn't ignore the feeling that what she was about to say would carry grave consequences if not worded carefully. But what better way was there to say he'd left her with nothing? How could she make it sound less despicable than it was?

"He usually leaves me some money, but he was in such a hurry this morning, he forgot." She shrugged, trying to make light of the situation.

"Careless man." Mrs. Jennings pinched her lips together and her cheeks reddened. She looked around the shop as if the books might be able to help the situation. She faced Amelia again. "Perhaps this is a good thing? Once you find work, you won't be dependent on that ... father of yours."

Amelia had the distinct impression Mrs. Jennings meant to insult her father, but stopped herself just in time. Amelia wasn't sure how she felt about that. It felt good to know someone cared. But did she really? Or was this simply distaste for her father in general? He hadn't made many friends in town because of his being gone so often and his arrogant attitude toward anyone with less wealth than what they used to have.

"But that's the problem. I first need to find work."

"Why don't you try the dry goods store?" Mrs. Jennings nodded, a light of hopefulness in her eyes.

"They might need someone to work in the shop part time."

"Thank you, Mrs. Jennings." Amelia nodded, glad there were other possibilities, but disappointed that it wouldn't be at the library.

As she neared the dry goods store, she remembered how the last time she walked this way she'd made a fool of herself before the handsome stranger. She giggled at the thought, and her mood lightened.

She pushed open the door and the bell jingled, announcing her presence.

Mr. Percy came to the counter, his thin frame and long neck reminding her of a pole.

Forcing a smile, she walked up to him.

"What can I do for you, Miss Taylor?" He straightened his already tall self and raised a condescending brow. "We're all out of dime novels. I'm expecting more to arrive next week."

Amelia cleared her throat. She wouldn't be able to buy one anyway. "I'm looking for work, actually. Would you happen to be hiring?"

Mr. Percy's small chin disappeared into his thin neck, clearly surprised by her request. "Not hiring today or any other day, for that matter." He arched a brow. "Why would you be needing a job?"

Sighing, she looked around. "Are you sure you don't need any help? Mrs. Jennings thought you were hiring."

"Mrs. Jennings?" Again, his chin aligned with his neck. "Been making the rounds, have you?"

"Isn't that what one does, sir, when a person is

looking for work?"

"Don't take that tone with me, child." Mr. Percy leaned his palms on his counter, his eyes narrowed.

Amelia stepped back, unaware that she'd taken a "tone." She sighed. "Forgive me." With that, she turned to go, feeling his eyes boring into her back as she left.

Finding work wasn't going to be as easy as she thought.

Chapter Three

Amelia had already tried several more shops with no success as she made her way down Main Street. No one was hiring.

"Amelia Taylor! Is that my sweet girl?" Widow Forester came bustling toward Amelia, her arms open wide.

A smile broke onto Amelia's face, as always when she saw the plump widow. She hugged the woman and giggled, chasing away some of her anxiety. Amazing what a bit of laughter could do.

"Why are you all made up like this?" Mrs. Forester patted Amelia's tight bun. "Your hair." She shook her head. "It doesn't suit you, dear. It's much too ... constricting ... so unlike you." Patting Amelia on her cheek, she said, "You're not happy. What's wrong?"

Leave it to the widow to read Amelia's thoughts before she voiced them.

Mrs. Forester took Amelia by the arm and they walked down the street as Amelia relayed everything. She knew what she shared would be safe with the old widow. Amelia would visit her, like she did the old widow Hawkins in Denver, and read stories from her dime novels. It was Mrs. Forester who gave her the idea to read to Mrs. Samson's daughters and teach them to read.

When she finished, Mrs. Forester stopped and faced her. "Amelia girl, you're doing the right thing." She nodded emphatically. "Times are changing, dear. More and more women are working, and it's about time your father realized this."

If Mrs. Forester felt any animosity toward her father, she didn't show it, and that put Amelia at ease.

"Now, have you tried the library?"

"That's the first place I went to."

Soon they were compiling a list of all the places and people left to solicit.

Later that day, Amelia met Violet when she finished sewing for Mrs. Nebel. Instead of walking away with Violet, Amelia stood inside the door. Slowly, she walked up to Mrs. Nebel who was hidden behind a hanging dress, the scent of cotton and crinoline filling Amelia's senses.

"Would you happen to need an extra seamstress?" Amelia asked, her voice small even to her own ears.

Violet gasped from the door, but Amelia waved

her to be quiet.

Mrs. Nebel peeked at her from behind a sleeve. "I'm afraid not, dear." She continued sewing.

Amelia sighed, surprised Mrs. Nebel didn't ask about her father. She clung to Violet's arm as they made their way outside.

"I thought you weren't allowed to work?" Violet said as soon as they were on the walkway.

"My father forgot to leave me money."

"He's gone again? Didn't he just get back?" She stopped, as if what Amelia just said finally sunk in. "He didn't leave you any means to get by? Nothing for food?"

Amelia told her the story, and by the time she finished, Violet's face had paled. "If I didn't have to help my family, I'd quit my job so you could have one."

Amelia squeezed her arm. "Thank you."

"Hi there, ladies." Jeb removed his hat and bowed to both of them, his brown hair falling over his forehead. As usual, on his way up, his gaze raked over Amelia, his hat hiding his face from Violet.

Amelia shuddered.

"We better be going, Violet." Amelia tugged on her friend.

"Oh …" Violet's face bloomed pink. "I never had a chance to tell you." She looked from Jeb to Amelia. "Jeb is walking me home today."

Amelia's heart plummeted to her feet. "He's what?" she whispered.

"Jeb came by the house yesterday and asked if he could walk me home today." Violet's eyes flitted up at Jeb.

He smiled, a boyish grin. For the first time Amelia could see why Violet found him attractive, but Violet didn't know what the man was really like. How could she convince her friend that she was allowing herself to be courted by a scoundrel?

"We'll talk more later." Violet squeezed Amelia's arm as she walked away, hanging onto Jeb's arm.

Speechless, Amelia watched them go.

"I'm interested in the Taylor's place," Nathaniel said to the bank manager.

The man's eyes narrowed behind his spectacles. "You mean Frank Taylor's place?"

"I believe he lives in a small cottage in the woods just south of town?"

The man nodded.

Nathaniel didn't want to give away too much information, but he had to know who owned the land. "And doesn't he have a daughter? What was her name again?" He rubbed his whiskers to make like he was thinking.

"Amelia Taylor?"

"Yes, that's it." He breathed deeply, unable to prevent the smile from taking over his face.

The man raised a brow.

So much for trying to hide it. Nathaniel leaned on the counter. "I'm looking to buy some property. Can you tell me who owns that land?"

The man frowned. "That dense forest? There's not much there worth buying."

"I like trees." He spoke the words between his

teeth. So, the land wasn't exactly what he was looking for, but the girl sure was. He'd already planned on combining business with pleasure when he came here. He also needed a place to stay while he was here, and maybe there was another house in the area close to her? If not, he'd hire someone to build one.

"Well, that would be Matt Lawson. He lives at the top of Lawson Road from the Taylors."

Nathaniel tipped the brim of his hat. "Thank you very much."

Nathaniel bought a horse and named him Jack. He liked the feel of the animal beneath him. The horse dealer didn't hide his shock very well when Nathaniel picked out what he wanted and purchased it on the spot. Now that he knew where Amelia lived, he had to wait things out and get to know her.

As he approached Mr. Lawson's property, the trees opened to a clearing where a large house with a barn and a shed stood. Maybe the Lawsons could tell him what he'd like to know about Amelia and her father. A woman tended a garden on the far right side of the house. He reined in and dismounted, leading his horse while he approached the woman.

Remembering his manners, he removed his hat. "Mrs. Lawson?"

The woman looked up, shielding her eyes from the sun. "Yes?"

"I'm Nathaniel Ward." He motioned with his hat to the trees. "Come to inquire about some property."

"What can I do for you, Mr. Ward?" A man's voice came from behind him.

"Mr. Lawson?"

"That'd be me." He stretched out his hand to shake Nathaniel's, his sleeves rolled up above his elbows.

"I'm looking to buy some land." He motioned toward the woods in the direction of Amelia's home.

The man chewed on a toothpick, flipping it to the corner of his mouth. "I've got some territory that I've been wanting to get off my back. I got renters right now, but the man's failed to pay. Still owes me for two months."

Nathaniel tried not to appear too eager. "And where might that be?" he asked.

The man pointed to the trees in the general direction. "Just northeast of here. It's dense forest though. Not much you can do on it."

Nathaniel nodded. Could it be the same cabin? "Who lives there now?"

"Well, I got two. One's empty, and Frank Taylor and his daughter live in the other." The man frowned. "He's out of town a lot and leaves his daughter to pretty much fend for herself."

Nathaniel's jaw tightened. How often did he leave Amelia alone in those thick woods? Come to think of it, when he carried her home, no one else was around. Where was her mother?

"I'd have evicted them a while back. This ain't the first time he's been lagging on his rent. But I can't wrap my mind around putting his girl out on the streets." He eyed Nathaniel. "I just can't afford it none. I gotta pay the bank, but when the renters don't pay, I can't pay."

46

Mrs. Lawson cleared her throat. "Or it makes things awfully tight."

Nathaniel nodded, ready to purchase the property. "Mind showing me the place?"

That Sunday, Amelia thought she'd die of misery, especially as the hymn about caring for the poor rolled off her tongue. She never did find work, and Widow Forester had given her some food to carry her through the week. She'd also had Amelia over for supper every evening. So, the widow wasn't exactly needy, thank goodness, but didn't the Good Book say the church was to care for the widow, and not the other way around? Mr. Forester had left Mrs. Forester very well off. She was quite rich, actually, but never flaunted it like the people Amelia remembered in Denver. Not to mention, like her father would do if he were still wealthy.

After the last hymn, everyone took their seats. That's when Amelia spotted Mr. Ward sitting not far from the front pew on the right side. He didn't wear his hat, but his broad shoulders and tall frame gave him away. Amelia sat in the second to the back pew on the left side next to Mrs. Forester.

Concentrating on the sermon proved to be difficult, especially when she noticed Betty McGillis eyeing Mr. Ward from her pew furthest to the right. Amelia had a good view of the hungry grin pulling on Betty's perfect pink lips. Amelia shook her head. Why would something like that bother her when she had absolutely no interest in the tall handsome stranger? She straightened, grateful she didn't need to succumb to such games of vying for a beau. It was silly, anyway. She barely knew the man. Although, his being in church these last two weeks was a good sign of his moral character. Amelia wanted to knock herself upside the head. She sounded like Mrs. Samson trying to marry off one of her daughters. What had gotten into her? She knew a handsome face wasn't a reliable factor when finding a husband. And more so, she wasn't even looking. She released a frustrated growl, only to have Spinster Bruster, the plumes flailing on her hat, turn her way to admonish her with a condescending gaze. Amelia coughed into her gloved hand and cleared her throat. She never could do anything right in that old woman's eyes. Amelia wondered what she might have to say after services today. She always had a mouthful for Amelia.

Sighing she looked straight ahead, and that's when she spotted Violet sitting next to Jeb Parker. Amelia's heart plummeted. She still hadn't been able to speak to Violet about Jeb. Ever since that one afternoon, he'd picked her up from work every day. Amelia didn't know what to do to warn her friend. Nothing she said convinced Violet of his questionable character. Why wouldn't she listen?

After missing the sermon entirely because she was so distracted with her worries, the preacher called for the final hymn. When that was finished and a prayer was said, the preacher asked the parishioners to wait because he had an announcement. This was new, and suddenly he had her attention.

"As most of you know, we'll be having a box

social next week. Mrs. Forbs expects all our ladies to prepare a special lunch for the gentlemen, and men, please be willing to offer a great price for those boxed lunches as the funds will go to helping our local orphans at the Olive Tree Orphan Asylum in Denver."

With that, everyone was dismissed, and Amelia stood beside Mrs. Forester as parishioners walked up the center aisle to the door. When the aisle cleared, Amelia began to step out and make room for Mrs. Forester, but Spinster Bruster came their way, pinning Amelia between her and Widow Forester.

"Will you be attending the box social, Miss Amelia?" Miss Bruster puffed up her chest and looked down at Amelia, her plumes waving atop her hat.

"Why … I …." Really, Amelia didn't know how she could attend when she had nothing in her cupboards to prepare.

"She'll be attending," Mrs. Forester said, coming to her rescue. "As a matter of fact, she has a wonderful box already picked out. I'm sure she'll bring in the most money for it."

Amelia looked at Mrs. Forester. She hadn't picked out any box, but the widow winked at her and nudged her forward. "We better be going."

Amelia squeezed by Miss Bruster who continued to glare at her, her mouth so pinched Amelia suspected she was gritting her teeth. Why did the woman dislike her so?

They stepped outside onto the steps, the bright sun winking at them from a big blue sky. Amelia turned to Mrs. Forester. "How could … I mean … what made you —"

"The box social was my idea." She cast her a sly grin. "I've already got the perfect box for you to take to the social, and I didn't want Miss Bruster to coerce you into explaining that you had no means to be able to take part in the fun." She shook her head.

"But that means … a gentleman will have to buy my box." Amelia swallowed and leaned in closer to her. "I'll have to share a meal with the man who buys my box."

"And that makes you frown?" Mrs. Forester looked at Amelia as if she'd lost her senses.

Amelia took in a deep breath. "What I'm about to say may surprise you, but I have no intention of ever marrying." There, she said it. Never had she voiced the words out loud to anyone. Holding her breath, she shielded herself from a harsh rebuke.

"Why ever not?" Mrs. Forester's concerned gaze swept over her as she took Amelia's hands in her own.

"You mean, you're not angry with me, shocked … mortified?" Amelia asked, surprised that Mrs. Forester hadn't berated her for making such a scandalous proclamation.

"Why, Amelia Taylor," a voice interrupted their conversation. Amelia turned to see Preacher Forbs and Mr. Ward. The men stood there watching them as Amelia's last words still hung on the air.

Surely, they didn't overhear what she'd just confessed. "That was a fine lesson," Amelia said, desperate to find conversation, if only to get the echo of her own words out of her mind.

"Oh, really?" Mr. Forbs straightened his lapels, lifting his chin and studied her with suspicion. "What did you like the most?"

Amelia's cheeks burned. She searched her mind for anything she may have picked up during his sermon, but nothing came, other than her wicked thoughts of Betty. "Why ... I ...." Amelia took a deep breath, stammering to come up with something, anything that may have been in his lesson. "You see ...."

"Was it the part about how we should spend more time reading our Bibles?" Mr. Ward grinned down at her, his eyes twinkling as if he knew she hadn't paid an ounce of attention. "The part where he spoke about dime novels, and how so many young people are wasting valuable time pouring over cheap romance novels when they could be reading God's Holy Word?"

Had he actually said that? "Yes, of course," Amelia said with hesitation. She eyed Mr. Ward and suspected he was trying to make a point as he fixed her with a mischievous grin. "I really needed to hear that one." She smiled pleasantly at Preacher Forbs, and then looked away from Mr. Ward.

"I thought you might," Mr. Forbs said, nodding his approval. "When I see you walking around with those Yellow Backs, I just have to shake my head, knowing it should be the Good Book you ought to be carrying around in that basket of yours."

Amelia stifled a gasp, feeling as though he were peeking at her ankles.

Preacher Forbs straightened. "Of course, we all know what's in that basket you carry around, Miss Amelia." He clucked. "But I'm proud to hear that you took my words to heart today. It'll do you good." He nodded, his double chin bobbing up and down. "Much good, indeed." Then as if realizing he'd forgotten something, he motioned to Mr. Ward. "My apologies, ladies. Have you had the honor of a formal introduction to Mr. Ward here? He's new in town. Been here about two weeks. Right?" He looked to Mr. Ward who nodded.

"It's a pleasure to meet you. I'm Lillian Forester." She held her hand out to Mr. Ward. He took it and bowed appropriately. She smiled.

"And this here is our Amelia Taylor." Preacher Forbs motioned to Amelia, then to the gentleman. "Nathaniel Ward."

"It's a pleasure," Amelia said, straining a smile onto her stiff face as she held out her hand. She didn't dare say they'd already met because then she'd have to explain where and how.

"The pleasure is all mine." Nathaniel tilted his head, taking her hand, his large fingers closing over her gloved ones.

"Who is this?" Betty's shrill voice rang through them like a dog whose tail was stepped on. "Why, I don't believe we've met," she said to Nathaniel.

He faced Betty McGillis whose smile hid none of her admiration of the man before her and slowly released Amelia's hand.

Strange how empty it felt when he let go.

Nathaniel nodded to Betty and straightened, but

he barely took hold of her outstretched fingers.

"Mr. Ward here," Preacher Forbs continued to hold his lapels, "has come to town on business. Says his plans to stay are indefinite."

"Where are you from, Mr. Ward?" Mrs. Forester's voice chimed into the conversation.

"Chicago, ma'am." Mr. Ward turned to face Mrs. Forester directly.

Betty's pink lips puckered into a frown. "You're not here to stay, then?"

"Not permanently," he said, staring at Amelia so intently that she looked down at her dress, pretending to remove a fleck of dust. Doing that made her all the more aware of her simple dress compared to Betty's bright crinoline fabrics and puffed sleeves.

"Well, you must come have dinner with us," Betty said, pulling her mother into the group and away from another conversation. "We have an extra place setting, do we not, Mother?"

"Why, yes." Betty's mother looked to her daughter, then to her friends, then back at her daughter, moving her body into the conversation. Her eyes swept from Mr. Ward's boots to his face. "Do, come have dinner with us, Mr ... Mr ..." She looked to her daughter for help, but Betty was too busy smiling up at Mr. Ward to notice.

Preacher Forbs introduced Nathaniel.

"And what is it you do, Mr. Ward? What brings you to our neck of the woods?"

"Land and real estate ... and other prospects." His eyes flickered to Amelia, and she quickly looked at

Mrs. McGillis.

"Did you not just buy a horse from old man Tucker? It was his finest horse from what I understand," Betty said, nudging her mother.

Betty's mother beamed up at Nathaniel, her interest suddenly piqued. "Where are you from, Mr. Ward?"

"Chicago, ma'am."

"Oh?" Her brows rose. "And you had the means to come all the way out here? My my," she said as Betty moved a little closer to Mr. Ward. "Perhaps we can entice you to stay?"

Betty's closest friend and conspirator ... er ... confidante, Georgina, joined them. She too flashed a big grin up at Nathaniel Ward, and by then, Amelia had had enough.

"Shall we go?" Amelia asked Mrs. Forester. She usually escorted Mrs. Forester home after services.

They turned to leave as Mr. Forbs called above the clamoring women who were asking Nathaniel repeated questions, "Don't forget to come to the box social next weekend, on Saturday!"

Amelia turned to nod to Preacher Forbs, and her eyes met Nathaniel's. Despite being bombarded with questions, his gaze held hers in a meaningful regard, so severe that Amelia nearly tripped as she turned back toward Mrs. Forester.

"Not all marriages are cruel," Lillian said to Amelia over her cup of tea.

Lunch had been delicious meat sandwiches. Now, they sat together in Mrs. Forester's ornate dining room with a dainty flowered tea set. Amelia set her cup on its saucer, taking care that it not chip or break. A carved, wooden clock ticked above them, emphasizing Amelia's silence. She had already been quite open with Lillian, so why not go all the way? Amelia took a deep breath.

"I've never seen a pleasant marriage where everyone was happy. Why be miserable with someone when you can be happy alone? A person who isn't married can make her own decisions, do what she wants when she wants to do it, without worrying about upsetting her husband. She's not tied down by children and slaving to the needs and wants of her man." What she said was scandalous, but Amelia refused to conform.

Lillian set her teacup down, and placed her hand on Amelia's. "I had a wonderful marriage, dear. You can too. I'm sure of it. And when you love someone, it's a joy to do things for that person, whether it's something they need or just because you want to."

She squeezed Amelia's hand. She wanted to pull away, but didn't dare hurt the woman's feelings. "Forgive me for saying so, but you had wealth. Therefore it was unnecessary for you to slave away at keeping house."

Lillian chuckled. "We didn't always have money, dear. At one point we lived in a two-room house. Imagine raising three boys in such confined quarters." Her smile was bright, telling Amelia she hadn't offended her with her words.

Amelia knew of only one son, and assumed that was all she had of children. "Where are they now?"

she asked.

"Well, as you know, George remained in Green Pines, but William and Harry moved away, taking their father's business elsewhere." She patted Amelia's hand and pulled her napkin to her lips. "They wanted to branch out, and so far, they've been quite successful. It's a shame they're all married. I would have loved to have you as a daughter."

Amelia's face warmed. She would have loved to have had Lillian as a mother. The thought ignited a longing in her heart, a dull ache as she recalled her mother's passing and the lack of affection her father had at the time when her mother gave birth to her stillborn brother, and the anger he expressed at being saddled with a girl and a dead son.

Lillian scooted out of her chair. "Now where did I put that box? I have some beautiful lavender fabric and some ribbon somewhere that we can use for decorating your box. It will be lovely." She set her napkin on the table and bustled away.

What would it have been like to have a mother? Another reason she should never marry. With no example, how would she know how to be a good mother? Yes, that was definitely reason enough not to marry.

Chapter Four

Later that afternoon, Amelia made her way home with a basket full of goods from Mrs. Forester: canned peaches, canned beans, and four potatoes. She also had her partially decorated box hidden under the towel that Lillian provided. The food was for Amelia to get through the next few days. It wouldn't be until later in the week that Mrs. Forester promised to help her with the meal for the box social. She was to finish the box at home, which would give Amelia something to do until she could find work. It was something to look forward to, something fun.

Thankfully, it was still light enough outside to make it to her home without having to walk in the dark, which was why she left when she did. Delighted, Amelia would work on her box, cook up some food, and have a peaceful evening … alone. She was good at being alone. Besides, didn't she just tell Lillian that she could be happy while being alone? She could reread another one of her dime novels if she finished the box too soon. Or as Preacher Forbs suggested, she could read her Bible. She nodded to herself. Yes, that's what she would do.

"Why, hello, Miss Amelia." Jeb took off his hat before Amelia.

She tried to walk around, but he scrambled in front of her.

"What's the rush?" he asked.

"I need to get home." Amelia sidled around him and marched along the walkway.

Jeb hurried next to her.

"Where's your father? I couldn't help but notice he wasn't in services this morning."

"Need you ask?" she said and picked up her pace.

"Come on, what's the rush?" He moved to jump in front of her, but his elbow knocked the basket from her hands.

She fumbled with it, but the contents tumbled out. The canned beans broke open and the peaches rolled ahead of them, while the potatoes thudded on the ground. One rolled under Jeb's boot where he caught it under his heel.

"No! Now look what you've done!" She dropped to her knees to retrieve her goods, her box for the social and its contents lay open, revealing the lavender colors and ribbon.

Jeb bent down. He grabbed the two potatoes and tossed them carelessly into her basket. He flung her fabric and ribbon back in. "Now I know what box to bid on."

"Just leave me alone!" Amelia gritted her teeth, seething with the sight of her food scattered all over the sidewalk and his filthy hands on her pretty things.

"Miss Taylor, is this man bothering you?" A baritone voice came from above.

Jeb straightened to his full height and shoved the man, creating a scuffle.

Amelia jumped to her feet, and stumbled backward as Mr. Ward lifted Jeb by his collar and britches and tossed him into the street.

Nathaniel brushed the dirt from his hands. He then turned to Amelia, bent and helped her gather her belongings, placing them in the basket, while Jeb shouted obscenities at him.

"Watch your language," Nathaniel said. He held out her box, the box that no one was supposed to recognize as belonging to her during the social. She hid the fabric and ribbons under the towel.

Jeb charged at Nathaniel, barreling into his side.

Amelia screamed, springing back several feet.

Nathaniel grabbed Jeb and lifted him off his feet by the collar. Jeb held on as Nathaniel carried him away from Amelia. When they reached a safe distance, he set Jeb down, dodging his swing.

Amelia hugged her basket as Jeb threw a punch and Nathaniel plowed his fist into Jeb's jaw. How did such a pleasant walk turn into such a disaster?

One last swing to the jaw threw Jeb backwards. Nathaniel stood over him as he backed off. Jeb glanced at Amelia, hatred in his eyes, just before he turned to run, stumbling as he regained his footing.

Amelia stood in stunned disbelief as Nathaniel walked back to her, his panted breaths breaking the silence between them. Amelia glanced around them, wondering who else may have witnessed the event. Mr. Percy ducked back into the dry goods store from up the street. A hint of Mrs. Nebel's hair shone through the window, then disappeared. Other than that, there was no one.

"Are you all right?" Nathaniel asked as Jeb tore off down the street, his boots kicking up dirt behind him.

"I'm well," Amelia said, her voice strained from the shock.

Nathaniel turned his sharp gaze on her. "You're not hurt, are you?"

"Oh, no. I'm fine." She hugged her basket tighter in an effort to control her trembling. "Thank you for your help."

"I'll walk you." He looked over his shoulder to where Jeb had bolted. "I don't trust him as far as I can throw him."

Amelia peered up at him from the corner of her eye. "But you did throw him," she whispered.

Nathaniel studied the road where Jeb had landed. "I suppose you're right." He shrugged.

Amelia simply nodded and swallowed. He wiped his hands off on his britches, and Amelia stopped to give him her towel.

"Here, use this." He wiped the dirt from his hands, and that's when she saw the cut and blood. "Oh, no. You're hurt! Put pressure on it." Stopping, she set her basket down. She grabbed his hand and wrapped the towel around it, tucking in the end. Picking up her things, she pushed a loose lock of hair behind her ear. "You should go home and take care of that."

"I'm fine." He studied her makeshift bandage and made a fist. "Just fine."

Was that a hint of satisfaction in his eyes as he made a fist?

They strolled in silence until they reached the woods. "You don't have to take me any farther."

"I'll see you safely to your doorstep." He motioned with his chin to the woods before them. "I don't trust that fellow. What was his name?"

"Jeb. I've never felt easy around him," she said. But she didn't dare tell him why. To talk about his leering glances made her feel ashamed, even though she couldn't do anything about it.

They continued walking and Nathaniel offered to take Amelia's basket. She handed it to him, relieved from the weight of it.

"Where's your mother?" he asked.

"She died when I was seven."

The crunch of pinecones under their feet echoed through the trees.

Nathaniel's jaw ticked. "How'd she die?"

"Childbirth. She had a son, but he was stillborn." Amelia always believed her mother also died from a broken heart. Father made her mother cry so often. She recalled hiding behind a plant when her father slapped her mother, telling her she'd better give him a son. Well, she did, but neither one of them had survived.

"Both my parents are gone too."

"Oh, I'm sorry." They came to the drive that would take her home. The branches from the trees stretching over it seemed to bow in sorrow. "What happened?"

"I lost them in a fire." He kicked a clump of dirt, the basket in his hands seeming to weigh nothing.

"That's terrible." She wanted to probe him with more questions. What kind of fire? Where? When? How? But noticing the grief pulling on his face, she didn't push for details. "Do you have any brothers or sisters?"

He smiled, but it didn't quite reach his eyes. "A younger brother and a sister."

"So you're the oldest?"

He nodded.

"Where are they now?"

"I don't know." Nathaniel cocked his head. "I've tried to find them, but I haven't had any success. We were separated during the fire."

It was better not to voice the next question, but curiosity got the best of her. "How do you know they're still alive?"

"We were separated at the orphanage. They sent Rachel to a girl's home, and I was too old, so they sent me away, but Michael stayed."

"Where did you go?" She couldn't imagine how he managed to survive into adulthood.

He cast her a side-glance, as if he was studying her, testing her. "I took to the streets. There was no other place. I worked odd jobs, saved money, caught the train when jobs were scarce."

"Oh my." She released a long breath. "I don't know how you managed to survive. I can't imagine living a life on the streets, with no home, no parents." She shook her head. "Your poor brother and sister."

He smirked. "You're sorry for them, but not for me?"

She giggled and waved her hand in the air. "Well, you seem to be doing well now." She crossed her arms. "I hope the same for your siblings."

Again, Nathaniel's jaw ticked and he didn't say anything.

"I'm sorry." She stopped and stared at the ground. "Forgive me."

"No need to apologize." Nathaniel walked on, placing his hand over hers and on his arm. "There are countless times I've wondered the same."

They walked on in silence, a breeze carried through the trees, covering them with the scent of pine, like a whisper to them both. Amelia gently pulled her hand away.

"What about you? Do you have any brothers or sisters?" he asked, not seeming to notice that she moved away from him.

"Nope. I'm the only one."

"How did you come to be in Green Pines?"

"What do you mean?"

"I mean …" he shrugged and moved a branch out of her way, "have you always lived here?"

"No." Amelia shook her head. "I was fourteen when we came. We used to live in Denver where my father owned a restaurant and had some investments." She grabbed a twig and broke it off from one of the trees hovering over them. "I'm not really sure what happened. His restaurant caught fire, and it seems everything else went downhill from there." She used the twig to hit other branches. Dare she reveal so much information about her father? "I think he made some bad investments." Really, that was all she knew, and how could telling this man cause any trouble for them now? "I'll never forget the day we lost our house."

Amelia recalled the memories of coming home that day, allowing her mind to take her from Green Pines all the way back to Denver City, to the day she went from riches to rags. "I was out with a friend," she said to Nathaniel as she relayed the story to him.

"It's not far." Amelia tugged on Rowena's arm.

A wagon full of laughing women covered in paint—but not so covered in clothing—and men with lopsided cowboy hats drove by.

"Whooot, whooot!" one of the cowboy's shouted at them as he lifted a bottle of drink.

"This isn't the nice part of town." Rowena held her hat in place, her eyes growing wider the closer they got to Holliday Street.

"We'll be fine," Amelia said, realizing how the disappearance of shiny buggies replaced by wooden wagons carrying rowdy men and women would disturb her friend. "We're only going to the corner. That's where Widow Hawkins lives. She'll be so glad to see us." Amelia warmed, thinking of the joyous gleam in Widow Hawkin's eyes when they'd arrive.

She had tucked the latest copy of her dime novel in her basket before she'd grabbed Rowena and headed for Holliday Street, not far from her father's restaurant. Even though it was out of the way, she passed by here as often as she could on her way to and from school. She'd first dared return five years ago when she'd lost her calico purse. Like Father had said, it was gone for good. But upon her return, she befriended an old widow, Mrs. Hawkins. The woman's eyesight was still going strong, but a couple days ago she fell and hurt herself. Now it was too painful to walk. Amelia often gave Mrs. Hawkins her weekly allowance. It took much coaxing and prodding, but the widow finally gave in. On occasion, Amelia also brought her food. Recently, to Amelia's delight, she discovered she and the widow had something in common: they both enjoyed reading.

Father forbade novel reading, but Amelia could see no wrong in reading a Yellow Back. Not only were dime novels a wonderful escape from the realities of life, they certainly created a nice distraction for those who couldn't leave their homes.

Rowena jerked on Amelia's arm. "I can't!"

Amelia staggered to a stop.

Rowena crossed her arms and lifted her perfect chin. "I won't take another step."

Amelia blew out a breath. "Widow Hawkins is a nice lady. You'll like her."

"I refuse to soil my shoes on that side of town!"

"We've practically arrived." Amelia pointed at the small wooden house a few feet away. Obviously, it had been built before the street took on its present "industry" and unruly inhabitants. Poor woman had no other place to go. "Look. It's right here."

"When you said widow, I thought you meant one of the widows near Pennsylvania Avenue." Rowena lifted her gloved hands as if to catch the sky from falling. "Not here." She looked down her nose, and for the first time, her pink cheeks under her pink bonnet, darkened into something Amelia found all too familiar.

Arrogance.

But perhaps Amelia misjudged her friend.

Searching for the right words, she motioned down the street as carriages and wagons rolled into the formidable side of town. "I understand why you're afraid." Despite being fourteen, both their parents would whip them if they were caught in this area.

Rowena straightened. "Afraid?" Her lips turned down in what Amelia knew was disgust. "These people are nothing but criminals. Do you think I'd dare go into such a person's house?"

Amelia's basket sagged in her hands. "She's a poor widow. Not a criminal." She had hoped Rowena wasn't like the others. "I thought you were different."

Rowena pinched her lips, something she did when thinking. She looked at the house and then at Amelia.

Amelia dared hope.

Swallowing visibly, Rowena said, "You thought wrong." With that, she turned and marched away.

Amelia watched her friend—her only friend—go. The friend she had tea parties with when they were little, the one with whom she shared all her deepest secrets, including the one about the street boy. She thought because Rowena knew about him and was intrigued, she'd want to go with her to the place she met him. Clearly, talking about adventures was quite different than experiencing them.

Amelia had lost so many friends for the very reasons Rowena now walked away.

After visiting with Widow Hawkins, Amelia strolled toward Pennsylvania Avenue, but stopped as soon as she saw her home.

Men hauled furniture from the house, and several items were strewn in the front yard. One mahogany armoire—resembling her own—sat leaning to one side, threatening to topple over, while other expensive pieces were loaded onto wagons.

Familiar neighbors, men with top hats and canes, women with parasols, and couples in buggies, watched the commotion as if they were spectators at a lynching. They shook their heads, looking at her house. One high-society woman noticed Amelia, and turning up her nose beneath her plumed hat, she scowled a silent "tsk-tsk" her way, as if Amelia had done something wrong.

Rowena stood nearby on the sidewalk. Amelia started toward her, hoping to question her friend, but Rowena shook her head, her eyes motioning toward her parents who hovered next to her with their noses in the air. Beneath his top hat, Rowena's father looked in Amelia's direction. He placed a gloved hand on Rowena's shoulder, turned their backs on Amelia, and escorted their daughter away.

"Up!" The men loaded a bed—Amelia's bed— onto a wagon with their fine things. The brass headboard came down with a clang as the men moved around it.

Amelia ran inside, wishing she wasn't center stage in this spectacle. She found her father sitting with his face in his hands next to the hearth, his pipe between his fingers. She'd never seen him slump over like this.

"What's happening?" she whispered, afraid to hear the answer.

Father lifted his face, his eyes red and wide. "I've lost everything." The words came out as if he could hardly believe the truth himself. He raked his hands through his dark hair. "The bank's confiscating all I own," he said as if speaking to a friend, lacking the typical condescension she was accustomed to.

She stepped back. "Wh ...Why? How?"

"Don't ask." Father stood, his chest heaving, and he shook his head. "It's nothing you should worry your pretty head about," he said, choking. He paced, his stride wobbly. As he set his pipe down on the hearth, his hand trembled, causing it to rattle. "I've got just enough hidden," he mumbled, not to her, but to himself. "Enough to get us out of here. Avoid the shame." He leaned against the mantel, nodding and mumbling.

"Father ..." Amelia didn't know what to say.

He pushed off and faced her. Straightening, he tugged on his lapels. "Get whatever is important to you. As much as you can carry. We're leaving."

Amelia stepped back, keeping her eyes on her father, trying to comprehend his change. A moment ago he was a broken man, like none she'd ever seen before, and with the inhaling of a breath, he'd put his old self back on, like putting on a coat, back to the arrogant condescending man she knew and recognized.

He motioned again with his finger, telling her without words that she'd better not delay.

"Yes, Father." Spinning with confusion, Amelia rushed up the stairs. She reached the landing and scurried down the hall, but stopped herself at the doorjamb.

Men, dressed in black frock coats and white vests, stood in her room. Her almost empty room. She'd never seen a man in her room before, not even her father.

"I'm sure this will fetch a good price." Winnie's voice echoed off the bare walls. Odd to think paintings covered them as recent as that morning. She motioned to the vanity, showing it to the men.

Amelia crept inside, feeling like a stranger in her own home.

"Winnie?" Amelia's voice shook. Would Winnie scold her too, like the people outside? Despite her trepidation, she went to her. "What's happening?"

Other men pushed past them and lifted her vanity.

For the first time ever, Winnie took Amelia in her arms. "Your father couldn't pay off his debts. The bank is confiscating everything he owns."

"Where are my journals? My mother's pictures?" They were all she had of value and in her writing desk, which was now missing.

"I have them here." Winnie held her away and motioned to two carpetbags leaning against the wall. "I rescued as many of your dresses as I could."

"They took my dresses?" Amelia looked to the armoire, only to discover it too was gone. So, it was her armoire on the front lawn.

"All the servants have been let go." Tears filled Winnie's eyes. "Your father can't afford to keep any of us."

Amelia put her hands over her mouth. She'd never seen Winnie cry. "You're not staying?"

Winnie sniffed and shook her head, her grey curls bobbing beneath her hat. "I'm afraid not, dear."

The ground dropped out beneath Amelia's feet. Not just the house, but her entire world crumbled around her and she was falling, as if she were losing her mother all over again. Please no. She couldn't survive the pain.

"Don't be afraid." Winnie grabbed Amelia by the arms and held her, a stern expression on her features — the expression she was accustomed to, but never associated with love until now. She cupped Amelia's face in her hands. "God is with you, child. Remember that."

So many new experiences. She'd never seen a man in her room, and now Winnie shed tears of grief for her.

She embraced Amelia. "Give me your word, you'll remember."

"I'll remember." A wail almost escaped Amelia's lips. How could she forget? Jesus was all she had.

"Whatever you do, don't change who you are." Tears streamed down Winnie's wrinkled cheeks. "I've never met a girl so special. The Lord is with you, child. He'll take good care of you."

Amelia breathed in Winnie's words, soaked them into her mind, into her heart. Never had she spoken such kindness, such love. Trembling, she clung to Winnie, desperate to hold on to something—Someone solid and unchanging—to keep from falling.

The memories were so potent, so heart wrenching, Amelia's legs wobbled and her boot collided with a stone. Nathaniel caught her by the arm as she stumbled, righting her.

"Are you well?" he asked.

"Yes, of course." She shook her head trying to awaken from the memory, a knot filling her throat. "We're almost there," she said and skipped ahead. She didn't want Mr. Ward to see her tears.

"I'm sure you miss your home, especially if it was larger than what you have now." His voice carried through the trees.

"Oh, it's not the house." As the run-down cottage came into view, she tossed her stick, scurried further ahead and leaped onto the step. "It's the people. The friends I had." Although, those were rather scarce. Taking in a deep breath, she spun around to face Nathaniel. She never really felt accepted in this town, unless she was with Violet or speaking to Widow Forester. "I tend to spend my time with widows, much like in Denver."

Nathaniel lifted the basket to her. On the step, she was almost as tall as him. Almost. She took it, but he didn't let go, his blue eyes dancing. "Don't you know, the Good Book says that pure religion is to visit the fatherless and widows in their affliction?"

"No." Amelia shook her head. "I didn't know that."

Nathaniel released the basket. "I believe it's

somewhere in the book of James. Give it a read."

"I will," Amelia said.

He tipped his hat. "Good day to you, Miss Amelia."

"Good day," she said, almost in a whisper as she watched the handsome Nathaniel turn back down the gravel drive.

Chapter Five

Nathaniel came to the end of the drive and turned up the road toward his new home, his new home for now, anyway. The conversation he shared with Amelia made the sun shine brighter as he ambled to his own small house not too far away. From what he could tell, she was still the same, kind-hearted girl he met on the streets long ago. Her openness about what happened surprised him. Not many women would have shared so much.

If she only knew the memories she stirred while talking about the past, both painful and pleasant. He lifted his fist and the towel to his nose. He breathed in its scent. Just a hint of lilacs mixed with a foreign perfumed fragrance. Not enough to satisfy.

Would she remember him from that single day

when they met so long ago? His recollection pulled his mind to the Denver streets when he first set eyes on Amelia.

He was only twelve, and she was probably about nine, and he'd just been hit by the kiss, the sweet kiss she blew to him from across the street ....

The last time Nathaniel felt this good was in his dreams. The dreams he had when his parents were still alive. The girl's kindness burned itself into Nathaniel's mind. After being on the street for a whole year, he'd never met anyone who went to so much trouble to help him the way this little girl had. At twelve and tall for his age, he'd taken good care of himself. But this act of kindness was something he'd never forget.

Her parasol bobbed up and down, and her feet kicked up her dress as she scrambled along the boardwalk back up the street. A nice girl. Nothing like her old man.

He squeezed the coins in his fist. Where should he get his next meal? Thinking about food made his stomach growl. He could actually buy something at the bakery, not far from where he met the little girl and her rich father. The smell of fresh bread had lingered on the air, and his mouth watered at the thought of sinking his teeth into the hard crust and soft center.

Dodging the oncoming wagons, he crossed the street. As he came to the sidewalk, he spotted something yellow, blue and with flowers lying on the ground next to the wooden planks. The little girl's reticule. He picked it up.

Empty.

She'd given him all her money. He looked along the sidewalk, trying to find the bright parasol making its way through the crowd.

No sign of it.

Clenching the bag in his fist, he jogged up the street, searching the crowd.

Still nothing.

He picked up his pace and ran, hoping he could get to her before she made it back to her father. Otherwise, how would he explain having her purse — not to mention, her money.

No parasol and no signs of the pretty little girl in white ruffles. He rounded the corner and skidded to a stop.

The father.

Nathaniel pressed his back against the wall.

The girl's father jerked her along by the arm, her face white as she looked up at the stern man. "Don't ever do that again," he said between clenched teeth and shoved her onto the wagon seat. "When we didn't find you in the restaurant, I had no idea where you'd gotten off to."

Nathaniel should do something. But what? If her old man knew she'd been consorting with a street rat, he might make it worse for her.

The father climbed up next to the girl and sat down. "It's the last time you'll come with me, Amelia. Never again."

The driver clicked the reins and the horses jolted the wagon forward.

The girl cried in her hands as the wagon pulled

away. Her parasol, still open, lay as if it had been tossed in the back of the wagon.

Fury ate at Nathaniel as they left. His fists ached to pummel the man. He chased them down the street. But what would he do or say once he reached them? Anything he did would only increase the father's wrath—and the girl's punishment. Within reach of the wagon, he stopped, biting down his temper. He punched the air, wanting to hit something, someone.

Panting, he stood in the middle of the street and watched them go, shaking his head in frustration that he couldn't help the little girl. The sun caught her brown curls, lighting them up like gold, before she disappeared around a corner. He ran his hand down his face and was reminded of the reticule. If anyone caught him with the dainty bag, they'd think he stole it.

Hiding the purse in his fist, he ran to the nearest alley. He hurried between the familiar buildings and sagged against the wall. Yellow and blue flowers dotted the fabric and seemed to smile up at him. A white ruffle near its mouth waved at him, and shiny blue ribbon, used as a drawstring to pull it closed, fell over his darkened fingers. The bright, clean bag contrasted with his rough, filthy hands, making him realize how much he needed a bath. He opened it, his fingers awkward with the pretty fabric, and dropped the change back in. As the last coin fell, he spotted an embroidered script on the inside.

Amelia E. Taylor.

He ran his dirty thumb over the delicate writing. She must have sewn the text herself. The stitches were lopsided and the letters uneven. When they could afford it, his mother used to make pretty things like this for his little sister.

Rachel.

How he longed for her. He hoped and prayed she fared better than himself. Not to mention his brother. Michael's wide brown eyes and his screams of rage as the people at the orphanage tore them away from one another played through his mind. Like a nightmare, he could still feel his brother's fingers losing their clawing grip on his hand.

He lifted the dainty bag to his nose. Enjoying the scent, he breathed it in.

Lilacs.

His mother used to collect them. He hadn't smelled anything this good in a long time. Not since his parents were alive.

Now you can buy yourself some clothes. Amelia's voice echoed in his mind. Maybe she was right. He could always find scraps to eat behind the restaurants. A new pair of shoes would last a lot longer than a few meals. And with the weather growing cold, he needed to keep his feet warm. Gritting his teeth, he thought of the bully, Jordan, who stole the shoes right off his feet while he was sleeping. Jordan had beaten Nathaniel up thoroughly. Good thing he'd left town. But now he had enough money to afford shoes. New shoes.

Yes. That's what he'd do.

"Thank you, Amelia," he whispered.

Voices carried on the street around the corner from the alley. He wadded up the purse and stuffed it deep into his pocket. With his head down, he made his way to the nearest shoemaker.

It was later that day he caught a ride out of Denver City.

The train blew its whistle and soon began its trudge on the tracks.

Waiting in the dark, Nathaniel stayed as far away from the platform as he dared. He didn't want to risk the train picking up too much speed for him to catch it.

Soon the engine plodded by, leaving a trail of steam in its path. Still, Nathaniel waited. Once the dining and hotel cars passed, the cargo holds appeared.

He exploded out of the bushes and ran, letting the moonlight guide him toward the moving train. As comforting as his new shoes were, they felt heavy, and he couldn't run nearly as fast with them. He raced along the boxcar, avoiding getting too close so he wouldn't trip on the slats shooting out under the rails, but close enough so he could grab hold of a door.

He came alongside a handle and stayed with it. Soon the train would gain speed, and it'd be impossible to leap on. Now was his chance. He ran several more feet, sprang up and grabbed on to the handle of the boxcar. As he'd hoped, his weight caused it to slide open, just enough for him to squeeze inside. He pulled himself up and tumbled into the car where hay bales cushioned his fall. Good. Hay. The worst car he'd ever been in was one full of meat. Ice blocks were everywhere to keep the meat cool, and it got so cold, he finally had to jump for it. Thankfully, he hadn't broken any bones in his fall. He still wasn't sure what would have been worse: breaking a bone or almost freezing to death.

He closed the door, shutting out the moonlight, and the darkness swallowed him. If someone noticed a car door open, they would telegraph the station at the other end of the tracks. Then the men would search the boxcars for stowaways. So far, he'd managed to avoid being caught, and because of that, he had a feeling his time was coming.

Nathaniel sat back against the hay. Comforting and warm. Wood, hay, and the smell of the engine filled his senses. He might actually get some shut-eye. Mentally, he waved farewell to Denver City, as if he were leaving something — or someone — behind.

Back then, Amelia's money had come in handy, and still, her kindness overwhelmed him. Nathaniel's home came into view, leaving the memories behind as he approached what he hoped to be his future.

As he neared the door, the small outbuilding caught his eye, jolting him from his reverie. He'd forgotten his horse. He'd left the poor stallion at the livery in town. He laughed at himself.

Shaking his head, he reached for the door. He'd first clean up his hand, and then he'd head back to town for Jack.

Amelia hummed that evening as she decorated her box. She'd eaten a bit late because as soon as she entered the house, she grabbed her Bible while it was still light and looked up the text in James. She was afraid she might forget where to read. Sitting by her window and soaking up the heat from the sun, she ended up reading the entire book as she found the passage he mentioned.

What surprised her most was how much she gleaned from the rest of the book, especially the part about belief without works. She never realized how faith and works went hand-in-hand. Naturally, if one believed, they would want to do good deeds. She tried to do good all the time, and she knew God was with her, but she didn't realize how much her works were supposed to exemplify her faith. The fact that it came naturally for her to visit widows warmed her heart. It was nice to find something worthy in her actions, a quality of goodness she feared she lacked. But she knew it all came from the Lord, nothing about her or anyone was innately good, and any goodness was because of His love. Thankfully, the Lord had given her something worthy of praise, something she was totally unaware of. Amelia could still feel the admiration coming from Nathaniel Ward's deep, approving regard. She would no longer belittle herself for visiting Widow Forester or feel that she was lacking in friends. Really, his praise touched her deeply. Funny how approval from a stranger could affect her.

Speaking of friends, she wondered about Violet. Why was Jeb paying so much attention to Amelia if he was interested in Violet? The man worked on her nerves. She had to find a way to speak to her friend and warn her about the scoundrel.

As the evening progressed and the sun dipped

behind the mountains, the room grew cold. Amelia got up and stoked the dying flames. Her lamp was well lit, but seeing how few timbers were in the fire, she realized she would have to chop wood. She'd wait until morning, though. It was already too dark. Hopefully, she'd have enough to last the night. She also liked to keep the fire going for the light. Made her feel less alone. Although, she had to admit, she didn't feel quite as lonely this evening. Having read her Bible—and she was still reading despite the strain on her eyes in the dim light—a comfort enveloped her. A reminder that the Lord would never leave her really helped give her a bolster of joy. Something she hadn't felt in a while, not since her mother was alive.

There was only one section that puzzled her, and she read it again, only this time, aloud, "Count it all joy when you fall into various trials, knowing that the testing of your faith produces patience. But let patience have its perfect work, that you may be perfect and complete, lacking nothing."

She had a hard time considering her situation joyful. But she'd do her best to make her difficult circumstances change her for the better. "Lord, I'm going to need your help with that one."

While she was up, she checked the door to make sure it was locked good and tight. She also checked the windows and pulled the curtains closed. She went to the back room and did the same. There were two beds, one large one for her father, and a smaller one by the window. A curtain divided the room. She usually slept in her father's bed while he was gone. Sleeping under the window usually gave her a chill.

With the curtains closed, she changed into her nightdress and put on her throw for extra warmth.

A shadow sputtered against one of the windows. Her gaze darted to the closed curtain. Was that really a shadow or was it the light flickering from the other room? She remained still, ears alert. A tree perhaps? The quiet stillness outside told her it couldn't be the wind. Perhaps it was a bird? But this late? She didn't usually hear or see the birds after dark. Not hearing anything, she moved back into the kitchen and prepared to sit down with her lamp at the table. She was near the window, so she collected a blanket and her things and moved to the hearth next to the warm fire. As she set everything down, she tossed in a large rock. After waiting a few minutes for it to heat up, she used the large poker to roll it out. She then wrapped a thick towel around it. The warmth made her shiver with delight. Curling in her blanket, she sat down on the hearth, and rested her feet on the rock.

Now that she was done decorating the box, she grabbed her Bible and decided to read the Psalms. As she sat quietly on the hearth, a scratch sounded on the door. Amelia froze. She stared at the handle, watching to make sure it didn't move.

Nothing.

Could it be an animal foraging for food, or an animal seeking warmth? She'd experienced that plenty of times.

Continuing with her reading, a bang exploded on the door. She waited for a knock. Again, nothing. It definitely had to be a person and not an animal. She leapt to her feet and grabbed her father's rifle.

Holding the rifle, she stood with it aimed at the door. Again, another bang echoed through the small house. Her arms trembled from the weight of the firearm.

"Go away or I'll shoot!" she shouted, her voice weak as she forced the air through her tight throat.

Silence.

In the not-so-far distance, a wicked cackling echoed through the trees.

A shudder skittered down Amelia's spine.

After long minutes, frozen like a statue, she finally sat in the rocker, back straight, with her father's rifle still aimed at the door.

The silence stretched out like an unending slingshot ready to snap. Suddenly, a knock reverberated through the house. Amelia jerked with tension. "Go away! I'll shoot!"

"Amelia, it's me, Nathaniel," came the breathless but urgent voice from outside. "I heard commotion in the woods. Are you safe?"

"How would you know?" Her voice was still strained, tight with tension. It could have been Nathaniel at the door, and then that laugh … she shuddered at the recollection of it.

"I live on Lawson's property."

So, he knew the name of the landowner. That could mean he was telling the truth. But what if he was the one trying to scare her? She shook her head. It didn't make sense. He'd had plenty of opportunities to do her harm.

"Amelia, just tell me you're safe. Is anyone in there with you?"

It was the first time he'd used her name, at least

since they'd first met, assuming he actually said it then, which of course, he didn't.

"Answer me, Amelia. Is anyone in there with you?"

She looked frantically around the kitchen and into the dark bedroom. Could someone have broken in through one of the windows? No, surely they were shut good and tight. She'd checked them before she settled in.

With an explosion, the door shot open and slammed against the wall. Nathaniel bolted inside, gun drawn. Amelia screamed as he grabbed the rifle, causing it to go off into the roof, bringing down woodchips onto his head. Nathaniel whisked her into his arms and pushed her behind him as he headed into the bedroom, his large footsteps causing the wooden planks to creak and moan with each step. Amelia's gaze darted from the front door, still swinging open, to the dark bedroom where Nathaniel had disappeared.

Finally, hands down at his side, he came out of the room. "All is clear," he said. "No one's broken in. He set the gun on the mantel above the fireplace and inched toward her, his hands lifted. "I heard a strange noise coming from this way. I thought you might be in danger."

Seeing that he was in a loose shirt and britches, with no shoes and no coat, she knew he had to be telling the truth. She shook violently and fell against him, her hands trembling on his chest. "I was so frightened!" she said, practically shrieking the words. "I was so scared!"

He pulled her close, his palm on her back. "You're safe now," he murmured. "No one's going to hurt you."

She wept quietly on his shirt, wrapped in his strong arms, with the scent of sweat, leather and pine enveloping her. As her trembling calmed, and her weeping subsided, she pushed away. Breathless, she glanced to the open door fearful someone else might appear.

Nathaniel turned and closed it, the lock now broken and two loose hinges causing it to hang. He lifted it and jarred it back in place, then faced her, his blue eyes wide with concern. His height made the cabin look small, and in just a pace or two he grabbed the rocker and slid it under her quivering form. She dropped into the chair, hands trembling in her lap as she shivered uncontrollably. He snatched up her blanket and flicked it over her shoulders, and she curled into the quilt, pulling in as much heat as possible.

Nathaniel squatted in front of the hearth and stoked the fire.

"There's a rock," she said, her voice small.

He glanced over his shoulder at her. "Rock?"

"There in the towel. It keeps my feet warm."

He lifted the towel and the rock thudded to the floor.

"If you put it in the fire, it'll warm up." Shivering, she pointed at the towel and the poker. "It gets hot, so be careful."

Nathaniel studied the rock and the towel, then realization reflected from his face. He tossed the rock into the flames. "Out of all those years on the streets, you'd think I would have thought of this."

After a few minutes, she motioned to the fireplace. "It should be hot enough by now. Sometimes it gets too hot."

He worked it out onto the hearth, and jerking away from the heat, he wrapped the towel around the stone.

Gingerly, he set the rock on the floor by her feet. Thank goodness she had her stockings on. The heat from the stone emanated up her legs and into her body, sending more warm shivers to her chattering teeth.

Nathaniel stood, grabbed a chair, and straddled it next to the fire. Then as if realizing something, he got up and moved her closer to the fire. He sat back down across from her, his pistol on the mantel above her head, within easy reach.

Warming to the flames, she looked at him, at the strength of his arms as he leaned against the back of the chair. He stared at her, studying her face, his blue eyes shimmering light. Her gaze darted back to the fire.

"It must have been Jeb." Nathaniel continued to study her, his foot perched on the hearth. He leaned over and tossed one of the woodchips from the roof into the flames, shaking the rest out of his hair. "It had to be."

Amelia, barely able to think, barely able to accept the fact that the new stranger to Green Pines was sitting in her house, tightened the blanket around her. "Why would he do such a thing?" She knew Jeb to be a scoundrel, but this was beyond anything she could imagine. Then she gasped. "He knew Father was gone."

Nathaniel raised a brow, casting a side-glance her way. "He was mad enough to do it. It was him." Clearly in Nathaniel's mind it was settled as he leaned forward, his dark hair mussed in such a fashion that made him endearing, like a young boy, and suddenly familiarity hit her, and she recalled the moment on the street so long ago with the street rat. She shook away the memory. Why would she think of such a thing at a time like this?

"What should I do?" She hugged herself. How could she keep this from happening again? What would she do if he came back? And now, with her door broken.

"Don't worry. I'll fix it."

That's when she realized she'd been staring at the damage. "I ..." She shook her head. "I don't know how to thank you."

He ran his hand down his face. "I'm sorry I broke down the door. I thought you might be ... I thought you were being attacked."

His words stunned her. She'd had nightmares about wild animals possibly getting into the cabin, but not a person, not a man out for revenge. Could Jeb truly be so wicked?

"I'll fix that too." He motioned with his thumb to the roof.

"Thank you. I just ..." What could she say? Really, she didn't know what to say, what to do.

"We should tell the sheriff."

"We don't have one."

"What?" He straightened, his eyes narrowing. "A marshal then."

She shook her head. "We're such a small town, nothing ever happens here. The men of the town simply work things out when something goes wrong, and like I said, nothing really does in these parts." She shrugged. "At least not since I've been here."

That news was met with silence. The quiet carried on for so long that Amelia eyes grew heavy. Then she remembered she wasn't alone, and she forced her head up.

"Go on. I'll stay here," he motioned to his chair, "for the night. That way you can get some rest."

"But ..."

"I'm not leaving." He said the words so firmly and decidedly, she didn't dare argue.

With the blanket around her shoulders, she shuffled into the dark bedroom. There was no doorway between the room and the kitchen area, so she decided to sleep on her small bed under the window so she could pull the curtain closed. Though, she knew a small curtain wouldn't protect her from anything about Nathaniel Ward, it would at least protect her from any peering eyes.

She crawled into the bed, wishing she'd brought her hot stone with her to curl around. What did it matter? She'd likely not get any sleep anyway.

Chapter Six

The smell of coffee, sausage and eggs floated on the air, and the sun's rays pierced through Amelia's thin curtain. Her eyes flew open. Someone was in her kitchen. She bolted up in bed, hair falling into her face. She forgot to braid it last night. Since when did Father cook? Then she remembered: the shadow at the window, banging on the door, Mr. Ward in her house, trembling in his arms.

It wasn't Father in the kitchen.

Was he still here?

Hidden safely behind the curtain, she slipped into her old dress as quickly as she could. Since when did she sleep in so late? Usually the cold would wake her before the sun came up, but the house was toasty warm. She grabbed her brush, put her hair up in a hairpin, and let some of it fall freely down her back and over her shoulders. Taking a deep breath, she slowly pulled the curtain back and poked her head out. Heavy boot steps creaked along the wooden floor. She crept out and peered around the door.

"Good morning," Nathaniel said, lifting a skillet from the fire. He turned and filled two plates on the table by the window. The open curtains allowed sunlight to penetrate the room. "Lock and hinges are fixed. So's the roof." He thumbed toward the door. "Got us some breakfast from my place."

"So, that's where the food came from," she said, under her breath. As she sat, she noticed Nathaniel's horse tied to a tree and grazing in the nearby grass. How strange to have this man in her house, and for the entire night! What if someone saw?

The chair scraped on the wood as he sat down. "I'll just stay long enough to eat." Even the table looked small with Nathaniel sitting at it.

Amelia picked up her fork, staring at the width of his forearms. So much larger than her own. So much larger than her father's.

Nathaniel removed his hat, tossed it onto the rocker, and bowed his head.

Catching the hint, Amelia dropped her fork, folded her hands and closed her eyes.

Nathaniel prayed, thanking God for the food, for His protection the night before, and asked Him for continued protection over Amelia.

It touched her that he would pray for her like that.

"Amen." He took a swig of coffee, then scooped up his fork and dug into the food. "I saw the peaches and thought you might like to save those for later."

Surely, he saw that she had only the food she brought from Mrs. Forester's house. She took a small bite of the eggs, the flavor tantalizing her mouth and empty stomach. The scent of the sausage sent her stomach to squealing.

Nathaniel looked up from his plate.

Amelia's face heated.

He cast her a lopsided grin, and together they chuckled.

"Miss Taylor, keep what little food I brought over this morning. I've no need for it." He took another bite and downed some more coffee.

Savoring the sausage and unable to speak with a mouthful of food, she simply nodded. After swallowing the succulent meat, she said, "Thank you, Mr. Ward. I can't thank you enough for your help last night, and now this morning." She would have just had peaches for breakfast, wanting to save what was left of the potatoes for an evening meal. A shame she lost the beans.

Before she knew it, Mr. Ward finished his food, shoveling the last bite into his mouth as he got up. Surely, he was in a hurry to remove himself from this compromising situation. She ought to feel the same, but the company was wonderful. She'd never had a visitor other than Violet, and then the preacher when they first moved to town. Her father had made it loud and clear that the preacher wasn't welcome. They'd see each other at the church house and that was enough for him.

Nathaniel scooped up his hat and thumped it onto

his head.

"Good day, Miss Taylor." His blue eyes held hers for a moment more, and then he turned to leave. The door closed behind him with a sound click.

The small house felt empty without the large presence of Mr. Ward. For some reason, Amelia wanted to weep into her plate. But the food was so good, and so filling, she forgot decorum and shoveled the rest into her mouth before it got cold, chewing and savoring the delicious flavors, the coffee warming her from head to toe.

As she sat alone in the now warm house, she noticed a tall stack of wood by the fireplace, a bag of flour and sugar on the high cupboard next to the small cupboard, a bag of coffee beans, some spices and flavorings, which surprised her because those could be pricy, and to her delight a loaf of bread wrapped in paper from Mr. Percy's dry goods store.

Amelia watched through the window as Mr. Ward sauntered to his horse. He stroked the animal's nose and offered the beast a small treat from his hand. Nathaniel didn't seem to be in as much of a hurry to leave now that he was away from her. He mounted and ambled away, looking over his shoulder at the house.

She rushed to the front, swung open the door and was greeted with an even higher stack of wood next to the porch. As she watched him go, their eyes met as he turned around for one last look.

Amelia lifted a tentative hand and waved. Whispering under her breath, she said, "Thank You Lord for people like Mr. Ward."

Nathaniel hated to leave Amelia alone again. He'd already made one major trip to buy some food to put on her shelves while she slept. He couldn't believe she only had what she was carrying with her the day before. Where was her father? He should have thought to ask. It seemed all the excitement from the night got his mind in a tangle. Seemed whenever he was around the woman his mind was in a tangle. He ran his hand down his face. The night had been long. When he'd heard that cackle through the woods, he instantly knew it was Jeb. The man had already proven to be addled in the head. What made him think he could get away with this? Then Nathaniel remembered Amelia saying Jeb knew her father was gone. How often did her father disappear? And where did the man go, leaving his daughter alone? What made the man think his daughter would be safe left alone in a cottage in the woods? Unbelievable.

He wanted to take care of her, but he had to be careful. He feared ruining her reputation, especially after spending the entire night in her cabin. If Jeb was still nearby, which he believed was likely the case, the man could spread gossip and rumors about Amelia. He had to find a way to keep Jeb away from her. He'd been up all night chopping wood, anything to keep himself awake, and since Amelia needed the kindling, it kept him busy. Once there was a hint of light in the sky, he got on the roof. He was careful to hammer lightly so as not to wake Amelia.

Nathaniel got what he needed at the bank and then went up to Mr. Lawson's place to take care of business. Upon his return, he went through the forest, avoiding the roads, to check out the woods near and around Amelia's place. He could set some traps to keep Jeb from getting too close to the house, but then what if Amelia got caught in them? As he moved deeper into the woods, the sounds of a river carried to him.

Birds whistled and twittered above, and a gentle breeze floated through the trees. As he broke through a small clearing, the rush of a river greeted him, along with a beautiful dove perched on a large boulder.

Amelia.

She sat above the sparkling water with a notepad in her hands, scribbling something on the page. Soon, she looked out over the water, taking in the sun.

What was she writing? Or was she drawing? Curious, he moved in closer, careful to keep enough distance so she wouldn't see him. He feared he'd frighten her, and she'd had enough of that in the last several hours. It was good to see her out of the cabin. Although, he would keep a wary eye out for Jeb.

As he moved in closer, he saw lines on the pad of paper. So she was writing. Hmm. He wondered what she could be writing about? Was it a journal?

She picked up a book next to her and opened it on her lap. Looked like a Bible. She read a while then flipped to the next page. Soon after, she set the Bible down and jotted something on her notepad.

It looked like she was taking notes from her Bible, which made her lovely form that much more beautiful to Nathaniel. A woman with a heart for God.

Slowly, he backed away, carefully easing himself from her view. He steered his horse into the trees, praying that what he just witnessed, the angel floating above the water, was a shadow of things to come.

It had been a disturbing week for Amelia, and already it was time for the box social. Normally, she would have despised the boredom with little to do and no job to be had, but after the terrifying evening of last week, she'd had enough excitement to last a lifetime. She'd contemplated staying inside until her father returned, but she knew that wasn't a good idea, so finally she'd ventured to her favorite rock near the river, praying for God to protect her the entire way there. The bright sun and comfort from the scriptures gave her courage, and she was able to enjoy being outdoors again. She also felt a bit safer knowing Mr. Ward was nearby. She knew he checked up on her on occasion, and it made her warm inside. She only hoped it wasn't a burden to him.

Now, she rode with Mrs. Forester in one of her lovely carriages. The appetizing aroma of the food wafted on the air. Amelia smoothed out the lavender fabric and straightened the ribbons on her decorated box, wishing her dull blue dress could look as beautiful. Lillian Forester helped her prepare the succulent meal, not to mention, provided the food for each dish. Amelia looked forward to eating the meat and pastries, but she didn't look forward to the company she'd have to keep while doing said act. She reminded herself that it was for the orphanage, which made it easier, especially thinking about the scripture Mr. Ward told her about.

The buggy entered a clearing where they were to have their picnic. A long table and a large, white tent greeted them, contrasting with the green grasses of the field. Several people were already gathered, and children played with a ball away from the boxes already lining the table.

The carriage came to a stop behind the tent and Mr. Forbs was there to greet them with one of his bright, warm smiles. "Welcome, welcome!" he said and helped Mrs. Forester and Amelia out of the carriage. "You're the last ones to arrive."

His wife bustled about the long table, arranging the boxes in an organized color-coded fashion. Amelia rushed to the table to deposit her box, keeping it under a towel so no one could see it.

Mrs. Forbs took Amelia's meal and placed it with two other purple boxes. The others didn't have lavender and white flowers, only hers, which made her cringe. If Jeb remembered the fabric, he might try to buy it.

"It's a perfect day for a picnic," Mrs. Forbs said, moving Amelia's box neatly into position, turning it until it looked just right. "As you can see, we have plenty of meals for the auction today, and the men are ready to fill their bellies, I'm sure. So, before things get cold ...." She faced the field where children played and men waited, and rang the cowbell, lifting it high for everyone to hear. "Let the auction begin! Hot meals are waiting and ready!"

The children clamored close, excited chatter filling

the tent as they pressed to get a peek at the decorated boxes.

Betty McGillis and Georgina stood off to the side in their bustled gowns, their eyes riveted and then coyly looking away from Mr. Ward, although his back was turned to them. Amelia always felt a bit lighter on her feet when she saw him, and seeing him now, all dressed up in his waistcoat and trousers, she could understand why Betty and Georgina couldn't take their eyes off of him. It brought memories of the time he left her cabin so abruptly that one dreadful, and oh-so-wonderful, morning. She admired Mr. Ward as his gaze casually drifted over the colorful boxes on the table.

Violet grabbed Amelia's arm, pulling her out of her reverie. "I'm so glad you're here!" She hugged Amelia, moving in close. "I wasn't sure you'd come because of ... well, you know."

Amelia blushed. "Mrs. Forester made it possible."

"I'm so glad!" Violet said, releasing her friend. "Mine is the yellow box there in the center."

Amelia spotted the sunny box. She grabbed Violet's hand. How she missed her friend. "It seems an age since I've seen you."

"I know, I know." Violet shook her head with a wide smile beaming from her eyes. "I've been busy."

Amelia took a deep breath. "Violet, I must speak to you about," she leaned closer so only Violet could hear, "about Jeb. There are some things you need to know."

Violet straightened, her lips pinched. "I know you don't like him." She pulled away from Amelia. "I think you're jealous."

"What?"

"You've always played hard-to-get with him and his brother, lifting your nose every time he comes around. Well, now you're simply paying for your rejection of him, and he's courting me."

"Violet, how dare you say such a thing." Amelia's voice rose, and they looked anxiously toward the crowd.

Miss Bruster eyed Amelia and shook her head in that condescending way of hers.

Clearing her throat, Amelia straightened, suddenly cold from the rigid stance of Violet next to her. If only she could pull her friend aside and tell what happened that horrid evening. Not giving up, she leaned toward her, eyes still on the crowd as Mrs. Forbs walked to the front of the table. "There's something I must tell you."

"Mother approves of the match," Violet snapped, keeping her gaze on the table as the crowd continued to chatter around them.

"Well, that doesn't mean much." Amelia half chuckled. "Look at the man she married."

Violet turned on Amelia. "My father is a good man," she said, between clenched teeth. "Shame on you!" Tears flooded Violet's eyes. "You're always outspoken, so I thought I could be the same with you. Now you're going to allow your jealousy to ruin our friendship."

Amelia's throat burned. "I only want to help," she said, just loud enough for her friend to hear, and barely able to get the words out.

The voices in the crowd settled down, and the children running around were reigned in by their parents or a nearby adult.

"Ladies and gentlemen, welcome to our annual box social! Many of you already know the rules, but I'd like to go over them again. The men are to bid on a lady's box," Mrs. Forbs motioned to the colorful packages on the table decorated with fabric, ribbon and colored paper, "with the anticipation of a meal with the lady who brought the box. The question is," Mrs. Forbs raised her brow in a suggestive manner, "which box belongs to your lady?"

The men whistled, some so shrill it hurt Amelia's ears, and some danced a short jig. She spotted Sam slapping Jeb on the back.

Laughing, Mrs. Forbs motioned for the men to settle down and shouted, "Remember, all funds raised during this event will go to the Olive Tree Orphan Asylum in Denver. Please remember the orphans as you place your bid."

The bidding began, husbands voting for their wives' boxes, and men voting for their sweethearts' boxes, until all that remained were Amelia and Violet's box and one other.

Mrs. Forbs lifted Amelia's box high into the air.

Mr. Forbs shouted, "Let the bidding begin at one dollar. Who bids a dollar and a half?"

Jeb raised his hand. "I bid a dollar and a quarter."

"Dollar and a quarter it is. Dollar, dollar, who bids a dollar and a half?"

"Two dollars," a firm baritone voice carried from

the other side of the tent. It was the first Mr. Ward bid on anything.

Amelia swallowed, feeling exposed with Jeb's sneer and Violet's shocked expression.

"Two dollars! Two dollars it is, do I hear two and a quarter? Two and a quarter."

Jeb raised his hand.

"Two and a quarter it is. Do I hear two and a half? Two and a half, two and a half."

"Three dollars," Mr. Ward said, his thumbs in his belt loops.

Jeb's head jerked in Nathaniel's direction as Violet tried to get Jeb's attention, motioning to her box still on the table. "Five dollars!" Jeb shouted, his chin thrust at Mr. Ward.

Mr. Forbs continued on with his auctioning tone.

"Ten dollars," Nathaniel said, not even looking at Jeb but focusing on the box in Mrs. Forbs' hands.

After that, Jeb waved the box away as if he didn't want it.

"Ten dollars! Ten dollars it is! Sold!" And the gavel came down on the table.

Mr. Ward went to Mr. Forbs, paid him the cash, and took the box. He then walked over to Amelia, who stood frozen in place. Wasn't this man tired of her? Jeb followed right behind him.

Violet rushed over to Jeb. "Why were you voting for her box?"

"I thought that one was yours." Jeb turned toward Violet, chest puffed out defensively.

She hit him on the arm. "I told you mine was yellow."

"Oh." He shrugged. "I thought you said lavender. You know, like your name."

"That one's mine!" Violet grabbed Jeb's arm and tugged him to face the table. "There, the yellow one in Mrs. Forbs' hands!" She clapped and jumped up and down, and the bidding began.

Nathaniel stood before Amelia with the box. Funny how it looked so small in his strong hands, while it felt so large in her own. "Shall we eat?" he said.

She nodded. Nathaniel led them to a shaded area under a tree. He took off his coat, spread it on the ground and motioned for Amelia to sit.

"Why did you pay so much for my box?" Amelia finally asked as she got comfortable on his warm coat.

"Well, it's for the orphanage, isn't it?" He sat down next to her. "It's a good cause."

"Oh." Amelia nodded, realizing that it wasn't because it was her box that he made such a high bid. "But you didn't bid for the others." She said the words only at that moment realizing what they might imply.

"I recognized it from your house." He led them in a prayer of thanks, praying also for the children in the orphanage. When done, he opened up the box and took a big whiff. "Delicious!" He handed her a chicken leg and pulled out the other for himself.

Amelia took a deep breath. She had to be honest with the poor man. "Mr. Ward, I appreciate all that you've done for me, please know that. I'm beyond grateful for everything. But I need to tell you something."

He stopped mid-bite and looked at her.

"I don't plan on marrying." The words were so shocking, even to herself, but she had to say it. "I realize this is just a box social," she motioned to the couples around them, spotting Jeb and Violet across the grass, "but things like this tend to lead to ... more."

Nathaniel chuckled, then his chuckle built into a laugh, and his wonderful baritone voice sent a warm tingle down her arms and back. He finally gathered himself, pulling up a knee, and leaned his elbow on it as he took a bite of his chicken. He lifted it and said, "This is good." And took another bite.

Amelia didn't know what to make of his glee. "Are you laughing at me, Mr. Ward?" She gathered her skirt and rose to her knees. "Because I'm serious. Dead serious, I might add."

Nathaniel touched her arm, he didn't grab it like she expected, he simply lay his fingers on her elbow, and the soft gesture brought her back down to a sitting position. "I know you're serious, Miss Taylor. I wasn't laughing at you. Let's just say, it was a laugh of relief, relief at what an honest, forthcoming woman you are."

Amelia shifted on his coat. "Well, I suppose you're used to women clamoring after your money." She waved her hand in the direction of Betty and Georgina. "After all, it's quite clear you are wealthy, Mr. Ward. Everyone can see it, and no one paid higher than three dollars for one of those boxes. To pay ten is just ... unheard of."

"Anything to help the children." He took another

bite from his chicken. Again, he said, "This is really good."

Amelia smiled, happy to move on to a new subject. "Well, Lillian is the one to thank. She made the chicken, while I made the desserts."

He raised his brows in what she assumed was surprise. "I'm really looking forward to the sweets then." He winked at her.

Her mouth gaped at the daring gesture. Finally, she shook her head at him and chuckled. "Shame on you, Mr. Ward."

"I just happen to like dessert, lots of dessert."

Settling down and feeling more comfortable, she said, "Well, I think it's a good thing to support the orphans. Thank you for doing that." She chewed on her food and enjoyed the succulent flavors.

"I know what it's like to have nothing."

"Dare I ask what it was like living on the streets?"

He licked his fingers. "Cold and lonely," came his reply and he took another bite.

She sighed. "I'm sorry." She wiped her mouth with a napkin, recalling the one boy she'd helped so long ago. Ever since that experience, she tried to help other boys or girls. But her efforts were never as successful as that one moment in time. Such a grand experience. She'd never realized how wonderful it could feel to do something good for others. And to give away everything she had, that was spectacular. She smiled at the memory.

But immediately her smile faded. It was also during that time she lost something most precious to her. A small reticule her mother had made. She never saw it again since that day. How she cried when it was lost. The more she cried, the more irritated her father got. She'd never forget the day she lost it. It was the same day she'd given the boy all her money ....

Amelia was doomed. With each trod of the horses hooves and bump of the carriage, her world crumbled. Father had been looking for her when she chased after that boy. Not only would Father whip her when they got home, he'd tell Winnie what happened. Thankfully, Father didn't know about the street boy. That gave her some consolation. She hoped the boy would find something good to spend his money on.

"Enough sniveling." Father shook his head. "Just like your mother."

His words stung. It wasn't a compliment. If only Mama were still alive. She had been gone for two years, which felt like a lifetime. Amelia dried her eyes and, taking a deep shaky breath, reached to squeeze her purse for comfort. After all, Mama had made it for her, and it was one of the few special mementos Amelia had left.

It wasn't on her lap. She felt beneath her skirt. It wasn't there either. Perhaps Father was sitting on it? Or maybe it fell when Father yanked the parasol out of her grasp? Maybe it was in the back of the wagon?

As the driver reined in before the stately house on the elite Pennsylvania Avenue, the wagon lurched to a stop.

Father stepped off the buckboard.

No purse on his seat. Nor was it clinging to his

backside. She looked on her seat and on the ground.

Nothing.

"What is it?" Father asked as he helped her down.

"I can't find my reticule."

"Well, it's no wonder. You wander off like that, then someone stole it."

Amelia stood on her tiptoes to look inside the wagon near her parasol.

Father grabbed the umbrella and handed it to her. She looked inside of it. No purse. She closed it and shook it out. Nothing. She squeezed the wood of the wagon. Splinters dug into her fingers and her knuckles turned white. It couldn't be gone. It couldn't be.

"Father, may we go back to the restaurant?" she asked, desperate. "Maybe it fell on the sidewalk?"

"We're not going back." Father exhaled. "If you dropped it, which I highly doubt, someone has taken it by now."

"It wasn't stolen," she whispered. She knew it wasn't stolen. Why would someone take an empty purse? Unless someone didn't know it was empty. But she had it in her hand the entire time. She would have noticed if someone had snatched it. She'd embroidered her name inside so if it ever got lost the person who found it might return it. But now she doubted anyone would take the time to return a little girl's reticule.

"Come, Amelia girl." Father's voice softened as he motioned her toward the front door. "We'll get you another one."

She wanted to tell him she didn't want another

one, but she didn't dare mention Mama. He always became angry when she brought up Mama. She trudged up the steps to the wide porch and shuffled into the house.

"Hurry it up, girl. We don't have all day." Father walked inside as the butler held open the door.

The familiar scents of pipe tobacco and cedar wafted over her as she entered her home with the burgundy curtains and low-hanging chandelier. "Thank you, Henry." Amelia tried to smile up at the silver-haired butler, but it was no use.

"You won't be whipped," Father said as he handed the maid his hat and gloves. Henry helped him out of his coat. "You're confined to your room."

"Yes, Father." Amelia's voice choked, not because she was confined, but because her precious reticule was gone. She'd never see it again. Never again hold the fabric that her mother so lovingly picked out and sewed for her. *Dear God, please bring it back to me.*

"No need to cry about it." Father faced her as another maid handed him a cigar and stood ready with the light.

"Yes, sir." Amelia lifted her chin, trying to keep it from trembling. *Didn't he know that purse had come from Mama?*

Father motioned up the stairs. "Off with you now."

Henry took her coat, and she made her way up the stairs, staring at the burgundy runner lining each wooden step. How could she have lost such a precious gift?

"What's wrong?" Nathaniel's voice broke into her

thoughts and brought her back to the present, children playing in the distance while other couples sat or walked through the field.

"Nothing." She shrugged. "Just remembering something that happened when I was young."

"Want to share?"

She shook her head, brushing a stray lock from her nose, feeling silly for allowing herself to get caught up in bad memories when she should be enjoying the day.

He studied her, his blue eyes searching her face.

Her cheeks warmed, as if he touched her, tracing over her chin, her mouth. His intense stare drew her in, tempted her, whispered to her with the tantalizing smell of lavender and pine. She must … she must break the spell he had over her. She tore her gaze from his and forced her attention to a flying ball in the distance. "Let's go play with the children." With that, she leaped to her feet and ran.

For her life.

Sandi Rog

Chapter Seven

Nathaniel watched Amelia run, her heels kicking up her dress behind her—much like the day they met. A simple blue dress with no bustle to hinder her. So free and alive compared to the other women who wore bonnets, bustles and carried parasols.

As the birds twittered above in the trees, Nathaniel watched her run with the children, catch the ball and throw it back, laughing with delight. A slow grin lifted the corners of his lips. When she made her declaration of becoming a spinster, he knew she was the woman for him. Never in his life did he expect to hear that from her, or from any woman. And it was clear she still had the thoughtful heart he remembered from so long ago. For none of the other women, or men, dared to run through the field with the children for all to see. He thought Amelia's friend … what was her name? Violet. He thought she would have joined her, since she also wasn't dressed as pristine as the other women, but her attention was on Jeb, who kept glancing over at Amelia. It made Nathaniel grit his teeth, fists itching to take him down. But his moment would come, and he'd wait for it. Now was the time to enjoy being with his Amelia. Yes, his Amelia.

Now to woo her. What could he do to convince her to marry him? He could tell her who he was—the boy she met on the streets and gave money to so long ago. No. If he did that, she'd think he was a stalker. He chuckled to himself. In essence he was, he couldn't deny that fact. Besides, just because he revealed who he was didn't mean she'd want to marry him. Perhaps she didn't even remember that moment in time. So, no. That idea wouldn't do. He snatched two of the little cakes she made for him and got to his feet, strolling toward the playing children. The sweet, sugary snack melted in his mouth. He brought the other one for Amelia, but he really didn't want to share. Boy, those cakes were good. Yes, he liked dessert. Especially when made by Amelia. The ball sailed toward him, and he snatched it out of the air with his free hand. The children clamored around his legs, and he laughed. He tossed the ball to the other end of the field and the children ran, giving him a moment with Amelia.

She laughed as they raced away, throwing her head back. "I could never throw the ball that far!" she shouted.

He sidled next to her and lifted one of the cakes near her lips. "Want one?"

Flushed from the exertion of her play, she nodded and snatched it from his fingers and took a bite.

"They're good. What do you call them?" he asked.

"Oh these?" She studied the half-eaten cake in her slender fingers. "Well, they came about by accident. I intended to make a cake, and half the dough was spilled by my clumsiness—I'm really not a good cook," she added as a firm aside. "So, I thought I'd try making mini cakes by cutting them up like this."

Eyeing her as she looked away—her chin lifted and the wind blowing strands of hair across her rosy cheeks—he knew she mentioned her poor cooking abilities to disparage her eligibility as a wife. Little did she know, cooking for him wouldn't be necessary. The children neared, and she ran to them, leaving him by himself. She caught the ball and kicked it away from Nathaniel. She and the children ran in that direction.

"She's a hard one to catch." The familiar voice of Preacher Forbs carried over Nathaniel's shoulder.

He turned to face the man.

"Jeb and Sam had set their caps on the girl, and she rejected them both. Poor boys." He motioned toward Jeb and Violet behind him. "But there are plenty of girls to be had."

Nathaniel turned to look back at Amelia. She was too good for those men. But what made him think she wasn't too good for him? What'd Nathaniel have to offer that those men didn't—other than wealth? He wanted to give her more, not just money and fancy clothes. He pushed his hat back on his head as he watched her run, the wind catching her long, golden brown hair.

"She's got some growin' up to do, that one." Mr. Forbs stepped closer to Nathaniel. "Keeps her nose in those cheap books. And what's worse, she reads them to the children." He shook his head in disapproval. "Violet's little sisters, no less."

Nathaniel had sensed the censure from some toward Amelia, but to Nathaniel, that was probably a good sign. It meant she didn't conform to the mold. Too often he found little he liked about those who did, those who lived up to society's rules, and left God behind: a starving child on the streets, a hungry boy stretching out empty hands, refusal to let a street rat do some work just because he had no shoes. "Why do you think that is, Mr. Forbs? Why do you think she reads those books?"

"There's no tellin'. Nothin' else to do, perhaps." He grabbed his lapels and puffed up his chest. "Nothin' worse than puttin' foolish ideas into the starry-eyed heads of those little girls, givin' them false ideas, false hopes for a handsome prince to rescue them from poverty when they should have their minds set on a decent, hard-working dependable future."

Nathaniel kept his observations to himself. He used to read Yellow Backs, and he knew what was in them. Nothing sinful. Just adventure, and yes, romance, but the kind of romance that wasn't practiced often enough where heroes died for their women daily as Christ taught husbands should do for their wives. Instead, he witnessed men belittling their wives, using them to bear children and slave in their home, while they warmed the beds with prostitutes. It was rare to find a couple that truly loved each other. Rare indeed. Usually the ones in love were those with less money. Funny how that worked, that folks who were poor in material goods were rich in love. Their minds weren't on their wealth, but on each other, struggling to survive and feed the ones they loved. Yellow Backs were a great escape, an escape from reality when one was starving for food, or in Amelia's case … love.

That was it. That's when the revelation hit him. What he had to offer.

Love.

A swelling of emotion nearly exploded from his chest as he stifled a shout. Yes. That's what he had to offer. And most happily.

He would make her feel his love.

Amelia played with the children, the children she'd usually teach to read, the children who had few who paid them any mind. She knew what it felt like to have little attention, so if she could be an encouragement to these little ones, she was happy to do so. Despite this being her motivation for all other occasions, she had to admit in her heart, avoiding Mr. Ward was her greatest incentive at this time. He'd laughed at her honesty and it took her by surprise. She felt certain he might have a secret hope of courting her, especially after all they'd been through together. On the other hand, she wasn't sure if that was his desire at all. Why would he laugh and not express disappointment of some kind? Unless he was sure of himself? But that wasn't it. He didn't act needy like Jeb and Sam.

As Violet said, Mr. Ward was certainly a handsome man, but appearances only ran skin deep, and after years of marriage and being bound to each other, no amount of handsomeness on either part could hold a marriage together—or so she'd witnessed both in her father and mother, and Violet's parents who were absolutely miserable. Yes, they were still together, but they might as well be apart, considering the lack of affection that was shared between them. They hadn't even come to the box social.

She imagined Mr. Ward would tire of her sooner than later, as so many men did with their women. She kicked the ball and the children ran as she caught a glance of Lillian laughing and chatting with the preacher's wife. Amelia thought of the sweet widow's marriage. According to Mrs. Forester it wasn't as bad as the others. If anything, Lillian had been a very happily married woman, and she didn't have her riches to thank for it since she had been happy even during their years of poverty.

Amelia ran to fetch the ball out of the trees. Well, perhaps some marriages were happy, but in Amelia's book, too few were, and she'd rather not risk a lifetime of endless misery. She'd be content to enjoy the happily-ever-afters in her dime novels.

In the end, she was grateful, oh so grateful to Mrs. Forester for making today possible. Without the sweet widow, Amelia would have had nothing to do but stay in her dingy house. On Monday, she would resume her search for work. She only had one place left to try, and that was the local hotel. Surely, they could use a maid.

Amelia was right, the hotel did need a maid as the previous one took a leave of absence. No one knew why the previous woman had been so sick, but the other maid's loss was Amelia's gain.

Grateful.

That's all Amelia could think as she scrubbed the porcelain sink in the hotel room on the third floor. Grateful to have work. Grateful to have money. She patted her pocket holding the wages she'd collected that morning after having worked with the hotel for four weeks. She got a weekly salary and to her delight, she'd built up some savings. Perhaps she could be on her own and moved out before her father returned, then she could at least hide from his wrath.

Drying the pitcher with a towel, she smiled at the shimmering porcelain vase. It'd been years since she had the joy of seeing such fine things. Too bad she couldn't experience the approval from a customer for her job well done, but the satisfaction she felt for bringing out a shine on the bowl was more than she thought possible. And the money in her pocket made her sing.

There were so many rooms. So many rooms. Either containing a brass bed or a wooden frame with intricate carvings, each with its own porcelain pitcher set on a stately commode, and some even had a fine bathroom with a sink and tub. The hotel's elegance reminded her of the fine things of luxury she used to enjoy as a child. Sometimes, she liked to pretend she was someone's wife while making each bed, tidying each room, and scrubbing each commode. She'd immediately shake off the thoughts with a flick of her towel, reminding herself that a life of solitude was much safer than catering to an ungrateful tyrant.

She pulled back the curtains and gazed down on Main Street. Dust carried up from a horse-drawn buggy, bringing to mind her ride to the box social. To think, Mr. Ward had stayed in this very hotel. She wondered which room had been his. She'd caught a glimpse of him every so often, riding to his cabin along their shared road or talking to Betty McGillis and Georgina, listening to their numerous tales and taking up their mothers' invitations for lunch. Their traps were set, and the decoys placed. Which one would be so lucky to snag the oh-so-handsome Mr. Ward? Once he took the bait, would he be satisfied with the pretentious smiles of his new wife? Even Violet had batted her eyelashes at the man, despite the fact that Jeb was supposedly her beau. Amelia tied the curtain back with a jerk. What did it matter anyway? She wasn't interested in the man, and the last thing she wanted in this life was marriage.

Stomping to the other side of the room, she grabbed her bucket and tossed in the wet towels. Her hands were raw and calloused from the soaps and rags and all the cleaning she had to do, and she wondered if they'd ever get used to the work as the few blisters she still had stung. In fact, the sores made her think of Violet's mother's hands after doing all the laundry and hanging it on the line. Her mother's hands didn't look blistered, but calloused and often red. Her weary smile and drooping face filled Amelia's mind. She shuddered at the thought that Violet might end up in a similar situation with Jeb. And what of Violet? She avoided Amelia like the plague, and Jeb continued to pick her up from work, leaving Amelia without her friend.

Perhaps having a job like this, scrubbing day in and day out, wasn't much different than being a wife, but one good thing happened every day. She got to go home to peace and leave the work behind. Although, going home also meant preparing dinner, cleaning the house, and doing the laundry. Perhaps working for a living wasn't much better, or maybe even worse, than taking care of a home. But at least she didn't have an angry husband to answer to.

Amelia left the hotel, her pocket full of money, and started for home. As she walked by Mrs. Nebel's sewing shop, she came upon Jeb and Violet walking ahead of her and not toward Violet's home. They were in deep conversation and between the muffled sounds Amelia captured "baby" and "not mine" bursting from Jeb's vehement mouth.

Amelia gasped and the two turned around. Jeb seized Violet by the arm and spewed words into her face, "Not mine!" He released her from his grip, practically throwing her away from him, and stormed off down the boardwalk.

Amelia stood frozen as she watched bewilderment flood her friend's desperate expression.

"Violet?" Amelia moved toward her. "What's wrong? What happened?" Even as she asked the questions, she had a sick feeling that she likely already knew the answer. Surely, Violet had not given herself to that monster? Surely, she had more sense than to do such a thing outside of marriage?

However, the shame reflecting on Violet's face spoke volumes. "We were supposed to get married." Violet took in a shuddering, gulping breath. "He promised!" With that, she cried and bolted passed Amelia.

"Violet! Wait!" Amelia raced after her friend, but Violet was too fast and made it inside the gate to her house, through the door and slammed it behind her, all before Amelia could catch her. Violet's mother looked out from behind her clothesline, the children swarming around in playful banter.

Terrified of giving away this dreadful secret, Amelia ran away from the house before Violet's mother and the children spotted her. She darted around the corner and pressed her back against the wall of one of the shops. Panting, Amelia fought to steady her breaths. What happened to her closest friend? How could this be? What would Violet do? What could she do for her friend? How dare that nasty Jeb! She knew he was no good! Why didn't Violet listen to her warnings?

Eyes welling with tears, Amelia marched home, gripping her pocket to make sure her money was still there and hadn't fallen out.

Her money. That's what she could do. She could help Violet by giving her all her savings.

What was she thinking? Her friend ... surely Violet could not be expecting a baby. It all seemed so unreal. In reality, how long had Jeb been secretly courting Violet? What —

"Miss Amelia." Betty McGillis's voice cut into her thoughts. "Why, you're a working woman now, I hear." Betty sauntered toward Amelia with parasol in hand and Georgina on her arm, the sway of her voice a stark contrast with Amelia's leaping thoughts.

"Why, what's wrong with you?" Betty closed the parasol. "You look like you've just seen a ghost."

"Just heading home." Amelia marched passed Betty.

"Home?" Betty caught up to Amelia's side. "You realize that your 'home' might not be your home much longer."

Amelia kept walking as thoughts rummaged through her mind. What could she do to help Violet? What would Violet's parents do to her? How would her father react? Oh my!

"It doesn't concern you that you soon might be homeless?"

"What are you saying?" Amelia stopped, clenching her fists at her side.

Betty's smile looked all too satisfied beneath the transparent veneer of mock concern. "During an evening meal last night at my house, Mr. Ward informed us that he recently purchased Mr. Lawson's property. He's your landlord, and according to Mr. Lawson your father hasn't kept up with the rent."

Amelia looked away from Betty's satisfied smirk and stared off down the road. Didn't her father keep up on the rent? How could she have known he didn't pay? Was it possible he left for good? Was he ever coming back, especially knowing he was in debt to Mr. Lawson? Shaking her head, she started walking again. This was too much. Too much to take in. Her friend was in dire straights, her father had deserted her, and now she might end up on the streets.

She glanced over her shoulder at Betty and Georgina. Their heads were close together as if conspiring their next evil deed, and thankfully, they didn't follow Amelia as she marched toward home. If Mr. Ward now owned the land, why hadn't he told her? Or asked for the rent? Would her savings be enough to cover the rent? Perhaps he didn't have a chance to ask her for the money, as she hadn't been home during the day now that she was working. Fact was, she hadn't seen much of him since the box social, although he did try to walk her home on occasion. Perhaps her constant refusals and her declaration of not wanting to marry had finally sunk in? That's what she wanted, wasn't it? Of course! She reminded herself of all the men who were cruel, which wasn't difficult. All she had to do was think of her father.

Chapter Eight

Nathaniel kept his distance as he followed Amelia home. The word stalker entered his mind on numerous occasions, but he had to protect her. He'd already caught Jeb more than once in the woods not far from her house. When was that ne'er-do-well father of hers going to return? How could the man leave his daughter behind to fend for herself for so long? He wanted to break the man's self-serving pride. But how?

Nathaniel had already heard tales from others about the man's many trips and leaving Amelia behind. That was one of the reasons he took in more of the conversations from Miss McGillis. She liked to talk a lot. She belittled others to make herself look intelligent or more sophisticated. What she didn't realize was she gave Nathaniel vital information about the horrible state of Amelia's life. He clenched his jaw. He had to find a way to get her out of this place without kidnapping the poor woman and forcing her to be his wife. Although, if push came to shove, he might be willing to do just that.

Today, she was troubled. He could see it in the way she stomped home, striding between trees and thrusting through branches as if they weren't there. What happened? Did Betty and Georgina say something to upset her? That wouldn't surprise him. But she rarely let what the girls say bother her. There seemed to be something else wrong. Something especially disturbing.

The following day, Amelia left work and the heavy clouds in the sky seemed to sit right on her shoulders. As she headed down the street and neared Mrs. Nebel's sewing shop, Violet stood alone, wringing her hands. Amelia stopped by her friend's side.

"He's not coming," Violet said, desperation in her whispered voice.

"I'll walk you home," Amelia murmured.

Violet shook her head. "I'm not ready to go there yet. Jeb used to walk with me up the street a ways so we could have more time together before he took me home."

Amelia shrugged. "We can do the same." She didn't remind her of the fact that they used to do the same together on a daily basis.

And so they walked.

"I suppose you know." Violet eyed Amelia then

her gaze swiftly focused on the boardwalk as their shoes clumped on the wood.

Amelia nodded, her heart sinking with each motion downward. How she prayed it wasn't so, and now she felt cold with the truth spoken out loud.

"We've actually been courting for some time in secret. I didn't want you to know because he said it would trouble you as he felt you had your cap set for him."

"What?" Amelia halted. "You know that's not true."

"He said we didn't have to be so secretive when I told him I thought you were playing coy."

"Absolutely not, Violet." Amelia's chest suddenly felt heavy as they resumed their steps. "I thought you knew me better that this."

"He was so convincing."

"Evidently, in more ways than that."

"Don't do this to me." Violet stopped and stared at her feet. "Please." Tears fell to the ground. "You're all I have. No one else knows."

Amelia took hold of her friend. "Forgive me! I'm so sorry." She hugged her. "I'm just so shocked. So angry." Amelia looked around. The dry goods entrance was just a few feet away and Miss Bruster stood nearby, her gaze darting away from them as she studied the shop window. Amelia guided Violet between the buildings so they could talk in private. "I just can't believe what a lying, conniving scoundrel he is," she whispered between clenched teeth. "I always suspected he was up to no good, but nothing this dreadful."

"I'm so frightened. What's Father going to do to me?"

Amelia didn't know how to answer. Would he force the reprobate to marry her or put her away somewhere? She took a deep breath. "If you ever need a place to go, you can come to my house."

Violet smiled with relief, but the ease quickly left her eyes. "What will I do when your father returns?"

"We'll figure that out when and if that time comes." Amelia took Violet's hand and held it tight. She didn't dare tell her that her father possibly deserted her. She hugged Violet close. How lovely it was to have her friend back, but not so much under such dreadful circumstances. "When will you tell your parents?"

"I don't know." Violet's cheeks went pale. "I can't tell them."

"But you'll have to eventually."

"I can't. I can't think of that right now." She shook her head. "I know when my mother was with child, she didn't show for several months." Violet sank into Amelia's arms, trembling. "With child! Oh, this can't be me. What will I do?"

Amelia held her friend, fearful not just for her reputation, but more so because of the dangers of childbirth. Violet's mother had a strong constitution and bore children just fine, maybe Violet would be the same? But seeing her in such a desperate state forced Amelia to recall her mother. The terrible screams of death during that time she gave birth. No one knew Amelia had hid deep in the closet in her room where the wall butted up against the birthing bed.

Would Violet scream from the pain? Would she cry out for God to take her? Would He then honor that request?

The following day, Amelia worked in the basement by a small window and lamplight. She had just enough light to make sure each sheet and pillow case lay flat without creases, but whether or not they still had stains, that was up to the women next door in the big room with larger windows and more light.

As Amelia folded sheets just outside the laundry room, the voices of her fellow workers carried to her as they echoed off the bare walls.

"How's the new girl comin' along?" one woman asked.

"She's good. Don't got no complaints here. Sure miss Mary though. Any news on her? Is she gettin' better?"

"You haven't heard?" one woman said followed by a gasp.

The shock in the woman's voice caused Amelia to pause, but she picked up her pace, wanting to keep on top of her work.

"Heard she's expectin'," the woman whispered loud enough for all to hear. "And not even married!"

Amelia collected the folded laundry into her arms.

"I'm tellin' you. It was one of them nasty brothers. Sam or Jeb. One of them boys, all right. They're always up to no good. Flattering young ladies, making promises of marriage so they can have their way with them. After that, they move on to the next gal."

Amelia stumbled but caught herself in time.

The women continued their gossiping, but Amelia couldn't bear it any longer. To know her closest friend was a victim of Jeb made the room cave in around her. She lifted the last folded load onto the shelf, untied her apron, signed out, and headed for the door. Thankfully, her day was over.

As she stepped outside, the bright light blinded her. She squinted and saw a man's shadow move to block the sun.

Mr. Ward. She'd recognize his towering form anywhere.

"Allow me to walk you home?"

"Thank you for the offer, Mr. Ward, but I'll go alone today." Mr. Ward stood his ground. Usually he listened when she said no, but this time he didn't turn to stroll off like he so often did. Did he wish to claim his rent?

She hurried away.

As she hastened toward Mrs. Nebel's sewing shop, there was no sign of Violet. Where could she be? She'd hoped to meet her again today. Spotting Mr. Ward following her from the corner of her eye, she picked up her pace and nearly collided with Miss Bruster.

"Oh, pardon me," Amelia said, stopping in her tracks.

"You ought to be ashamed of yourself, young lady. You disgust me!" Miss Bruster turned her back on her and marched away.

Amelia stood frozen, watching her go. "What was

that about?" she whispered. Again, she caught the shadow of Mr. Ward, so she moved along as quickly as she could, but not too fast so as to catch up with Miss Bruster.

What if he wanted his rent? How would she pay for it? She doubted she had enough money, especially if her father was so far behind on his payments. What was she to do? And here she offered for Violet to come live with her when she'd likely be out on the streets in no time. She glanced back, and Mr. Ward strode up easily beside her.

"What's the rush?"

"I can walk alone, thank you." It wasn't the first time she refused to allow him to escort her home, why was he being more persistent this time?

Nathaniel laughed, his booming voice carrying off the side of the buildings and causing Miss Bruster to stop and look at them.

"What do you find so funny?" Amelia faced him, hands on her hips.

"Nothing." Nathaniel lifted his palms. "Nothing at all."

"Then why are you laughing?"

He stared down at her, his blue eyes twinkling. "You're one of a kind, Miss Amelia. One of a kind." He tipped his hat, a teasing grin tugging at the corner of his mouth. "Enjoy your walk." He strode away from her, crossing the street.

Amelia shook her head. Well, at least he didn't ask for the rent. Taking a deep breath, she turned and rushed home, but her mind couldn't escape the terrors Violet would have to face.

Two weeks later and no signs of Violet, Amelia headed home from work.

"Miss Taylor!" a male voice shouted as Amelia neared the sidewalk. She turned to see the postmaster waving her down with an envelope in his hands.

She walked up to his window. Could it be a message from her father?

"This is for you," the postmaster said as he handed her the envelope.

"Thank you."

The postmaster nodded and turned to the counter, busying himself with piles of paper.

Amelia looked at the envelope with her name addressed on the front in neat penmanship. She opened it as she walked down the sidewalk, passing by Mrs. Nebel's sewing shop with no Violet waiting there to greet her. Where could she be? She had to work, didn't she?

As Amelia got the small paper open, she spotted Mr. Ward leading his horse up the street, with Betty and Georgina by his side. Thankfully, he was caught up in conversation with Preacher Forbs and didn't take notice of her. What did that man do all day anyway? Didn't he have a job? And look at the way Betty fawned over him. Leaning so close to him was unseemly. He didn't seem to mind it, especially if he was having so many evening meals at her home.

She shook her head as she unfolded the paper.

Dear Amelia,

I'm sure you've noticed that I've been absent. I don't have much time as I'm being sent away. I told my parents. Mother cried and Father struck me. He was so angry. I'm terrified as they're sending me to a home for unwed mothers in Denver. I'll have no friends. I don't know if I'll ever return. Please don't tell anyone. My parents plan to tell folks I went to live with an aunt. I wonder how convincing that will be considering I was contributing financially to the family. My heart is breaking. I need to end this letter so I can mail it. I want to make sure this reaches you.

I love you, my only friend.

Sincerely,

Violet

Tears filled Amelia's eyes as she reread the heartbreaking words.

Her closest friend. Gone.

Sent away.

Banished.

Amelia folded the letter and stuffed it back in the envelope. What would she do without her? She'd already spent numerous days without her, but there was always a hope they'd be together again. They'd had arguments in the past and worked through them. She knew all would be well with Violet despite her relationship with Jeb. Relationship. It hadn't been any such thing. How horrific! What would become of her friend?

She marched up the street toward home. How could this happen? Why couldn't Violet see the true nature of Jeb from the beginning? Why? And now Violet will be the next topic of gossip at work. How will Amelia endure it when they voice their disgust of her dear, sweet Violet? And what will become of her?

Will she survive childbirth? Who will be there for her to comfort her? Offer her support? Who will be there to put her in her grave? Amelia stifled a sob and tried to shake the thoughts from her mind.

Now she had no one, and now her precious friend had no one. She sniffed back her tears. Who would Amelia share her confidences with? Who would listen to her prattle on and on about the stories she's read? There was no one else who loved her like Violet did.

"Something troubling you?" Nathaniel's smooth, baritone voice swept over her shattered heart. Preacher Forbs, Betty and Georgina gone.

"I'm afraid …" Amelia held the letter to her chest. She couldn't speak.

Nathaniel bent closer to her, the rim of his hat casting her in his shadow. "What's happened?"

"I can't say," Amelia said, her voice broken. She couldn't betray her friend and reveal what the scoundrel Jeb did to her.

"I'll walk you home," he murmured, his tone soothing and compassionate.

Amelia nodded, and they turned to walk. Wiping her eyes with the ends of her sleeves, Amelia spotted Miss Bruster standing in front of the dry goods store, lips pinched with disgust as she eyed Nathaniel. Amelia looked up at him to see if he noticed, but his gaze was forward as he tugged on his horse's reins.

Nathaniel wanted to take Amelia into his arms and carry her away from this town. He gritted his teeth at the thought of her having to work to take care of herself, but the fact that she was willing to do it, and so happily, encouraged Nathaniel and made him worry less. But now what could be bothering her? Something happened, and he intended to find out what.

He'd been so busy watching out for her, protecting her from Jeb who became more and more daring in his efforts to invade her house, it was a bit of a relief when she was confined to the hotel. But his greatest fear was that Jeb might try to harm her while she walked home. So, even when she refused his escort, he followed her from a distance. He'd already had two confrontations with the man, and when Nathaniel told him he owned the property and Jeb was to stay away, the man refused to listen. Not that Nathaniel expected him to adhere to his demands. But the time was drawing near for Jeb to make his move, a big move, and Nathaniel needed to be ready.

Amelia sniffled by his side as they entered the woods, their silence carrying into the light wind and the singing birds. Jack ducked beneath the branches as Nathaniel tugged him along, his hooves crunching on the pinecones. Seemed silly that he purchased a horse when he rarely rode the animal. He spent so much time walking because that's what Amelia did. But he came in handy for quick errands to town. He didn't like leaving Amelia unguarded for too long, and Jack made it possible to get back in good time.

They broke through the trees that bordered her house, and he stood by as she trudged up the wooden steps in silence. Still holding the envelope to her chest, she turned to face him. "Thank you, Mr. Ward. I appreciate your kindness." Her voice was broken, still revealing the distress she felt.

"Good day, Miss Amelia." He tipped his hat and waited for her to go inside.

He'd checked her house just before he came to meet her when she left work, but he knew Jeb could still try something during his absence.

Once the door was closed, he headed in the direction of his own house, but cut back around to peer through one of the windows.

Amelia sat at the table with her head in her hands.

If only she'd talk to him, open up to him. He'd just have to be patient. With that, he dropped Jack's reins and climbed one of the trees. He found it helpful to survey the woods from a higher viewpoint.

From one of the high branches, he spotted Jeb creeping through the woods, dodging from one tree to another, crouching each time he reached a trunk. This time Jeb was so close Nathaniel feared Amelia would hear the commotion when he reached the good-for-nothing.

He climbed down from the tree and mounted Jack. He patted the horse's neck. "Let's go get him."

They galloped over the forest floor, dodging low branches and fallen logs. Jeb hid against a thick trunk, but Nathaniel caught sight of him. He leaped off Jack and tackled Jeb to the ground, holding him down.

"I told you to stay away," he growled between clenched teeth.

Eyes wide and face red, Jeb twisted, trying to knee him.

"Don't fight me." He shoved him deeper into the pine needles poking around his head, his hat off to the side. "Come here again and you'll hang from one of these trees by your ankles. Hear me?" He shook him for emphasis. "All night. For the wolves, coyotes, and mountain lions." He yanked Jeb to his feet and shoved him away. "Git!"

Leaving his hat behind, Jeb stumbled away. Once he got his footing, he ran.

"What happened?"

Amelia's voice prickled down Nathaniel's back. He turned. "Nothing." He grabbed Jack's reins.

Amelia put her fists on her hips. "What do you mean, 'nothing?' Who was that man?" Spotting his hat, she straightened, her eyes wide. "Was that Jeb?"

Nathaniel nodded.

Amelia swallowed visibly. "What was he doing here?"

"Can't say. But he's gone now."

Amelia hugged herself, her petite form looking all the more delightful and vulnerable. She bit her lip, and he saw a hint of wariness in her eyes. She knew something was wrong, especially because it involved Jeb.

"Well, I'm not quite sure what to thank you for, but something tells me I owe you my gratitude. Again."

"You're welcome, Miss Amelia." He tipped his hat.

She turned and hurried back to her house, still hugging herself. As soon as she was inside, he strode toward his house.

Tonight, there'd be no sleeping at home.

Sandi Rog

Chapter Nine

That night, Nathaniel lay on a thick bed of pinecones with his back against a tree and his eye on Amelia's house. As soon as she doused the light, he sat up and rested his elbows on his knees. Funny how this brought back memories. He'd spent several nights outdoors, sleeping under the stars or sandwiched between two brick buildings or in a narrow stairwell. Constantly wondering where his next meal would be. Only this time, his stomach didn't grumble or feel like it was clinging to his spine, but having his senses on high alert was the same. Every sound made his gaze flicker to the slight noise. A flutter of a bird's wings, the scurrying of a chipmunk or a squirrel, the hoot of an owl, the heavy scent of pine cloaking the air, and Jack's grazing on the forest grasses several feet away.

Thankfully, no signs of danger.

Yet.

He wished he didn't have to hide out so close to Amelia's home because that meant Jeb would get too close for comfort. But the only way to catch him was to take cover near the house. He didn't want to risk missing the rat if he camped too far away.

Moonlight glimmered between the thick trees, the dense forest he now owned. What use was it? He supposed the many trees would provide timber for lumber companies. He could clear out several acres. Or he could use it to build more homes in town. Green Pines might appreciate that … or not. The only reason he purchased the land was to gain Amelia. As if he was purchasing her. He shook his head. It'd be best not to tell her that.

A twig snapped. The hairs on Nathaniel's arms stood on end. Slowly, he got to his feet, his hand resting on his pistol.

A crunch of pinecones.

A whisper on the air.

Low voices echoed between the tall trees. There was more than one. How would he take them all down? Knowing Amelia's life could be at stake would do it. He'd take down the entire town if they were headed this way.

The steps and whispers neared.

After making herself ready for bed, Amelia finished tidying up and reluctantly went to douse the lamp. She never liked being in the dark, especially when she felt so alone, but the light and warmth from the hearth would help. The emptiness of the small house was suffocating. The forest seemed eerily quiet this evening, and she didn't dare peer through the window curtains for fear she might see a strange shadow. My, how her imagination got the best of her, but ever since that awful night with the wild screams carrying through the forest, she couldn't help but worry that Jeb might be lurking outside her house. Every night was the same, and this time weariness from the hard day at work and Violet's horrible fate completely wore her down. Perhaps she'd finally get some rest, which was what she desperately needed.

She slipped beneath the covers, and just as she began to lose herself in a deep, comforting sleep, a sleep to escape the worries of life, gunshots ricocheted through the woods, jolting her upright. Her ears rang. That was close. It had to be right next to her window. She leapt out of bed and in the dark, groped for her father's rifle.

Falling into the rocking chair, she aimed the rifle at the door.

Scuffles echoed through the quiet night just outside the kitchen window. She jerked the rifle in that direction, hands trembling.

"Sam!" Jeb shouted outside, but his voice was quickly muffled.

That scoundrel! What was he doing here in the middle of the night?

She dropped the rifle and ran to the window. Two men cloaked in shadows moved around each other in the darkness, the moon casting shards of light on fists, shoulders and fallen hats. The larger man moved like

Nathaniel, but where was Sam?

Another shot fired, partially shattering the window above Amelia's head and sending needle-like pain onto her temple. She ducked from the window and dove for the floor. More shots fired.

Was Nathaniel getting shot? Was that Sam?

Cowering on the floor, she felt tiny shards of glass against her temple. Blood trickled down her cheek as she tried to pick them out, plucking them with her fingernails. Silence filled the night air. Was Nathaniel dead? Was Jeb or Sam coming for her?

Someone slammed against her door and it flew open, crashing into the wall. Nathaniel towered above her, but a shadow stood behind him.

"Look out!" Amelia shouted.

Nathaniel turned, grabbed Sam's wrist as his gun fired into the air. He cracked his knuckles into Sam's face and the man dropped, unconscious.

"You all right?" Nathaniel rushed to Amelia, lifting her off the floor and glancing over his shoulder at Sam's still form.

"Yes," Amelia said, brushing the dust from her nightdress.

Nathaniel pulled away hair from her bloodied cheek with his large fingers. He grabbed a rag from the table and held it against her temple.

"It's nothing," she said. "Just glass. I got it all."

Jaw pulsing, he rushed to Amelia's bed, whisked off the top blanket and draped it over her.

"Be right back." Nathaniel marched toward Sam, lifted and hoisted him over his shoulder, and carried him away.

Amelia slumped into her rocker, closing the blanket tightly around her trembling body.

Nathaniel yanked the last knot of the gag around Sam's mouth. That should do it. Both Sam and Jeb now hung from their feet, each in his own tree behind the house. That should keep them out of trouble. For the time being, anyway.

Now to tend to Amelia. The blood on her face. The blood. He had to get her away from here.

Now.

Enough was enough.

He entered the little house and found her curled up in her rocker, shivering uncontrollably and pale as the moon outside. He lit the nearby lamp and knelt by her. Bracing her head in his hands, he examined her golden-brown hair for fragments of glass.

"Is there any water in the house?" he asked, his tone gentle, controlled, tamping down his rage at her father for neglecting her.

Hand shaking, she pointed to a pot hanging in the hearth.

From the nearby shelf, he grabbed a folded cloth and dipped it in the water. Gently, he cradled her head in his hand, patting the blood from her hair and face. She winced from the movement.

Glass was still lodged in her skin. "You didn't get it all." He angled her head just right for the light to reflect off the tiny crystals glimmering behind bloody strands. One by one, and piece by piece, he plucked them out, dragging them through her hair, pulling the soft strands aside as they caressed his fingers. After what felt like an hour of tedious work, it appeared he'd finally gotten them all.

He grabbed another clean rag, and let her scrub her face.

She patted and gently rubbed up and down, sighing with relief.

"Better?" he asked.

Eyes closed, she nodded as tears glistened on her rosy cheeks. Finally, her color had returned.

Still kneeling, he shifted a little closer and slowly pulled the cloth from her hands, purposely brushing his fingers against hers. With great care, he wiped back the hair from her face with smooth, gentle strokes.

Amelia released a long drawn-out breath.

The door burst open with a crash. "I knew it!"

Nathaniel leaped to his feet, tossing the rag in the stranger's face. He grabbed the rifle and wielded it at the man's chest.

"How dare you!" the older man said, ripping off the rag. "What's the meaning of this?"

Nathaniel stared down the barrel of the rifle into the eyes of the man who once refused to help him on the streets when he was young.

Amelia's father.

Nathaniel lowered the rifle and set it against the hearth.

"Papa," Amelia whispered, all color lost in those once rosy cheeks and eyes so wide it was as if the rifle was aimed at her.

Her father's jowls shook in rage as he marched toward her, stopping just short of her chair. "She told me everything!" he shouted, pointing a finger so close to her nose he almost touched it.

Amelia's breathing became visibly rapid as her chest rose and fell, her gaze darting from side to side as if she might find an answer to her obvious confusion somewhere in the room. Then a light dawned on her countenance, and she looked up at him with a guilty expression.

"I'm sorry, but there wasn't any money."

Her father stepped back. "What?" He didn't seem to know what she referred to.

"I tried to catch you, but you were already gone." Amelia waved her hands in supplication. "I didn't have any other choice. I had to find work." Her eyes were pleading.

Mr. Taylor shook his head. "What are you talking about?" Red-faced, he pointed his finger at her again, then at Nathaniel. He swiveled, grabbed the rifle and aimed it at Nathaniel. "Spinster Bruster told me everything! I had her look out for you, and she sent me word, revealing everything you've been up to while I was away!"

Nathaniel raised his hands up to his chest, palms out. "What did she say?" he asked with forced calm. What in the world had gotten into this man? Didn't he realize he left his daughter destitute? Was that not what she was just telling him? And even worse, she acted like it was her fault.

"Get in the wagon!" He shook the rifle toward a wagon sitting outside. The driver leaned against the back of his seat, watching the scene inside the house. He quickly turned and grabbed the reins.

Amelia didn't question her father. She slowly stood, stared at the ground and trudged in her bare feet and blanket toward the door as her father eyed Nathaniel, not taking his eyes, or the rifle, off of him.

"If I may, sir." Nathaniel could have easily wrenched the rifle out of the man's hands, but he didn't want to upset Amelia any more than was necessary, so with as much politeness as he could muster, he said, "May I ask where we're going?"

"We're gonna go see Preacher Forbs, and he's gonna make a gentleman out of you." He lurched toward him with the rifle. "Now, git!"

Nathaniel, more curious now than ever, decided to do what he was told. That's when common sense smacked him upside the head. The only reason they'd need the preacher was if he thought his daughter was with child. His head spun. Had Jeb actually gotten to her? No, no. That didn't make any sense. Nathaniel had been with Amelia—unbeknownst to her—the entire time he'd been in town. No, she was innocent.

Nathaniel climbed into the wagon, leaving Jack behind, tethered on the side of the house, along with two scoundrels hanging in the back. He leaned into his seat, moving in close enough to cover Amelia with some of his warmth, that was, until her father climbed up and squeezed in between them, rifle still aimed and its butt before Amelia's terrified face.

"Get on!" he said to the driver, and the wagon lurched forward. "Amelia girl. You do what I say now. If you don't, this man dies."

Amelia gasped, her face so ashen in the moonlight, he thought she might faint. After everything she had been through, who could blame her? Didn't the fool-of-a-man see that she had blood on her scalp and in her hair? He clenched his fists, resisting the urge to hammer him. But what a great thing to come, if he indeed forced them to marry. Hopefully, the preacher wouldn't talk sense into him.

After they arrived at Preacher Forbs's house, Amelia's father bounded from the wagon and banged on the door. "Open up! We have an emergency!"

The man had no shame.

A sleepy Preacher Forbs finally came, and Mr. Taylor barged in, his back against the door. "Amelia, get in here!" He turned and kept the rifle trained on Nathaniel.

"What? What … is going on?" Mr. Forbs ran a hand down his drooping face, his nightcap falling sideways.

Clearly dazed and terrified, Amelia scurried to do her father's bidding. As she reached the threshold—Nathaniel following close behind—she tripped over her blanket. He caught her around the waist, helping her to her feet.

"Get your hands off my girl!" Mr. Taylor lunged toward Nathaniel with the rifle.

He grabbed and shoved its barrel, and it fired, creating a hole in Preacher Forbs's parlor wall and a ringing in his ears. Nathaniel moved toward him, but he stopped himself just in time.

Wait.

Wait until Amelia was his.

Suddenly, Preacher Forbs was awake, as was his wife. Screaming, she came rushing down the stairs with a lantern in her hands. "What in heaven's name?"

"You need to marry these two fornicators!"

Preacher Forbs looked from Mr. Taylor to Amelia. When his gaze met Nathaniel's he gave the preacher a subtle nod, and that made Forbs move. He snatched up his Bible from a nearby table and began reading a passage.

"Oh, get on with it!" Mr. Taylor shouted. "Get it done!"

Jaw pulsating, Preacher Forbs looked at Nathaniel.

"Do you, Nathaniel Ward," Forbs cleared his throat and scowled at Mr. Taylor, "take Amelia Taylor to be your lawfully wedded wife?"

Amelia's father cocked his rifle and aimed it at Nathaniel.

"I do." Nathaniel straightened against the barrel of the rifle, towering over Mr. Taylor and contemplating what he was going to do to the man as soon as Amelia was his.

Amelia stared at her bare feet, her face ashen and pasty, as if frozen in place. What was the poor woman thinking?

"Do you, Amelia Taylor, take Nathaniel Ward to be your lawfully wedded husband?"

Amelia stood paralyzed.

The preacher cleared his throat. His wife, holding up the lantern, cowered behind him.

Amelia swallowed visibly, darting a glance at her foolish father.

With a snarl, he glared at Nathaniel and pressed closer with his rifle.

Nathaniel waited with bated breath—say yes Amelia—ready to hammer the man.

"Amelia, girl." Mr. Taylor's voice echoed through the quiet house. "You know, I always keep my word."

"I do," she finally said, her voice small and trembling.

"I now pronounce you man and wife." Preacher Forbs slammed his Bible shut and pointed it at Mr. Taylor. "Now get out!"

Nathaniel made a move toward Frank, but Amelia wobbled and swayed, and her legs crumpled beneath her. Nathaniel caught the feather-light angel in his arms.

"Oh, dear!" Mrs. Forbs covered her mouth. "Bring her over here."

Nathaniel lifted the lifeless maiden. Her golden-brown hair draped over his arm as her thin nightdress revealed every curve and burned his hands, despite her cold, sweat-soaked body. As he scanned her face, it looked like death had taken her. He gently laid her on the settee. She sighed. Thank the Lord she was still breathing. Anger scorched through him as his shaking fingers brushed a strand of hair away from her white cheek. "Rest peacefully my wife." Yes, finally my wife. "Your nightmares are over."

With that, he straightened, methodically taking in a slow deep breath, and turned to face Amelia's father. Like an incessantly yapping dog, he still aimed his rifle at him. Nathaniel marched toward him, grabbed the weapon, yanking it easily out of the man's hands, and socked him with the butt of the rifle.

Mr. Taylor dropped to the wooden floor, out cold.

He turned to Preacher Forbs and motioned to the hole in the wall. "I apologize for this. I'll cover the damages."

Mr. and Mrs. Forbs blinked, mouths agape, staring at Nathaniel as if seeing him for the first time. Then they looked down at Mr. Taylor lying on the wooden floor.

"He'll be fine. I'll take him home." He emptied the magazine and the bullets clattered to the wooden planks at his feet. "She's innocent." He motioned with his chin to Amelia.

"We know." Preacher Forbs nodded. "It was her friend, Violet, who is with child. Apparently, Mr. Taylor hired Miss Bruster to spy … er—I mean, look after Amelia, and she sent him telegrams. But it was actually Mrs. Forester who took the young lady under her wing."

"We heard gunshots!" A man burst into the house. He stopped when he saw Mr. Taylor on the floor. "Is everyone all right?"

Preacher Forbs took the man aside. "Everyone is fine. We just had a little incident."

Nathaniel snorted at that. Shaking his head, he turned to take care of Amelia's father. He hoisted him over his shoulder and heaved him into the wagon waiting outside.

"He was supposed to pay me," the driver said, looking aghast at the lifeless Mr. Taylor.

"I'll cover it."

When they arrived at the house, Amelia's father

was still out. Nathaniel carried him in and dropped him onto the larger bed in the back room, his vest and coat wrinkled in the lamplight. He could afford nice clothes for himself, but not for his daughter. Nathaniel wanted to spit.

He marched out of the room and onto the front porch where the driver set Mr. Taylor's trunk. Remembering Jack, Nathaniel strode around to collect his horse. He'd make a nice gift for Preacher Forbs. It was the least he could do for damaging his house and upending his evening. Between the pines, the two men still hung from the heavy branches. He cut them down, and tied them to the front porch, eliciting a shocked response from the driver as he dragged them around. "They were up to no good."

Wide-eyed and nodding, the driver stared at the men sitting next to Mr. Taylor's trunk, tied to a wooden post. Taylor would hear their shouts and wails soon enough.

Now to collect his bride.

Sandi Rog

Chapter Ten

Amelia lay on the hard wooden floor of the cottage, her ears ringing from the shotgun. Steps neared. Black boots.

Her father.

He shouted words she couldn't understand. She couldn't hear him above the ringing.

Finally, the words cleared through the din, as if moving toward her, her father's face inches from hers.

"Amelia! You fool!"

She whimpered.

"Amelia!"

Head still ringing, Amelia tried to move away from his raging words, but couldn't.

"Amelia?" His voice calmed. "Amelia, girl."

Amelia turned away.

"Dear child." The voice suddenly changed. No longer her father.

"Wake up, dear." The owner of the voice patted her cheeks. The hard ground became like pillows beneath her body.

"Amelia, dear. Everything's going to be all right."

She opened her eyes.

Lillian hovered over her, brushing a wet cloth over her forehead. A chill swept over her and she shivered. Where was she? People moved about the lamp-lit room. Footsteps and voices carried off the walls. Slowly, she turned to look. Several people from town were in the room. Not a room. This was Preacher Forbs's parlor. What were they all doing here? The moon barely cast its light through the window, revealing a hole in the wall not far from the simple curtain.

Then she remembered.

Her father. The threats. The shot of the rifle.

Her husband.

And she wept.

What would become of her? Forced upon Mr. Ward. Bound to a man who didn't love her!

"All is well. We all know you're innocent." Lillian motioned to the others. "Mr. Forbs came and got me. Those gunshots woke the entire town."

So … the entire town was there to witness her mortification? How she wanted to crawl under the blankets. Under the settee. Maybe she would? She buried her face in her pillow, and the scent of Mrs. Forbs's perfume nearly suffocated her.

"Do you think you can walk, dear?"

Slowly, Amelia lifted her head from the pillow, and she nodded.

"Try sitting."

Amelia pushed herself up, her matted, bloodied hair clinging to the side of her head.

"You look awful!" Betty's mother sang out. "What happened to you?" She rushed toward Amelia and grabbed her by the shoulders. She'd never before showed her any concern. Why now?

Amelia didn't have the strength to pull away from the probing hands on her arms and shoulders.

Lillian pushed her body between the woman and Amelia. "Control yourself." She spoke in a chastising tone. "Let her be." She waved her hand to shoo her away.

Betty's mother straightened, eyes wide and practically bulging. "Well!" She turned and strode away.

Amelia sighed with relief, and Mrs. Forester patted her on her back. "Feeling dizzy? The sooner we get you out of here, the better. Do you think you can stand?"

The chattering in the room was too much. How could she shut them out? "Must I?" Amelia's voice was a small whisper as she croaked out the words. "Where will I go?" Her eyes filled with tears again.

"I'm taking you to my place, get you cleaned up."

"And then … what?" Amelia whispered, wondering if Mr. Ward would be joining them. She trembled at the thought.

"We'll figure that out later." She pulled Amelia to her feet, holding her steady around her waist.

As she stood, regaining her balance on such wobbly, unreliable legs that worked just fine earlier that day, a hush filled the room. Amelia, trying to catch the blanket as it fell from her shoulders, looked up to see what caused the silence.

Nathaniel stood in the doorway, his hard gaze locked on hers. He strode toward her, jaw pulsing beneath his whiskers, and everyone made a path, clearing his way. As he towered over her, Amelia felt as if she shrank several feet beneath him.

He'd beat her. She was sure of it. As soon as he got her alone, he'd beat her.

He grabbed the blanket and wrapped it securely around her, then without warning, he scooped her into his arms and marched for the door.

Trapped.

Trapped in his bulky arms! Doomed to live with this man for the rest of her life.

"Mr. Ward, if I may ... " Mrs. Forester thankfully stepped forward. To rescue her? Yes, please! "You and Amelia are welcome to stay with me."

Nathaniel stopped and turned to face her. "I have a home."

"Oh, I don't doubt that!" Mrs. Forester laughed, smacking him on his large arm adding a little levity to the situation. "But do you have a bath?" She raised a brow. "A large tub perhaps? So that ...." She looked around with her brows raised high, and the people who had been gawking turned away and began a nervous chatter amongst themselves, and then she continued in a hushed tone, "in order for your new bride to bathe properly?"

"That I don't."

"Then, if it pleases you, you're more than welcome to spend this evening at my house."

Amelia's hopeful heart galloped in her chest, so much so she feared Mr. Ward could feel it. Would he allow it? Please allow it. Please!

Perhaps she could use this as a chance to run away, to escape? Would Mrs. Forester dare assist her in such a feat? But where would she go? She had no home. And her money. All of it was back at the cabin. How would she get to it?

As Mr. Ward carried her into the crisp night air, Amelia was reminded that all she had for clothes were what she now wore, her thin nightdress. Despite her fears, she soaked in the heat from Mr. Ward as he carried her to the wagon. The driver seemed quite intrigued by all the events as he watched them get into their seats. Mr. Ward set Amelia between him and Mrs. Forester, and Amelia shivered from cold, nestling as close to Mrs. Forester as she dared. At last, the carriage lurched forward, and made its way to Lillian's house.

Upon arrival, Mr. Ward helped Amelia out of the carriage as Lillian hurried to open the door. "I have a spare room upstairs," she said to Mr. Ward. "If you don't mind, I'll need your help preparing the bath. There's a large pot in the mudroom, and it needs to be filled with water. Once that's heated we can start preparing her bath. I'll get Amelia settled while you take care of those things for me." Mrs. Forester pointed the way for Mr. Ward as she led Amelia up the wooden stairs. The smells of wood and Lillian's perfume made Amelia feel at home and helped her to relax a little. But only a little. She had to find a way out of this horrible situation.

Once they reached a room, Mrs. Forester lit a lamp next to a large bed. She then swung open the doors to a large armoire, revealing a sparse set of garments. "I'm afraid it's not much, but I'm sure I have a robe in here somewhere. We're going to have to get you some clothes."

Amelia stood just inside the door, trembling. Laying out the robe on the bed, Mrs. Forester looked at Amelia. "You poor thing." She walked over and brought her next to the bed. "Sit a spell." She readjusted Amelia's blanket as Amelia slumped onto the soft bed. "You're cold as ice. Let me get you something warm to drink." She bustled away, leaving Amelia alone on the bed.

What a relief to be away from all those peering eyes. All she wanted was to be left alone. That they would act like they cared for her when really few of them did. Betty McGillis's mother had been awful. How could she suddenly pretend to care? Why would she do such a thing? Thank the good Lord for people like Mrs. Forester. She knew how to be a true mother. Amelia slumped down. If only her mother were here. If only she had a mother to soften the blow of this horrendous situation. But wasn't that what Mrs. Forester was doing? Wasn't she acting just like a mother, bossing Mr. Ward around and taking care of Amelia? She almost giggled at the thought, and she might have if her situation wasn't so dire.

Thank you, Lord. Thank you for Mrs. Forester.

Please help me. Please protect me from Mr. Ward's wrath.

The opening and closing of cupboards carried up the stairs from the kitchen, and soon Mrs. Forester was back. "Drink this. It should help calm your nerves and warm you up a bit till the water's ready."

With trembling hands, Amelia took a sip from the cup. The liquid burned its way down her throat.

Mrs. Forester then grabbed a blanket out of the wardrobe and wrapped it around Amelia over her own. "Why don't you lie down a spell? Once the bath is ready, I'll come for you."

Amelia nodded, her arms and legs suddenly feeling heavy from the drink.

Lillian placed a small blanket over her clean pillow and tucked it beneath Amelia's bloodied head. "You just rest a while."

Amelia lay down, warmth cascading through her body. She lay there as Mrs. Forester stood by the door, shaking her head.

"The good Lord has rescued you, my dear. All will be well. You're in good hands."

Amelia wanted to protest. Sure, she was in good hands with Lillian. But as for her husband? As soon as he had her alone, away from prying eyes and listening ears, she'd be in danger. She shuddered at the thought of Mr. Ward's big hands and the harm they would inflict.

Mrs. Forester closed the door, and Amelia, despite her distress, closed her eyes, losing herself to sleep.

"Come, dear. It's time to get you cleaned up."

Amelia felt Lillian helping her to a sitting position, awakening her from a deep, dreamless sleep. How long had she been lying there?

Lillian pulled the blankets off of her, and guided her down the hall to a washroom with a large, porcelain tub. Steam came up from the water, and Amelia ached to get in. Thankfully, Mr. Ward was nowhere to be seen.

"Now, you get undressed and into the water. I'll come in after a bit and help you wash your hair." With that, Mrs. Forester left Amelia alone in the room.

She slipped out of her nightdress, letting it crumple at her feet, and gingerly stepped into the tub. As she sank deep into the warm, inviting water, she released a long sigh. Never had she experienced such extravagance. Not even when she lived in Denver off of Pennsylvania Avenue. What a blessing. What a luxury. What a comfort to soak her entire body at once. The hot water relaxed every tense muscle.

She sank beneath the water to warm her head and loosen the sticky blood from her hair. It wasn't long before Mrs. Forester returned with soaps and towels. She pulled up a stool and proceeded to wash Amelia's hair.

"You don't have to do this," Amelia said, finally breaking the silence. It felt odd, unnatural to be cared for, and she didn't want to burden Mrs. Forester.

"I'm happy to do it, and besides, I might need to take a comb through some of it. It's matted with blood."

Amelia didn't realize just how bloodied she was until the water gradually changed from a clear, soapy hue, to a pink, rosy color.

"Why that man didn't even notice what was done to you, is beyond me. How could he put you through that? Mr. Ward filled me in on what Jeb and Sam had done." Lillian mumbled as she gently combed through Amelia's knots. "Let me know if I pull too hard."

Eventually, the comb glided through Amelia's hair with ease, only nicking a few cuts along the way, causing Amelia to bleed yet again.

"It'll be good for you to wash your hair again tomorrow. Right now, I want you to get some rest. Mr. Ward went home so you could get some sleep."

Amelia nearly exploded into tears of joy. What a relief to know he was no longer in the house and that this night she wouldn't suffer. Yes. She would actually get some much needed sleep and build up her strength so she could face tomorrow.

Tomorrow. She dared not think of what the morrow would bring.

"Thank you," was all she could muster as Lillian helped her dry off. "I don't know what I would have done without you."

"Oh, my dear. It's all from the Lord." Mrs. Forester cupped her face in her hands. "Thank Him, not me."

That night, Nathaniel kicked off his boots, and fell onto his cot. Distant wails carried through the forest as he lay there. What was Taylor doing right now? Nathaniel knew he was awake as he saw the lamp lit in the cabin on his way home. He put his hands behind his head as he stared at the moonlit ceiling and thanked the good Lord. "I don't know how I would have done it. She never would have married me. Not even to get away from her father." Who would have thought her father would help make it happen. What a night. Despite being grateful for the man handing his daughter over to him without a fight, Nathaniel wanted to make him pay for how he treated Amelia tonight. The man didn't even care that she'd been injured. Didn't he notice the blood in her hair? The line of it on her face? How could a man be so stupid? Especially to his own kin? But ... it shouldn't have been a surprise after everything Nathaniel had seen her endure. It was obvious she was terrified of her own father. He'd never seen Amelia cower in such a way. He was sure the man could have wiped the floor with her ... and she would have allowed it.

"That will change," he said between gritted teeth.

More cries carried through the night air, and Nathaniel imagined Mr. Taylor finding the rascals on his front porch. What was the old man thinking by now? Did it occur to him that Sam and Jeb might have meant harm to his daughter? Did he care? Was he piecing the night's events together and realizing he'd made a mistake? What if he realized his mistake and tried to annul the marriage? Amelia would certainly agree to an annulment.

He sat up in bed. Time to pack. He couldn't risk losing her. He'd have her on the stage to Denver first thing in the morning.

Chapter Eleven

The morning sun filtered through the curtain and Amelia stretched out on the bed. What a restful sleep. She hadn't slept that well in … she couldn't remember how long. Amazing that she could sleep so well after what happened last night.

Last night.

Mr. Ward.

Her husband.

A shiver coursed through her veins and suddenly she was wide awake. She had to find a way of escape. But how? She had no clothes, just her nightdress. She couldn't just walk out the door. Even if she did make it out the door, where would she go? Certainly not home. Plus, she had no money. Her entire savings was at home. She fisted her hands and pressed them

159

against her forehead. Now what?

A quiet knock sounded on the door and it opened. Mrs. Forester came in with a tray of food. "Oh, you're awake. Wonderful. You need to eat." She set the tray down at the foot of the bed. "How did you sleep?"

"Very well, thank you." Amelia scooted up and swung her legs over. Really, she wanted to scream. It didn't matter that she finally got a decent rest. Nothing mattered because her life was ruined.

"What are you doing?" Lillian asked, her hands on her hips.

Amelia shrugged.

"You stay right where you're at. I'm serving you breakfast in bed."

Amelia sat there and stared. She'd never heard of such a thing.

"Come, come." She motioned for Amelia to get back in bed. "Get, get."

"I can't," Amelia said. "I just can't."

"Can't what?"

Can't live this life that was forced on me.

"Sit right here." Lillian fluffed up some pillows.

Amelia pushed herself against the headboard, and Mrs. Forester placed the tray of food on her lap. She breathed in the sweet scent of fresh fruit, warm eggs, and toast. Her stomach growled audibly and her face went hot. She hadn't eaten this much food since Mr. Ward fixed her breakfast.

Shivers coursed up her spine. How could she eat when she was now a married woman?

"I'll get you some tea," Lillian said as she left the room.

Amelia had to find a way to escape. As she nibbled on the delicious food—very strange doing such a thing in bed—she organized her plan. Who knew when Mr. Ward was due to arrive, and she would need to escape before he got there. But ... she needed clothes.

Clearly, the sun had just come up as it peered low in the eastern sky. Not many would be out-and-about quite yet. But how would she get past her father? How would she get her money back? With Father home, there was no way she could sneak into the cabin unnoticed.

Somehow, someway, she had to get her hands on her money. What she would do and where she would go after that, she didn't know. But she had a decent job. Surely, she could continue working, save enough to be on her own.

This was insane. There was no way this would work. Where would she live? Where would she sleep?

Mrs. Forester returned with tea and gently set the dainty cup down on Amelia's tray. The steam wafted over Amelia's trembling heart.

Could she live here? Would Mrs. Forester approve of such a thing?

Heavy footsteps bounded up the stairs.

Mrs. Forester turned to the door, and Amelia's breath caught in her throat at the sight of Nathaniel Ward.

"Get your things. We're leaving."

Amelia dropped her toast. "What? Now?"

"Now, come on. Get dressed."

"What's the hurry?" Lillian asked. "She's barely

eaten."

"I've got food. We need to leave now."

Amelia moved the tray off her lap, then slid out of bed, purposefully displaying her ankles to remind him that she had nothing but her nightdress.

His gaze burned at her foot and up her leg, which thankfully was still covered. He sucked in a long, slow deep breath. "Get dressed."

He turned to leave, but before he could shut the door, she called, "I am dressed." Speaking to him made her heart race, her breathing rapid. How could she run? How could she hide? Lillian stood not far from her as she collected the tray of food, and Amelia faced her. "May I stay with you? May I live here?" Amelia's whisper was desperate, pleading, and hopefully not loud enough for Mr. Ward to hear.

"Oh, dear." Mrs. Forester set the tray down on the nightstand, and her hand fluttered to her chest.

"Please." Amelia leaned toward her. "I can pay you."

Nathaniel stepped further into the room. "What's this about?"

"Just like a man," Mrs. Forester said, motioning toward Amelia. "Can't you see? She has no clothes. I'm sure I can find something, though it'll be too big. I'll have to take it in."

"There's no time for that," Mr. Ward said.

"She can't go out like this." Lillian motioned toward Amelia again.

"Fine." Mr. Ward's jaw pulsed. "Be quick. We don't have much time."

Mrs. Forester flew out of the room faster than

Amelia ever saw her move, leaving Amelia and Mr. Ward alone together.

Mr. Ward's face softened. "The stage leaves in half an hour."

"Stage?" Amelia stepped away from him, pressing against the bed. "Where are … we going?" The word "we" made her shudder.

"Home."

Amelia hugged herself, now wishing she wasn't so exposed to the man. She turned to find her blanket, but she didn't see it.

He reached toward her and she jumped away. He lifted her blanket from a chest at the foot of the bed, shook it out, and wrapped it over her shoulders, covering her.

Trembling, she attempted to thank him, but the words lodged in her throat.

Lillian entered the room, holding a lavender gown, which was clearly too big for Amelia. "I'll pin it," she said breathless. "It's the smallest one I own, and I haven't been able to fit into this for years." She draped it over the bed. "Get this on, and I'll find some thread."

Both Lillian and Mr. Ward left the room before Amelia could catch her breath, the door closing behind them.

Amelia got into the gown as quickly as possible. The sleeves and skirt were a bit long, and the bust, too wide. This would never do. But it was better than her nightdress.

The door flew open and Lillian burst inside, needles, thread and all. "Let's get this adjusted." She stuffed some pins in her mouth and went to work as Amelia lifted her arms. She turned round and round as Mrs. Forester adjusted the hem and tightened the bodice.

"A quick baste should do it."

"Please," was all Amelia could muster as Lillian busied herself with the dress. "I have money and a job."

Mrs. Forester shook her head rapidly. "We're almost finished." With one more tug on the bodice, she placed the final stitch. "There, dear." She straightened and faced Amelia, taking a deep breath and patting her arms. "You must trust in the Lord. Mr. Ward is a good man. He'll take much better care of you than … he'll treat you right, dear. Trust. Just trust." With that, she turned and left Amelia alone in the room.

Now what? Amelia panted. Where was this man taking her? She'd be far away from anyone she knew. Had he forgotten, she had a job here, not to mention payday was coming? What did it matter? What did any of it matter to anyone? No one cared. No one!

Amelia charged through the door, raced down the stairs, lifting her skirt so she wouldn't trip, but she still managed to step on the thing and went flying on the last step.

Mr. Ward caught her just in time, his large hands on her waist. "Watch yourself."

Amelia pushed him away and wrenched out of his grip. She ran for the door, but he caught her by the arm and yanked her against himself.

"Let go!" Amelia beat him on his chest, tears

flooding her eyes. "Let me go!" It was useless. She couldn't break free, and she crumpled at his feet. "Help me," she whispered, desperate for Lillian to rescue her from this man. "Someone, please help." She wept into her hands, no sign of Lillian, no sign of anyone to rescue her. And of course, no one would come. No one ever came. She went from being a possession of her father's, to being a possession of this man, this stranger.

Mr. Ward marched out the door, leaving it open behind him. A carriage stood outside, and he spoke to the driver. As the driver pulled away, Amelia pushed up into a sitting position, and Mr. Ward came toward her. Would he kick her or strike? She lifted her hand to block his swing, but instead, he took hold of it and lifted her to her feet. Once she had her balance, he tucked her arm under his, patting it. "Let's go for a walk." And he led her toward the door.

By this time, Lillian came out of hiding and reached for Amelia. She cupped Amelia's face in her hands, casting a hopeful smile with a quick nod. "Go." She kissed her forehead. "Be blessed." She released her, and nodded for them to go, encouraging her to leave with Mr. Ward.

Amelia swallowed, tears trailing down her face, as Mr. Ward led her out the door. He probably didn't strike her because he knew Mrs. Forester was there. What would he do to her once they were alone? Completely alone? She nearly lost her footing at the thought, and Mr. Ward righted her. A couple strode by with a smile. Mr. Ward touched the brim of his hat, and Amelia dropped her gaze to her feet, which were hidden beneath the overlong dress. Surely, he didn't want to look bad in front of the neighbors.

They walked in silence several blocks toward the post office where a stage was waiting. The driver of their carriage was already there, strapping down supplies onto the roof of the coach. Mr. Ward escorted Amelia to the door and opened it. Free of his grasp, Amelia grabbed her skirt and turned to run, but Mr. Ward caught her by the waist and swung her around.

"No!" she cried, not caring if anymore saw or heard her screams.

Without warning, Mr. Ward planted his mouth on hers, kissing her with such fierceness and forcefulness, she lost her breath. She tried to scream and pushed against him, but the kiss continued, invading her mouth, kissing the daylights out of her, until finally, she quit struggling, resting her hands on his chest, focusing on breathing. He slowly lightened the pressure, gradually softening the kiss to a tender, leisurely brushing against her lips, until it felt almost like … like … a caress. His assault ignited something within her, something she'd never felt before, something she couldn't even name, and slowly, as she became like liquid in his arms, he loosened his grasp. He cupped her face in his large hands, gently pressing his lips to hers, slowly, tenderly pulling away. Now dizzy and unable to keep her footing, he lifted her up and set her in the carriage, climbing in after her.

"Drive!" he shouted at the driver, and the stage jerked forward, jarring her deeper into the seat.

Dazed and bewildered, she grasped the couch to

keep her balance as her new husband sat across from her, his long legs reaching all the way to hers and their knees touching. She moved her legs away, her lips still swollen from his assault, and he watched her with such an intense stare, heat poured from the top of her head, all the way down to the tips of her toes.

Breathing heavily, he removed his hat and scrubbed his hand through his hair and down his face, then smashed his hat back on his head. Was that anger she saw?

Desperate to escape, she didn't dare leap from the carriage, but tore her gaze away from his and stared out the window, watching the pines pass by with such speed, she felt the loss of each tree, each rock and each nest, each friend and foe as she headed straight toward a terrifying unknown.

Sandi Rog

Chapter Twelve

Nathaniel ran his hand down his face as he stared at the beautiful, frightened Amelia sitting across from him. Getting her into the carriage sure was … interesting. How often would he have to fight her till they reached Chicago? And that kiss—if one could call it that—made him want to taste her lips more. He clenched his jaw, tamping down the craving that overwhelmed his senses.

He studied her profile as she stared out the window, rigid as a board. Her smooth, pale cheeks contoured into a perfect dainty nose, and luscious lips. He licked his own, remembering their taste. He forced his mind on safer areas, like … her chin. A chin that could lift just to the right height in confidence, but could also drop at one word from that lousy father of hers. He gritted his teeth. What a life. What a miserable, wretched life she'd led.

He'd change that.

After all, she was his wife.

Hard to believe. It happened so fast.

He had a wife. And it was the lovely Amelia. He got what he came for.

Although, as he stared at her rigid form, he remembered, they were only wed on paper, not in heart. He'd have to change that too.

She was drowning in the dress Mrs. Forester pinned on her. He'd have to remedy that in Denver. He doubted he'd find anything before then. As long as they were far away from Green Pines, he might be able to trust her not to escape.

Escape. From him! It was almost laughable. Didn't she know he offered a much better life?

The sun cast a jagged lance of light against her wavy locks — frizzy from having been braided — lighting her hair up like gold all the way down to her waist, and as the carriage turned, the light tantalized him as it brushed against her lips. Those perfectly formed lips.

Oh, no. The lips again.

This was going to be a long ride, even if it was only a day to Denver. How would he last all the way to Chicago?

Where was he taking her? Amelia didn't dare ask. She could barely breathe during this entire journey, let alone talk.

It had been several hours, and she didn't dare

utter a word. When he wasn't looking, she stole glances at the man, at her captor. At her husband. What a mess she was in. And no one to help her. No one willing to rescue her. Tears welled in her eyes and she forced them not to fall, but one lone tear betrayed her. She swiped it away before he could see.

After several hours, the carriage came to a stop at a small inn to exchange horses. She and Mr. Ward were the only passengers and they were allowed to disembark for a reprieve.

Mr. Ward helped her out of the carriage, his strong hand encasing hers. She wiped his touch off on her oversized dress as she got to her feet.

"The privy is there," he said, pointing with his thumb over his shoulder.

The buildings were few, certainly not enough to call it a town, with a small ticket office, stalls for horses, and like Mr. Ward said, a privy.

Amelia glanced around, desperately searching for a way of escape. The dirt road was narrow and nestled against the bottom of a cliff, while a steep ravine ran on the opposite side. Nothing looked hopeful, unless she escaped into the woods. And if she did that, where in the world would she go? It'd be foolish to try. She should wait until they reached a town.

After taking her time in the privy—anything to put off seeing her husband again—she walked around the buildings in search of some form of escape. As she rounded a corner behind the ticket office, she nearly collided with Mr. Ward's chest.

"Food?" He held something wrapped in paper

and eyed her with a lifted brow, as if he knew she might try to run.

From the delicious aroma of the meat and bread, her stomach growled, and she couldn't refuse.

They sat at a nearby table, apparently for travelers to dine at while on the road.

He joined her on the other side, straddling one leg over the bench as he unwrapped the food. He handed her a sandwich.

They ate in silence as Amelia savored her food. For the first time she studied Mr. Ward, studying the shape of his jaw as he chewed. His blue gaze flickered to hers, and she glanced away. From then on, he watched her as if examining the contours of her face, but she stared at the trees. Much like they did in the carriage.

Hard to believe they ever used to speak. Ever used to hold a conversation. Really, the most they ever spoke was at the box social. And now, they were bound together for the rest of their lives.

How much did he hate her for this? When would she experience his wrath?

"It's only half a day's journey from here," he said, interrupting her thoughts.

She cleared her throat, daring to speak for the first time since leaving Green Pines. "To where?" she asked in a whisper, barely audible to her own ears.

"Denver, of course."

Again, she stared at the trees, the scent of pine washing over her as a branch dangled not too far from where they sat. She wished she could grab hold of it, cling to it as her last hope, and that the tree would take her up, up so high Mr. Ward wouldn't be able to reach her. She sighed. Doomed to return to the city of her youth.

Denver. What were they going to do there?

After the stagecoach made the last stop, they cleared the trees, reaching the plains of Colorado. Why go to Denver? She knew Mr. Ward was wealthy, but didn't he just buy property in Green Pines? Why did they have to leave?

By the end of the day, they pulled onto the dark streets of Denver. The city had grown with more buildings springing up on all corners. Despite the late hour, folks dawdled along the wooden walkways being guided by the gas-lit lamps above and peering into the closed storefronts. The only positive thing about their arrival was that the evening shadows masked Amelia's wretched appearance. Her body had never ached so much, emphasizing the pain in her skull. Her head throbbed even more from the cuts, and she could still feel the matted hair against her scalp that she was supposed to wash that morning but never had a chance to do. Her back and shoulders hurt from her efforts to stay as far away from Mr. Ward in the carriage as possible.

They pulled up to the Silver Palace Hotel, the coach jarring to a stop. She remembered this place. Her father had several business meetings here. It wasn't terribly far from Pennsylvania Avenue where she lived as a child. Strange to be returning as a married woman.

Wasn't Denver also where Violet was sent? Maybe she could visit her? How would she even find her?

What was the name of the place they sent her, and would visitors even be allowed?

The door to the carriage swung open. Mr. Ward hopped out and held his large hand up for her. Where he got the energy, she didn't know. Amelia looked at his outstretched palm and slowly placed hers in his. He helped her down as she held her skirt, careful not to trip on its overlong hem. The doorman held open the front door as the driver took a carpetbag and wrapped packages from off the roof of the carriage.

Despite her weary state, walking into the empty lobby brought back memories of her father as she'd waited quietly on one of the couches for him to wrap up one of his long, boring meetings. Mr. Ward went to the maître d' and arranged for their room. She always wondered what it would be like to stay in the Silver Palace Hotel with all its shimmering, silver fixings, broad staircase and large rooms, with bellhops at one's every beck and call. She shook her head at the thought that now she'd have that chance, but why under such horrific circumstances?

The maître d' with a lantern beckoned them to follow, while the one bellhop on duty at this late hour took care of the luggage. They led them up the grand staircase, but they just as well had been walking down the stairs toward a dungeon. What would become of her in one of these rooms? What would he do to her in this magnificent palace? And would anyone hear her cries, her screams? Would anyone bother to rescue her? Likely not. She was his wife, after all. His slave. His property. With plodding steps, she followed as the bellhop turned down the long balcony with their luggage, her back rigid with the sensation of Mr. Ward's presence behind her, likely to keep her from running. The balcony wrapped around the huge atrium below, and normally she would like to stop and have a look, but she followed obediently as they were led down a corridor, the long hall stretching before them with flowered carpet and textured wallpaper, all matching that of the lobby below. If only she could enjoy the beauty and its grandeur. Instead, she might as well have been wearing shackles as she took each step toward her doom.

Soon, the maître d' stopped before a door at the very end of the hallway. His keys rattled in the lock before the door swung open. He lit all the lamps as she stepped slowly into the room that would likely become her torture-chamber. Soon after, he left, while the bellhop set down their belongings. She took in the magnificent tapestries, the royal blue curtains and ceramic bowl and pitcher sitting on a walnut stand covered in blue lace. While this room was ten times more elegant, it made her long for her job in Green Pines.

How could Mr. Ward afford such accommodations?

He gave a tip to the bellhop and the door closed with a thud that echoed off the walls in the room, and especially off her heart. They were left standing alone in the elegant space, and she stood frozen staring at Mr. Ward. Her chest heaved as she tried to control her breathing. He held her with his severe, unsmiling gaze, the lamplight flickering off the stubbly shadow on his chin.

It was the moment he waited for, and she prepared herself for the onslaught. He stepped toward her.

Amelia tried to scream, but it came out as a squeak, as she dashed to the other side of the room, ducking and crouching against the bed. She waited for his grasp, for his fists to yank her up by the hair as she so often experienced from her father, but nothing. Nothing happened. She peeked up, and Mr. Ward looked at her, studied her with such a queer expression, she wasn't sure what to make of it. Was it not anger the way his brows lowered over his blue eyes? If so, why didn't he reach for her? Why didn't he lunge at her? Or was he waiting for the right moment? She held her breath, but … he didn't move.

"I'll order you a bath," he finally said, breaking the silence, his voice resigned. With that, he walked out of the room and left her alone still crouching by the bed. Slowly, she straightened. It was his moment to unleash all the anger he'd pent up during their long trip, and he didn't raise a hand against her. Why was that? What was he waiting for? She sank onto the bed, grasping her hands together to ease their trembling, then hugging herself as she suddenly felt chilled. It was then that tears flooded her eyes and poured down her cheeks. As she sobbed, wailing at God for putting her in this situation, she fell on the bed in anguish and despair.

The door flew open with a maid carrying several towels, soaps and a brush. Mr. Ward followed close behind, stopping in the doorway. Amelia quickly pushed up from the bed, focusing her blurred vision on the man forced to be her husband. If she was angry, how much more was he? She took a slow, deep breath, trying to compose herself.

Mr. Ward took a step, and she straightened, but instead of walking toward her, he moved around the room as if searching for something. He grabbed a divider and positioned it just outside the washroom, then moved a chair and placed it behind the divider just outside the door. "You can change here," he said as he set the carpetbag inside. "I'll return when you're finished." With that, he left the room.

The maid hummed a soft tune in the washroom, and the sounds of pouring water filled the air.

Amelia stood and crept to the washroom, glancing to the doorknob where Mr. Ward just left.

To her wonder and amazement, water filled a large, four-legged porcelain tub. She'd never bathed in such a large basin before. The only time she ever dipped herself in so much water was when she was a child and lived in their large house off Pennsylvania Avenue and when she went for a swim in the pond near her house in Green Pines. At the hotel where she worked, they only provided large washtubs, but nothing this beautiful and elegant.

"I can help you bathe, ma'am." The maid had set one of the folded towels on a table in the tiled room and stood waiting on her with a large bar of soap and a cloth.

Speechless, Amelia simply nodded and turned to the divider where she proceeded to slide easily out of her oversized dress. It crumpled to the floor at her feet. She moved to the tub, stepped into the surprisingly warm water, and sank into its inviting depths.

Once she was finished, she dried off and opened her carpetbag as the maid lit the small fireplace in the room. "We only have fireplaces on the end rooms," the maid said from the other side of the divider. "You're blessed you got one. These rooms are also much larger than the others."

Amelia pulled on her nightdress, the one she got married in, and scrubbed the towel over her damp hair.

"Come sit by the fire, ma'am, and I'll brush it out for you." The maid pulled one of the chairs near the small hearth.

Amelia, still unable to speak, crept toward the flames. Never in her life had she been treated in such a manner, as if she were a queen or a princess. She wasn't quite sure how to respond. She simply did what she was told and thoroughly enjoyed, and even relaxed, beneath the deft hands of the lovely maid who took care of her.

Once the tangles were out of Amelia's hair, and it was dry, the maid pulled back the blankets on the bed. As she collected the damp towels, she asked, "Is there anything else I can do for you, ma'am?"

Amelia, still sitting in the chair by the warm fire finally found her voice. "No, thank you." She stood to see the maid out. "Thank you for everything," she said. "I'm afraid ... I'm afraid I don't have a tip."

"Oh, no worries, ma'am. It's been taken care of." She smiled and whisked away down the hall.

Amelia studied the corridor. Thankfully, there was no sign of Mr. Ward. She closed the door and leaned against it, sighing. Despite her terror and the long, aching ride, she felt refreshed and relaxed. She turned toward the bed and crawled beneath the covers, wishing she could tie down the blankets so no one else could get beneath them. For what felt like several long hours, with the sheets pulled to her chin, she watched the door and its knob. Nothing moved. As her lids grew heavy, she kept her ears alert for when her husband would enter, but he never did, and the exhaustion finally enfolded her, carrying her into a deep, restful sleep.

The door opened, jerking Amelia awake. She yanked on the covers, pulling them back up to her chin. A new maid flung open the curtains, the bright sun blinding Amelia as she tried to focus.

"Good morning, ma'am." The spritely maid spoke in a singsong voice. "Your husband sent me in here to have you get ready." She turned to Amelia with enthusiasm. "A gentleman is on his way up to fit you for a new dress." The maid clapped her hands to her chest, her face beaming with excitement.

Amelia glanced to the other side of the bed. The covers were untouched. Her husband had never returned. She released a long sigh of relief. But where was he? Where had he been? Didn't he sleep?

"Come, ma'am." She motioned Amelia to the chair near the dying embers in the hearth. "Allow me to brush your hair. Make you presentable."

Amelia almost chuckled. More pampering? It was

beginning to be a bit too much. "You don't have to. I can brush my own hair."

The maid's expression deflated into obvious disappointment.

"Well … never mind, then." Amelia said briskly, waving her hand. She didn't like disappointing the woman.

"Oh, thank you, ma'am." She ushered Amelia to the chair. "I've never seen a fitting before, and the frocks from this company are quite exquisite. Although, you're only being fitted for a traveling dress, it's still quite exciting." She brushed Amelia's hair, and despite Amelia's earlier refusal, she languished in the maid's gentle touch.

Soon, a stoic gentleman entered the room, carrying several garments of varying colors over his arm. He laid them gently on the bed and then proceeded to take Amelia's measurements over her nightdress, from her height, to around her waist, and the width of her arms. Amelia never realized there could be so many sections of the body that could be measured.

Shortly after that, he handed her a dress to try on behind the divider. She then stepped out and allowed him to measure her again, pinning in seams and hems.

"I believe these two will do," he finally said, holding up a dark-blue garment that matched the curtains in the room, and a light beige dress. Both dresses were intended for traveling, which meant they weren't going to stay in Denver.

Amelia's heart galloped with dread at the thought. Where did Mr. Ward plan on taking her?

Chapter Thirteen

Nathaniel had slept in a room next door to Amelia's. He hadn't planned on sleeping in separate rooms, but when he'd seen the terror she displayed when they'd just arrived, he knew he couldn't be in the same room with her. Neither one of them would have gotten any sleep. He could only hope she was able to finally rest since they had a long journey ahead of them.

A knock sounded on the door and he leaped to open it. It meant Amelia was finally ready, and they could catch the late afternoon train to Cheyenne. Exactly what he was hoping for. Thankfully, the dressmaker had found some pre-made dresses to refit for his bride.

The tiny maid smiled up at him, and with a lilt on her toes, she motioned to Amelia's room. "She's ready for you, Mr. Ward." Nathaniel gave the woman a generous tip, and she gasped as he dropped it into her hands. "Oh, this is too much, sir."

"Absolutely not," he said, as he motioned for her to go.

Grinning, she curtsied and traipsed away down the hall.

Nathaniel took a deep breath, preparing himself for a fight with his new bride. It was time. Time to go. It was bad enough getting her into a public carriage, how much worse would it be to get her onto a train? He'd just toss her over his shoulder if he had to. She could either go with him calmly or create a spectacle. It was her choice. Taking a deep breath, he knocked on the door before opening it, but he didn't wait for an answer. She was his wife, after all. Whether she liked it or not, he had every right to be in her room.

As he swung open the door, he walked in, but immediately stopped in his tracks. He gaped at the beauty standing in a ray of sunlight lancing from the window. A stunning woman in a dark blue dress, emphasizing a narrow waist and an hourglass figure, stood before him. The light played off her dainty hat trimmed with heavy silk and small plumes, which perched above golden-brown ringlets that brushed lightly against her neck and cheeks, a neck he longed to touch with his lips. No longer the "girl" he knew in Green Pines, but a beautiful woman with her chin held high—likely in fear of his presence—but giving off a confident air of sophistication and grace.

Amelia.

His gorgeous Amelia knocked the breath right out of him. And to think, this was just a traveling dress.

How stunning would she be in a gown? He meant to find out. Inwardly, he shook his head to bring him back to his senses.

He suddenly felt silly, inept as he tried to find the words to address her. Slowly, he stretched out his hand, palm up, reaching for her. Her gaze darted from it to his face. He smiled. "Shall we go?"

Amelia straightened, her chest heaving. "Where to?" she asked, her voice barely a whisper.

"Take my hand," Nathaniel said with a forced calm, burying the temptation to take her into his arms and press his lips to her perfectly shaped mouth.

With hesitation, she lifted her hand and carefully placed it on his. He wrapped his fingers around her cold, trembling ones. Gently, he moved her arm under his—so she wouldn't easily be able to get away—as he guided her through the hall. So far, so good. Now if he could just make it as far as the train depot without a fight, all would be well. As they walked along the balcony, he caught Amelia's sidelong glances to the atrium. Was she planning her escape or admiring the beauty in the sunlight, the silver vases and tassels winking at them? Perhaps both. He stopped to let her look, and as she studied the splendor of the hotel, he studied the loveliness of his bride: her rosy cheeks, her bright eyes. Soon, they descended the stairs in regal elegance. To have such a stunning beauty on his arm caused him to walk taller.

Somehow without a fight, they made it all the way to the train station. After purchasing tickets to Chicago, Nathaniel turned toward the luggage where he'd asked Amelia to wait. The luggage was there, but she was gone. Nowhere in sight.

He strode toward the nearest door, not rushing in order to avoid a scene. He caught sight of her just outside the doors. He marched toward her, taking her by the elbow. She stiffened beneath him as he escorted her back inside.

"Thank you for waiting, my dear," he said, patting her hand on his arm.

Face flushed, she didn't pull away from him as she spoke. "Where are we going? Where are you taking me?"

He guided her to their luggage and handed the conductor his ticket for the carpetbag and new trunk containing her dress. He could have easily carried them himself, but he wanted his hands free just in case she made a run for it. The man nodded, then preceded to take care of their things as Nathaniel then guided Amelia to the train between the bustling throng of travelers.

"We're going home," he said with a smile, praying she'd stay calm and wouldn't again try to flee.

"To where?" Amelia's voice lifted above the crowd.

Luckily the steam from the train and shouting people saying their goodbyes were good distractions and her outburst didn't draw any attention.

"Chicago." He maneuvered her onto the steps, keeping a firm hold on her arm so she couldn't break away.

He guided her down the aisle and toward a couch away from the other travelers then motioned for her to take a seat next to the window. He sat next to the aisle so she couldn't escape.

"I'll never see Violet again," she said, and broke down into tears. She cried quietly into her hands.

Nathaniel shifted in his seat, unsure what to do or say. "She's here?" He handed her a handkerchief.

Amelia dabbed her eyes, the plumes waving above her hat as she nodded.

"I'm sorry." Nathaniel sighed, feeling like a cad. Once the train lurched forward, he knew she wouldn't try to run, so he relaxed. He thought to encourage her by saying they could one day visit, but he wasn't sure that would happen, considering how much she fought him thus far. So, he kept silent. Not much he could do or say to offer any form of comfort as he listened to her quiet sniffles.

Since they were in the back with no one behind them, he leisurely stretched. She stiffened when his arm came down around her shoulders, but he kept it there as she wiped her eyes, gently rubbing his hand against her sleeve. To his surprise and utter joy, she didn't move away or try to remove his hand.

Progress. Already, he was making progress with his new bride.

Amelia had never been in a train, and as it moved away from the station the speed began to pick up. So much so, she pulled away from Mr. Ward and looked out the window. Trees, fields and homes moved by so fast with no bumps or jarring from her seat that she felt like she was flying. Truth be told, it was thrilling.

"Amazing," she whispered against the glass as they raced along.

"First time?"

"Huh?" Amelia glanced up at Mr. Ward then back again.

"First time on a train?"

She dried her tears and nodded, staring out the window. "It's so fast." Then she faced him. "Have you ever ridden a train?"

"Yeah. I rode them a lot when I was young."

"Really?" His parents must have been wealthy. Then she remembered his story of being on the streets, and the revelation hit her. "Oh ...."

"Yeah." He grinned, and her cheeks went hot.

"I'm sorry." She pressed her fingers against her forehead. "I should have remembered—"

"It's all right." He chuckled.

"I can't believe I forgot." She felt like a fool. How many conversations had they had about his past? This was the same man who offered to walk her home every day, who helped her in the night, who ... bid on her box at the box social. The very man she shunned and rejected. She stared at the plush seat in front of her and, facing straight ahead, she allowed her eyes to slide his way, studying his long legs as he sat comfortably beside her. She folded her hands in her lap, again noticing the amazing blue dress he purchased for her. And she had another one in their coffers. Taking a deep breath, she stared out the window again. He could have beaten her last night. Could have done horrible things, but instead, he let her rest. Gave up his bed for her. Where did he sleep last night? Downstairs in the lobby? On a chair? The man was used to sleeping on the street. A chair would

186

have been luxurious compared to that. Surely, the hotel never would have allowed such a thing.

She cleared her throat, curiosity getting the best of her. "So ... um ... where did you sleep last night?"

"In the room next door."

"Oh." Again, she looked out the window, watching trees fly by. Heat rose from the tips of her toes to the top of her head, realizing just how close he had been that entire time. She thanked God he never came back into the room. She thanked God that Mr. Ward didn't beat her. When would he, if not now? Was this not the worst possible situation they could be in where he could blame her, take his rage out on her? He may have bid on her box at the social, but that didn't mean he wanted to marry her. Forced upon a man was the worst possible thing that could happen to a woman. Or any man, for that matter. Then she recalled her father. He always waited till they got home to unleash his wrath. And that's where Mr. Ward was taking her.

Home.

Despite the obvious fact that everyone could see her father was neglectful, he always placed a high standard on appearances. That's why he'd wait until they were home.

The mountains looked blue across the big Colorado sky, much the way she felt. Distant and alone. Never again would she see those mountains ... or Violet.

Tears burned her eyes again, only this time she kept her gaze away from Mr. Ward. The comfort he'd offered was calming, but she still didn't trust him.

Surely, he didn't accept this union. He slept away from her last night. That certainly spoke of how he felt about the situation.

Her heart raced in time to the beat of the tracks. What strange places and horrors awaited her? Where would they live? How much would she have to slave for him?

When would he release his wrath?

They arrived at Cheyenne, Wyoming just over an hour later. The train spit out all the travelers and Amelia was left standing on the platform as Mr. Ward collected their belongings. She'd never been outside of Colorado. How strange to be so far away from home already. As he came toward her with the trunk on his shoulder and the carpetbag in his other hand, she couldn't help but admire his strength and stature, his long legs, and a hint of shadow on his chin. Didn't he ever shave? Or did his beard simply grow too fast for his razor to keep up?

"Ready?" he asked as he approached her.

Ready for what? She nodded.

She followed him over the wooden planks of the platform onto the dirt road toward a large hotel where other travelers gathered.

"The next train leaves at ten tomorrow," he said to her over his shoulder. He carried the trunk as if it were filled with air. She imagined her dress inside it. What a beautiful dress. Perhaps she'd be expected to wear it tomorrow?

They entered the hotel as Mr. Ward allowed her to go in before him, thoughts of escape nonexistent in this far-off land. Where in the world could she run? She had no money, no means to do anything on her own at all.

Again, they were led to a room where Mr. Ward set down the trunk and the carpetbag. The room was more similar to the rooms at the hotel she cleaned in Green Pines, not terribly large. Just the right size for a person needing a bed for the night.

Green Pines seemed so far away now. Almost like it was a dream. More like she was in a dream now. A nightmare, really.

"There's a restaurant downstairs." He cocked his arm. "Shall we?"

With no other choice, she took his elbow, and he led her back down to the lobby.

The evening meal was uneventful, neither of them having much to say. After a short stroll down the street, peering into shop windows that were closed, he led her back up to their room. Would he stay with her this time? She held her breath as he reached into his pocket for the key. The door squeaked as he held it open for her.

"If you need me, I'll be right next door." He strode toward the door. "Don't forget. Train leaves at ten. A maid will help you with your things. I'll meet you here for breakfast in the morning." He touched the brim of his hat and left.

Amelia stood in the empty room that boasted peach-colored flowers on its walls and a wooden floor with crimson rugs scattered about. She slumped onto the bed. A small table held a bowl and pitcher with a green hand-towel folded next to it.

What a strange new world.

She sighed and was grateful for the lamp that was already lit next to her bed as she got out of her new dress. Too bad she didn't have the help of a maid this time as she pulled and tugged the strings loose on her chemise. Finally free of the beautiful garment, she opened her trunk and pulled out her new beige dress to hang it in a small closet. Beneath the dress, she discovered a new nightgown. The color was a vibrant white, a striking contrast to the dingy, worn-out fabric of her old one. She pulled out the thin gown and held it against herself. The soft fabric was like silk against her skin. She rubbed it against her cheek. Perhaps it was silk? Lace flowers were embroidered along the cuffs and hem. It was too beautiful to wear to bed and wrinkle. Still, she eagerly slipped it on.

With everything put away, her hair brushed and her face cleaned, she crawled into bed and released a long sigh. Something was different about this evening. Something she hadn't experienced in a long time. As she lay staring at the ceiling, then at the door to make sure it was locked, she realized what was so different. For the first time in years, she felt safe. There was no need to sleep with her father's rifle nearby, no dark windows for strangers to peer into, no strange sounds in the night, other than a carriage or two going by. And the man she married clearly wasn't interested in her and had booked his own room. So, this evening, this night, she was safe.

Safe in her Father's arms, she thought, as she nestled deep down beneath the plush coverlet. Thank you, God. Thank you for this night.

Chapter Fourteen

Two days and two trains later, Amelia sat straight as a board on the last leg to Chicago. Shifting on the soft couch, she brushed off the dust from her fancy blue dress as Mr. Ward sat opposite her with his boots stretched out over the seat next to her. She would have thought it rude, but she understood the need. They were both exhausted, as neither one of them had slept a wink in the sleeping car. The couches pulled out into beds, but when he offered to open the bed for her, she refused. Made for awkward conversation the rest of the weary night and now throughout the day. A steward had brought them food, which broke the long, strained silence, but it didn't help ease the weariness that weighed both of them down.

Mr. Ward's attractive head covered in dark-brown

hair bobbed as he nodded off every once in a while.

She took a deep breath and sighed. "How much longer?"

Mr. Ward, handsome in his dark grey waistcoat and vest—quite a contrast from the mountain man she knew in Green Pines—took out his pocket watch. "Half hour." He eyed her with his stunning blue eyes as he slipped the watch back into his pocket. He'd purchased a suit at the last stop, and now he looked quite pristine, shockingly handsome. Although she missed the scruff along his square jaw, seeing the cleft on his chin made up for that loss.

Flashing by the window were farms and rich landscape, and in the distance the view of one of the Great Lakes broke between the fast-moving trees and hills. Hard to believe they were about to enter a large city with so much green surrounding both sides of the train. The rails continued on along the Chicago River, again chanting in time to the rapid beating of her heart. What would happen to her when they arrived at his home?

Before she knew it, the green disappeared, replaced by buildings shooting up like tall square boxes along the track's path. Warehouses, mills called grain elevators, and slaughterhouses went by so fast she barely had a chance to examine them, but the stench was awful.

Finally, the train began to slow, moving toward smoke and several soot-covered tracks on each side. Mr. Ward took his feet off the couch next to her and straightened, yawning and stretching. The canopy in the terminal shadowed the lowering sun as they slid alongside the platform, and the train finally rolled to a stop, releasing a long hiss that taunted Amelia's nerves. She closed her eyes. What awaited her once they were behind the closed doors of his home? She trembled as he stood and reached out to help her rise. Sucking in a deep breath, she allowed him to take her hand.

Amelia stepped onto the platform. Muggy air, throngs of people, their chatter, and train whistles bombarded her from all sides. Mr. Ward whistled for someone to fetch the luggage. He handed a young man his ticket stub, and the boy rushed away.

Taking her by the arm, Mr. Ward escorted Amelia to the stairs on the other side of the platform where they waited. Soon, the young man was next to them with the luggage, and Mr. Ward arranged for him to carry it to the cab. Amelia had never ridden in a cab before. What might that be like in such a busy city?

As they made their way through the arched doorway, she studied the intricate walls and windows above them. Chuckling, Mr. Ward gently tugged her along, and she tried not to trip over her own feet as they followed the young man along the soot-covered square with their luggage. They neared the cab drivers. Never had she seen so many coaches.

Mr. Ward waved one down. "North Astor Street." He handed the man some cash and helped Amelia in.

She sat on the plush couch, surprised that a coach could be so comfortable. Leaning toward the window, she realized most of the other cabs weren't quite as nice as the one she was in.

After the luggage was placed in the back, Mr.

Ward tipped the young man and swung in next to her.

"It's good to be home." His eyes sparkled despite their long train ride and his obvious exhaustion.

Amelia still wasn't used to his nearness, and when his leg brushed against her skirt, she moved away. How in the world was this marriage ever going to work?

"Get on!" The coach started forward with the driver shouting and snapping his whip.

It rumbled down the street, while other coaches with passengers drove across the road, turning down different lanes.

"How can so many people live in one city?" Amelia stared out the window and gaped at the soot covering the sidewalks, the smoke carrying on the air as buildings skyrocketed above it, reaching into the sky. Did they reach as high as the clouds? Peddlers shouted from behind their booths and beneath small tents of goods.

"What are those?" She pointed at what looked like railway tracks cutting through the middle of the road. Odd. Surely, trains didn't travel through the middle of the city.

Mr. Ward leaned over her shoulder to peer out her side of the window, his cologne wafting over her and teasing her senses. "Tracks. For cable cars."

"I've never heard of such a thing."

He grinned at her, and she imagined her puzzled gaze reflecting in his eyes. "They're like miniature trains to bring people and workers to and around the city. They're electric-powered trolleys. They opened the first cable car line this year."

"Why would you need those if you have horses?"

"Horse cars are too slow." He chuckled. "It takes longer to get downtown by horse car than to Milwaukee by train."

"I might like to ride one someday," she said, feeling childish. It sounded like fun.

He grinned at her, a gleam in his eyes.

The coach turned away from the commotion and up a bridge. Amelia stretched to see the water of the Chicago River moving beneath them—much deeper and wider than the South Platte in Colorado—and a number of bridges crisscrossing over the river while boats floated lazily along.

Coming off the bridge, they cantered down several blocks and into a neighborhood, passing by a large park and trees. In the distance, one of the Great Lakes stretched out as far as the eye could see.

They turned onto an empty neighborhood street and only one house greeted them, sitting grandly behind an iron gate, but the house … what a house. A mansion was more like it. Or even a castle. The person manning the gate opened it, and the coach trotted up a half-circle drive.

"What are we doing here?" Amelia asked. Surely, this wasn't his home. She knew he was wealthy, but ….

The coach stopped at the front of the house, and Mr. Ward swung open the carriage door and hopped out. "My lady," he said, offering her his hand and bending to her. "Welcome home."

Amelia gasped and blinked. "It can't be."

He helped her out of the coach, and she stared up at the white columns and spires.

She shook her head.

The driver brought their luggage to the door and rang the bell.

"This?" She motioned to the mansion. "This is your home?"

"Our home." He smiled, his wide chest pronounced.

The front door opened, and a tall butler moved to the side as an elderly gentleman in slippers and pipe in his hand scuttled down the stone steps and embraced Mr. Ward. "Good to see you, man! It's been too long!" The man stood in front of him, grasping his arms. Then he turned to Amelia. "So, this is her."

Amelia stepped back. Who was this man?

Mr. Ward broke away and put his hand around Amelia's waist. "This is William Goldman, my … he's like a father to me."

Mr. Goldman shuffled to Amelia, taking her hands in his big wrinkly ones, his pipe still between his fingers and smelling of peppermint. "Pleeeased to meet you!" His cheeks filled with color as he spoke. "My, my, you are lovely."

"And tired." Mr. Ward tipped the driver, took Amelia by the arm, and escorted her around Mr. Goldman toward the front door.

"Why wouldn't you let me send a carriage?" Mr. Goldman stomped up the steps.

"Didn't want to create undo attention for my new bride."

"Why not? She's lovely!"

"She's tired! You think I'm going to put her on public display after an arduous trip?" Mr. Ward sighed. "Come." Grinning, he tossed a glance at Mr. Goldman over his shoulder. "We'll talk more inside."

Amelia didn't know what to think. Suddenly, Mr. Ward had a voice. She barely heard a peep out of him the entire way from Green Pines, but it was clear he felt truly at home with this Mr. Goldman. They stopped in the doorway to let his friend pass. Who was this older man exactly? Did he live here too? How many others lived in this huge house? She arched her neck, taking in the magnificent door with its intricate designs and carved wood paneling. Mr. Goldman escorted them down a hall with marble tiles and a high ceiling. Was this truly a house? Someone's home? Mr. Ward's home? It couldn't be.

"After getting your telegram—which is hardly private, by the way, so I'm sure word is already spreading about your new bride—I hired a nice maid for your little wife. She's Irish, full-blooded Irish, I'm telling you!" He punched the air, laughing. "Boy, did I get a lot of uppity talk for taking her on, but she's a sweet little thing and deserves work just like the rest of us."

"I'm finally rubbing off on you, huh?" Mr. Ward said.

"Nope!" Mr. Goldman marched down the hall, his slippers quiet on the tiles while her and Mr. Ward's footsteps echoed off the high walls. "It's the man upstairs." Mr. Goldman wagged his finger to the sky as he continued to shuffle ahead of them, leading them into a large room with vaulted ceilings and a

197

grand staircase.

Another man lived upstairs? Up those beautiful white, marble stairs? "How many people live here?" Amelia finally found the courage to speak, even if it was practically a whisper.

Mr. Goldman stopped to face them, studying Amelia with one bushy eyebrow raised. "You have a voice. And a beautiful one, at that."

She swallowed.

"Just us, and the servants," Mr. Ward said. "How many are there, would you say?" Mr. Ward cocked his head to his old friend.

Mr. Goldman waved away the question. "Oh, how do I know? What does it matter?" He started walking again, turning his back to them.

"But you said," Amelia practically whispered, "'the man upstairs.'"

Mr. Goldman did an about-face, scrutinizing her with such shock and incredulity that Amelia was sure she met with his disapproval. She shouldn't have opened her mouth. Shouldn't have said a word, let alone asked so many questions.

Suddenly, Mr. Goldman barked out laughter and slapped his thigh. "The good Lord, little one! The good Lord is the Man upstairs." He chuckled pointing his pipe above his head. "Good heavens. For a moment there, Nate, I thought you brought home a heathen." He shook his head with an exaggerated sigh and led the way again.

He led them up the grand staircase, and as they walked along the balcony, Amelia couldn't take her eyes off the atrium below. Its white columns and suspended chandeliers twinkled pink, yellow and orange in the last gleaming rays of the sun that shone through the tall windows above. The effect was mesmerizing, nearly making her dizzy. It reminded her of the Silver Palace Hotel, but oh, how much more beautiful Mr. Ward's home was in comparison.

Mr. Goldman led them down a blue, carpeted hall to a set of oak double-doors. They swung open, their wooden scent wafting over her, revealing a bedroom so grand, she gasped, releasing all the pent-up amazement at such a magnificent house.

"How do you like it?" Mr. Goldman asked.

Mr. Ward set her trunk down at the foot of a bed, which reached out in all its grandeur as if standing at attention, yet offering up its plush cushions and pillows for a glorious sleep. Oh, how she needed sleep.

She walked toward the large bay window, looking out over land, hills and one of the Great Lakes. Sheer curtains hung in front of the pristine glass, and royal blue draperies, meant to block out the light, were swept aside, hanging with an elegance even the Silver Palace Hotel couldn't mimic.

"Well?" Mr. Goldman cleared his throat.

She looked to Mr. Ward who was standing with his arms crossed, watching her.

"Oh?" She put her hands to her chest. No one ever cared for her opinion before. "Me?"

"Yes, of course you." Mr. Goldman puffed up his chest and motioned to the room, the window, the bed, the oak armoire in the corner. "What do you think? Do you like it?"

"Why, yes," she said, breathless. "Of course." She slowly turned around the room, taking in the flower-print walls and grand fireplace. "I've never seen anything more beautiful."

"Well, good then!" Mr. Goldman clapped his hands. "Let's eat!" He turned on his heel and headed for the door.

Mr. Ward chuckled, his hands in his pockets. "Shall we?" He offered Amelia his arm.

She took it, and he escorted her through several more halls, past rooms and down stairs, until finally, after passing through another corridor on the main floor, Amelia found herself in a sizeable dining room with high windows illuminating the setting sun. The long table was already adorned with three place settings together at one end where a maidservant set a hot tray of steaming duck, potatoes and greens. Amelia's mouth watered.

Mr. Ward pulled out a chair for her, and she sat as Mr. Goldman took the seat at the head of the table. Mr. Ward sat directly across from her and smiled, his grin so contagious, even she was forced to smile back at him. The first optimistic exchange since their horrendous wedding.

"Let's thank the Lord," Mr. Goldman said as he bowed his head. "Dear Father, we thank You for the safe passage You gave to Nate and Miss Amelia, his new bride. We thank You for the fact that Nate found the woman of his dreams, and that she was willing to come all this way with him to Chicago. And I thank You, Lord, for the grandchildren that will come forth from this union."

Amelia gasped.

"In Your son's name, amen." Mr. Goldman grabbed his fork and knife and stabbed a piece of meat from the serving tray in front of him and plopped the roasted wing onto his plate. He cut off a piece and took a bite. "Mm, good!" He swallowed and took another bite. He motioned with his fork to Mr. Ward. "Eat! You two kids must be starving!"

A maidservant leaned over the table and placed some slices of meat, potatoes and green beans on Amelia's plate.

"Thank you," she said, taking in the delicious aroma. Her stomach growled audibly.

"See!" Mr. Goldman lifted his eyebrows at Amelia. "You are hungry." He pointed his fork at her plate. "Eat up. Eat up!"

Mr. Ward shook his head, chuckling, as he cut a bite for himself.

"I've arranged for the west rooms with the bay windows to be for the children and a playroom for them as well. I've already purchased a few toys, not much, mind you. Just enough to make the rooms pleasant."

Amelia nearly choked on her food. She picked up her napkin and coughed. A maidservant poured wine into her glass, and she took a drink, continuing to cough.

"Will, let's talk about those things later," Mr. Ward said, glancing Amelia's way.

"Why?" Mr. Goldman straightened, his napkin hanging from his collar, a fork and knife in each hand. "These things are natural, boy. I never understood why womenfolk evade the subject. It's a God-given occurrence with marriage. There's no need to be hush-hush about it." He looked at Amelia and then down at his plate, his cheeks reddened. Perhaps because of Amelia's horrified expression? "Forgive me, girl. You must know, surely Nate has told you, I'm eager to be a grandfather. Just need to hear the pitter-patter of little feet, voices of children. You know." He shrugged as if ashamed.

"You don't need to apologize." If only she hadn't choked, perhaps this subject might not have seemed so magnified. Amelia placed her hand near Mr. Goldman's plate, gazing into his forlorn expression. What happened so suddenly to make this delightful man so sad?

"You see," Mr. Ward's voice carried with a sympathetic tone from across the table, "William … well, he lost his family in the fire. He had three girls, and he misses their laughter." Mr. Ward stopped eating, but he didn't look up from his plate.

"He's right." Tears welled in Mr. Goldman's eyes as he nodded. "That I do." He began eating his food again. "But, just to clarify. I still have three girls and a wonderful wife. They're just waiting for me to join them in paradise."

"I didn't realize …" Amelia whispered, speechless. What fire? Was this the same fire Mr. Ward lost his family in, or was it two separate fires? She didn't dare pry. "I'm sorry for your terrible loss."

"Thank you," Mr. Goldman said, looking up from his plate and staring off as if into some distant memory. "They were good girls. Good girls. They'd be about your age now." He looked at her. "How old are you?"

"I'm eighteen, sir."

"Yep. Seventeen, eighteen, and twenty, they'd be. And they looked just like their mother. All three of them. I'll show you their pictures in the study. You can see just how beautiful they were, all four of them."

"I'd like that very much," Amelia said, meaning every word. This poor man. What a terrible loss.

After the meal, they sat quietly in Mr. Goldman's study as he shared his small photos with Amelia. They were small photographs he carried with him while away on business, and now they were all he had left of his family. What a kind man to share such intimate details of his life. She'd never experienced such openness and tender expressions of love.

"Well, enough about me. Did Nate ever tell you what an amazing blessing he's been to me?" He lifted his hands to the room and the house around them. "I was wealthy before I ever met him, but boy, I tell you, he knows how to turn a profit. All of this, all of what you see, was made possible by his talent for entrepreneurship." Mr. Goldman leaned his elbows on his knees. "Opened up the Goldman Department Store, biggest retail store in town! And the windows," again, he motioned around them, "he loves windows. And he put windows on his store fronts, filling the displays with goods that attract women from every class of life." He slapped his leg. "Who would have thought of that? Windows, so folks could see what's inside? Enticing them to come in! Why didn't we think of it sooner?" He laughed. "Who knew?"

Amelia smiled and glanced over at Mr. Ward sitting with his ankle crossed over his knee. He studied Amelia, his regard intense. Her gaze shifted back at Mr. Goldman who continued his tale.

"And you know what else he did?" He motioned to Mr. Ward. "Good thing I had the money to make it happen. He helped clean this city up of its slums. He got into real estate and built neighborhoods for the workers just outside the city so they could get out of the shantytowns. Now these kids have good homes to grow up in, and they even started themselves a baseball team called 'Goldman Boys.' Course, it was Nate who did it all, but he refuses to put his name on anything."

"It wouldn't have happened without your money."

"But it was your ideas that made it possible." Mr. Goldman pointed at Mr. Ward. "He's earned me more money than I ever thought possible, than I ever dreamed possible."

Amelia studied the two men, two complete strangers, despite knowing Mr. Ward in Green Pines. This was an entirely new man, a different man. Really, she never knew Mr. Ward while in Green Pines, and just from Mr. Goldman's tales, she'd learned more about Mr. Ward than she ever did after all those hours spent together.

It was all so overwhelming. She didn't know what to think, how to respond, what to say. This man, this stranger, was her husband. And this … this mansion … was his home. And now, here he was forced to marry a woman who had nothing to her name, nothing to offer him in refinement or education. She was out of place, out of her station, and she didn't belong. How frustrated Mr. Ward must feel to be shackled to a woman who had no talents, who had nothing.

"I'm afraid it's late, and—"

"Oh. Of course! You need your rest after such a long journey." Mr. Goldman and Nathaniel stood.

Amelia got to her feet. She looked for a servant or someone to take her to her room. "I don't know the way."

"I'll take you." Mr. Ward came to her side.

"Good night, sir," she said to Mr. Goldman.

"No, no. Please, call me Will, or William. But not sir." He walked over to her and took her hand into his, patting it. "As the new wife of Nate here, and because he's like a son to me, that makes you like a daughter to me. Please, don't call me sir."

Amelia nodded, deeply taken back by the sincerity of his tone. "Yes, sir ... uh—I mean, yes, Mr. William."

"No! Just William, no Mr. Please!" He smiled at her.

"Thank you ... William," she said, softly.

"That's a good girl," he said, patting her hand again then passing her to Mr. Ward.

As Amelia and Mr. Ward walked down the hall and they were quite a ways from William's study, Mr. Ward said, "You may also call me Nathaniel, Nathan, or Nate. Whatever suits your fancy."

"Really? You don't mind?"

He chuckled in reply.

He drew her to a stop just outside the bedroom door. His nearness in the dim light made Amelia feel small and breathless. What did he intend to do?

"I'll sleep elsewhere, but don't tell Will." His deep baritone voice resonated quietly off the walls. "He won't understand."

"I won't." She looked down at her feet. It was obvious Mr. Goldman—William—didn't know about the forced nuptials. Clearly, he thought Mr. Ward, Nathaniel—she liked that name—had chosen to marry her. "I'm sorry."

"Don't." He put his fingers on her lips to quiet her, and it did more than that, it made her knees feel weak in a way she'd never experienced. "Don't be sorry, because I'm not."

Amelia looked into his eyes. Was he telling the truth? How could he not be sorry? But the sincerity of his gaze in the lamplight spoke volumes, and her heart beat faster, so fast, she was sure he could hear it. "So, you're not going to beat me?" The words flew out before she had time to think.

"What?" Nathaniel straightened. "Why would I do that?"

Amelia bit her lip. "Because … that's what angry husbands do."

"First of all, I'm not angry. And second of all, that's not what angry husbands should do."

She'd never heard of such a thing. Her father made it clear a husband had every right over his wife, whether in the marriage bed or if he wished to "discipline" her. How could he not wish to beat her after all they'd been through?

"Do you mean it? Really?" she asked.

"Of course," he whispered, stroking her jaw.

With those words, and the affectionate way he said them, Amelia bent over, tears flooding her eyes and drowning her face. "I thought for sure." She gasped for air in her constricting corset. "I thought you were waiting all this time to … to get me to your home where no one would hear my screams …" She sobbed uncontrollably, completely shocked by her own reaction and the enormous release of tension.

Nathaniel pulled her against him, holding her, embracing her. "I would never raise a hand to you." He stroked her hair. "Never." He held her against his chest. "I … I—wouldn't do that." He released a long sigh as his heartbeat reverberated against her cheek, and the scent of his cologne enveloped her.

How odd to receive a hug instead of a beating. And what a comfort. A comfort she'd never before experienced. Not from a man, anyway.

Nathaniel took her face into his hands and brushed the tears off her cheeks. "I can't believe you expected me to beat you." His jaw ticked, his eyes studying her, bewildered. "Go." He motioned with his chin toward the door. "Get some rest. And know that no one in this house is ever going to harm you."

Sandi Rog

Chapter Fifteen

Dazed, Amelia walked into her room, leaving Nathaniel behind staring after her in the hall. In gratitude, she dipped her head toward him as she closed the door. After it clicked shut, she sighed against it, tears still hot on her cheeks. He wasn't going to beat her. The realization still barely took root in her mind, but now she felt as if a huge weight had been lifted off her shoulders. Dare she believe it? As she pressed her forehead against the wood, she noticed a dancing light reflecting off the doorpost.

Wiping the tears from her cheeks, she turned. A fire was lit and a small red-haired woman stood over her trunk, holding up her dress. Amelia gasped and the woman faced her.

"Forgive me for startling you, miss. I've been

hired as your lady's maid." She curtsied. "Me name's Claire."

"Oh." Amelia recalled Mr. Goldman—William—talking about hiring someone for her. How odd to find a stranger in her room. It did bring back memories from her former days, however, as a child when she had a nursemaid. "It's nice to meet you," she finally said, unsure how to behave when she'd just been sobbing outside her bedroom door. What should she do? How should she behave? Amelia glanced at the bed, longing to crawl under the covers.

"Tomorrow, a dressmaker will come, miss." Claire carried Amelia's dress to the armoire and hung it inside. "You'll be measured and sized for a new wardrobe. Mr. Goldman told me that Mr. Ward telegraphed him and said you'd be needing some clothes."

When did Mr. Ward—Nathaniel—find time to send a telegraph? Then she remembered their stay at the Silver Palace Hotel. That must have been when he did that. Or, perhaps he sent it from Green Pines?

"You look tired, miss. Will you be wanting your bed?"

Amelia nodded, calming to the lilt in the maid's singsong voice. That seemed to be the only thing she was certain about. Exhaustion. Sleep. This entire marriage debacle had taken a 180-degree turn. For the better, of course. Thank the good Lord. Oh, thank you God. Thank you that he's kind.

Claire came over to help Amelia out of her dress, and as awkward as it felt to have someone help her, she didn't mind. Those buttons were such a pain. She experienced that in Cheyenne when the maid fumbled to help her get dressed. And the corset. What a complicated contraption.

Claire shook out Amelia's old nightgown. It seemed to be from another time, another world. The entire day since they arrived in Chicago played over in her mind. It all came to one shocking revelation. Mr. Ward — Nathaniel — was a good man.

Despite her protests, Claire helped Amelia into her new nightgown. "I don't need help with this. I've dressed myself plenty of times."

"I understand, miss, but Mr. Goldman told me I should do everything, I should treat you 'like a princess,' were his words, because that's what you are." She looked up at Amelia, no sign of mockery on her face.

Amelia forced a smile as she put her arms through her soft sleeves. "You know," she said, motioning to her old nightgown that Claire had set aside on the bed, "that was my wedding dress." She brushed down the skirt with the soft, white hem of her new gown. Glorious to be against silk. "Do you like it?" Amelia lifted her old, cotton gown. Thank goodness she didn't have to wear it. She held it up to herself and twirled around, a slight giggle escaping her lips. The sounds of laughter, not only surprised her, but reminded her of her days with Violet. Her close friend was the only joy she'd ever experienced. And now, she laughed? How could she feel joy after the nightmare she'd experienced? After knowing she may never see Violet again? Perhaps this sudden joy came from relief? Relief that her husband wouldn't hurt her? Yes. That must be it.

Amelia draped her old nightdress over a nearby chair.

Claire either didn't believe her, or she didn't care. With a serious look in her eyes, Claire pulled down the royal blue blankets on the large canopy bed as if she were performing a task for a queen, or as she said, a princess. The sheets and cushions were white, and so fluffy, Amelia felt as though she were falling into billowing clouds.

"This is wonderful." She sighed heavily and stretched out as far as she could beneath the thick covers.

"As it should be, miss. I've made sure all was faultless for your arrival." Claire straightened out the blankets then stood straight like a soldier, hands folded in front of her.

Amelia pulled the bedding up to her chin, studying the woman who was probably about her same age, the pride on her face, something Amelia could relate to when she'd experienced a job well done at the Green Pines Hotel.

"Thank you, Claire," Amelia whispered, hoping the woman could hear the sincerity in her tone. "Thank you for this."

"You're that welcome, miss."

Amelia sank down and fell into a deep restful — safe — sleep.

Amelia was in his room, in his bed.

It was all Nathaniel could think about as he listened — or half-listened — to William prattle on about his new bride. But he wouldn't be sleeping there tonight. Or the next. He gritted his teeth at the thought. How long would it take?

"She's absolutely beautiful, man!" Will leaned back in his chair by the fire, propping a slippered foot on his knee and puffing on his pipe. "Where did you find her? Such quality, such fine character." He sat up in his chair. "Certainly not on the streets as you said?"

"No, of course not." Nathaniel swallowed his drink, hoping to cool down the thoughts of Amelia in his arms. "She lived with her father in Green Pines, Colorado." Nathaniel frowned. "Kind of."

William furrowed his brows. "What do you mean, kind of?"

Nathaniel sighed as he set his glass down on the nearby table and proceeded to tell him the entire story. During the telling, Nathaniel watched with amusement as William's facial expressions changed from sheer horror to outrage, which Nathaniel also relived as he shared what happened.

"A shotgun wedding." William shook his head in disbelief. "Never in my born days did I ever witness such a thing. I've heard of 'em, but never—you let him do this to you. Didn't you? You wanted her, so you let it happen. May the good Lord be praised! It's as if He orchestrated it. Ha!"

Nathaniel grinned. He'd actually had the same thoughts. Then he took a deep breath as he eyed Will. "You know, she's never experienced real love." He was determined to show that to her.

"No. No, she hasn't." Will studied the rug at his feet as he nodded thoughtfully. "This means we need to throw a ball."

Nathaniel shook his head. "What?"

"Introduce her to society."

"She doesn't need a party. She needs a father. And I was hoping ... you'd be that person."

"Well, of course, man!" He waved the air as if that information was a given.

"Like you've been to me."

William stopped carrying on, and looked Nathaniel in the eye. "Nate, you don't have to ask me that, or put it in my head. She's a Ward, and that means she's family. I've already taken her into my heart." He touched his chest, his pipe still in his hand.

Nathaniel smiled. "Thank you."

"Now for the ball."

"No ball," Nathaniel said.

"Most certainly, yes a ball!" he said, clearly perturbed. "I've got it all figured out. We'll have it here at the house. I think she'll be more comfortable here. And we'll invite everyone from Prairie Avenue, and—"

"Why are you pushing to throw a party? Isn't it enough I've got a bride, and I brought her back here? Now you'll get your grandchildren." Or so he hoped.

"Nathaniel."

He rubbed the back of his neck. The thought of those arrogant snobs, nosing around in his house, his home, made his pulse rise. Nathaniel knew they'd criticize Amelia, exaggerating every perceived flaw, when none of them could hold a candle to her. What was so important about a party anyway?

"I realize you have little care for what other

people think in this world, but for your bride's sake, give her a fair chance. If you don't introduce her to society in a fashionable, controlled environment, they'll tear her to shreds, and you know it." He sat back in his chair with a huff.

Nathaniel sighed. He was right. He hated to admit it. Would Amelia even want such a thing?

"I'm not sure she knows how to dance," Nathaniel said. "She's been living in squalor, and her father didn't do anything for her, let alone arrange for her to have clothes that fit properly."

"Well, that will be taken care of tomorrow." William puffed on his pipe with an air of confidence. "I've already made arrangements for a new wardrobe."

"That would be good." Nathaniel nodded. "She needs it."

"And we'll just have to teach her how to dance." William grinned mischievously. Nathaniel wasn't sure he could trust it. "It's been a while since I had the pleasure of dancing with a beautiful young woman." He tapped his feet on the carpet as he sat in his chair.

Nathaniel shook his head and rolled his eyes.

"And it's been too long since I've seen you dance with one as well." William raised an accusing brow at him.

"If you don't behave, you won't get to dance with her." Nathaniel smirked.

William harrumphed as he kicked his feet up on the ottoman and leaned back.

"She'll need a gown," Nathaniel said, conceding to the ball.

"Arranged." Will puffed on his pipe.

"And it has to be blue. Royal blue." Nathaniel nodded. She would be absolutely beautiful in his favorite color.

"It can be done."

"Good."

Chapter Sixteen

"This is for you. Finally done." Mama handed Amelia a reticule.

Amelia gasped and ran her fingers along the calico design, blue and yellow scattering over the fabric like prairie flowers. The ribbon drawstring shimmered blue in the sunlight coming from the window.

"And look." Her mother opened the white ruffles, revealing the inside. "This is where you can stitch your name. That way if it ever gets lost, someone will know who it belongs to and return it." Mama's smile beamed as she turned in her chair, her protruding belly blocking her way against the table. "Silly me." She pushed her chair, scratching against the wooden floor. "I always forget about my girth."

Amelia giggled, her voice echoing off the walls in

the brightly lit sewing room. Mama said the baby would arrive soon. How it got inside her belly, Amelia didn't know.

"What do you think you're doing?" Amelia's father stood in the doorway, fists on his hips. "I told you to put on a corset for the guests. Look at you!"

Mama's face turned pale, as it often did when Father shouted.

"Frank, I just can't. It's too—"

"Get out!"

Amelia looked up to see Father glaring down at her. She ran from the area, holding on to her new purse. She dashed to her room and heard what sounded like a slap, just before she shut the door. Resting against it, her back to the wood, Amelia covered her ears as her father's shouts and stomps carried down the hall.

"I'm not showing off a frumpy housewife to my colleagues!" Shuffling sounds came closer, and she knew her mother was being dragged to their room. How often had she crept to the closet next to her room and listened to her mama cry herself to sleep?

"Amelia!" Her father's voice shattered through the door. Amelia scurried to her bed and yanked the covers over her head.

The door swung open. "Get up!"

She tried to sit up, but couldn't move. Her body was paralyzed against the mattress. "Get up, now!"

Amelia opened her mouth to talk, attempting to explain she couldn't move, but her lips wouldn't work. Terrified of what he might do, she screamed and sat bolt upright in bed.

"Miss Amelia!" Claire jumped back. "Saints preserve us, I didn't mean to frighten you, miss."

Amelia looked around, the royal blue colors flashing from the curtains, the bedspread, and the chair. She wasn't a child in her bed on Pennsylvania Avenue. She was a married woman in a room that didn't belong to her. But the blankets and coverlets were warm and inviting. Just like they were when she was small. She fell back into the comfort of the sheets. It'd been years since she dreamt about that dreadful night. The night her mother died. Really, she hadn't slept this well as long as she could remember, which likely brought on the dream. She had too many nights waking to every little sound in the woods that might pose a threat.

"Miss Amelia." Claire's tone was gentle. "You must be getting up. The tailor's coming." Claire took Amelia's dress out of the armoire. "Now certainly, you won't be needing this. The tailor will be measuring you." She hung it back up, shaking her head. "I've never done anything like this before, miss. I hope you can be patient with me."

"Of course." Amelia curled under the covers, her cheek nestled on the pillow as Claire wrung her hands.

"Sure, I haven't a clue what's expected of me. They say this is the finest tailor in town. Having the grandest fabrics there are, and the loveliest, most fashionable patterns."

"So?" Amelia pushed to sit up.

"Miss. You don't mean it?" Claire helped Amelia out of bed. "That man's one of the best. I don't know what he'll be wanting of me." Claire had Amelia sit in one of the elegantly cushioned chairs.

Amelia rubbed her fingertips along the smooth wood. Mr. Ward didn't beat her last night. And he said he never would. How could it be possible? How could he not want to beat her for all she'd put him through? Yet, it wasn't her choice by any means, and somehow he saw that. He knew she didn't want the marriage any more than he did. So, of course, he's not going to blame her. Suddenly, she felt light. Like all her bone-deep fears vanished in that moment. It was as if the Lord came to her while she slept and stole them all away. She smiled.

"Why do you smile, miss?" Claire brushed Amelia's hair.

"I can do this, you know." Amelia held up her hand. "I've been brushing my own hair for a long time now." She frowned at being pampered by someone she felt should be a friend, not a servant.

Claire gripped the brush and knelt in front of her. "Ach, don't be saying that, Miss Amelia. 'Tis my job. I'd be out of work if you took over."

"It's just hair." Amelia flipped a few strands over her shoulder.

Claire cast her gaze to the floor.

Amelia relented. "Go ahead."

Claire jumped up and brushed as though her life depended on it, working gently around the tangles.

"You're doing a good job, Claire." Amelia still wasn't comfortable with all this pampering.

"Oh, thank you, miss." Claire responded with such delight, Amelia didn't dare try to steal her joy and allowed her to brush to her heart's content.

What a life. Amelia stared at the hearth in front of her, the bronze fire poker reflecting the light from the warm flames.

Claire finished with her hair and put the brush away.

"Today, you'll be measured for an entire wardrobe." Claire scurried around her, making the bed and straightening the curtains. "It's so thrilling!"

An entire wardrobe? She'd only owned two dresses for ... how long had it been since she got her last dress? Four years ago? She couldn't even remember. And now she owned two new ones to replace the old. She glanced up at the open armoire, the beige and blue dresses hanging stiffly from their hangers. Too nice to belong to plain old Amelia. How could those dresses really be hers? And now she'd get more?

Before they knew it, the tailor arrived, and as Amelia stood on a stool for the man to measure her — thankfully, she was allowed to keep her nightdress on — she still felt exposed. Like she was on display for all to see.

The man's spectacles slid to the tip of his nose as he had his assistant write down all her measurements. He measured in places that she never would have thought needed measuring: her wrists, her ankles, and even her hands.

"What are you measuring those for?" she asked, daring to speak, despite the arrogant, refined air about him.

Of course, he looked at her as though she were

daft, but quickly adjusted his face to regard her with respect. "Boots, my lady. Gloves, and the like."

Amelia nodded. "Oh." So she'd even get boots and gloves. How lovely. Never in her wildest dreams did she imagine marriage would be like this. To think, she was a married woman. What did he expect of her? Would she have to clean this enormous house? No. She knew he had servants for that. Claire smiled at her as the tailor's assistant jotted down the numbers.

He lifted up a ribbon by its ring and held it to the top of her head and let it fall all the way down to her ankles. "Help me with this," the tailor said. The assistant handed his tablet and pencil to Claire and grabbed the bottom of the ribbon.

"Take this down," the tailor said to Claire who stood holding the paper as if she didn't know what to do with it. He called out the measurements, but Claire didn't move.

The tailor huffed. "Tom, take it." With an exasperated wave he motioned for his assistant to take the tablet from Claire. "All you Irish are alike. Good lord, she can't even write."

Tom gently took the tablet, and Claire scurried over to help the tailor, despite his derogatory remark.

"You can leave now," Amelia said, calm fury seething in her tone. "You have enough." She reached for Claire to help her down from the chair.

"But ma'am—"

"You've measured everything but my eyeballs." Amelia marched toward the door and swung it open. "I won't abide by this sort of insolence. You will respect my—" What was she called? "My friend!"

There. That was the perfect title, even though they just met. She knew Claire would make a fine friend, and even if she didn't, Amelia would be hers. "Out!" Amelia's imperious tone shocked even her, and she felt like she was a heroine in one of her favorite dime novels. As the men collected their things and scampered to the door, trying not to trip over themselves, she noticed Nathaniel standing in the hall, witnessing the entire scene.

"Nathaniel." Amelia gasped as the men hurried past him.

"Amelia," he said, his baritone voice caressing her, along with his gaze as it swept down, resting on her ankles.

She ducked behind the door.

"You allowed strangers to see you like this, why not your own husband?" He cast her a crooked grin, and her cheeks went hot. "It's time for breakfast," he said, and motioned to the men leaving. "I thought they were taking too long in here, and I can see I was right." His jaw pulsed. "Did they … were they … inappropriate?"

"Yes, as a matter of fact, they were." Amelia lifted her chin, the fury of how they treated Claire reigniting.

Nathaniel stepped toward her. "What'd they do?"

"They insulted Claire!" Amelia felt like stomping her foot, and she might have if Nathaniel hadn't moved so close. She cowered further behind the door.

"They didn't … touch you?" He hovered over her.

"Well, of course they did."

"What?"

"They were taking my measurements, so they had to touch me," she said, catching her breath from his nearness. "I just didn't appreciate the way they spoke to Claire. What's so terrible about being Irish? Nothing but insolent cads!"

"What'd they do to her?"

Amelia glanced at Claire, her green eyes wide with fear. "Nothing." Amelia straightened. "Nothing I can't take care of." She moved with the door, and proceeded to close it with Nathaniel standing in the way. "Now, if you'll excuse us. I need to get dressed."

Nathaniel smirked and bowed slightly, touching his head. "As you wish, my lady."

Amelia proceeded to close the door, but Nathaniel caught it with his foot. "I've never been kicked out of my own room before." Then he closed the door himself, yanking the handle out of Amelia's hands. She stood there frozen, taking in his last words. His room? Of course this was his room. It certainly couldn't be hers. Oh, my. That meant … she slept in his bed. His lovely, wonderful, glorious bed. She'd think about that later. She turned to face her terrified friend.

"Claire."

"Yes, miss." Tears filled Claire's eyes, and she cried into her hands.

Amelia went to her and wrapped her arms around her. "You can't read, can you?"

"No, miss."

She knew it. Amelia recognized that blank stare on several of the children's faces when it was discovered they couldn't read. Amelia grasped her by the shoulders. "I can teach you. Do you like stories? I mean, romantic stories?" She bounced to her toes. "Stories about heroes and heroines and chivalry and … everything!" All the Yellow Backs Amelia had ever read flashed through her mind. Then she remembered, they were home in her cabin, far away from her grasp. She stopped short. "Oh, no."

"What is it, miss?"

"Never mind." Amelia took her by the arm. She'd find a way to get her hands on some. She always did. She sat Claire down in the royal-blue chair she'd just occupied.

"I'm going to teach you to read." She knelt before Claire and cupped her tear-streaked face in her hands. "You're going to learn to read. And the stories will excite you. They'll amaze you!"

"But, miss." Claire lifted her hands, her face dazed, confused. "I'm the one who's supposed to be looking after you. They'll only be dismissing me."

"It'll be our secret," Amelia whispered, feeling more alive than she had in a long time. "No one has to know." She giggled and hugged Claire.

Slowly, cautiously, she felt Claire's arms wrap around her.

Yes, Claire will make a wonderful friend.

At breakfast, sitting in her beige dress, and eating her eggs in as much a lady-like fashion as she could muster, Amelia took a deep breath, collecting all her courage so she could make her request.

"We've already had a caller," Mr. Ward said to William. "I had Nick send them away."

"You had the butler send them away? Who was it?" William looked up from his plate. "What'd you go and do that for?"

"You know folks just want to pry."

Mr. Goldman huffed.

"I was wondering ..." Amelia said.

Both William and Nathaniel stopped, William with his spoon halfway to his mouth, and Nathaniel with his fork down, watching her with eager anticipation.

"Yes?" Nathaniel said.

"Is there anyplace I can find some books?" She shifted uncomfortably in her chair. "You see, I used to have several Yellow Backs and ... well ... I—"

"Of course you can have some books!" William shouted as he always did. Perhaps he was hard of hearing? "We've got a whole library full."

"Oh! You do?"

"Why yes, little lady." He motioned across the table. "Nate'll show you the way."

As soon as breakfast was over, Nathaniel led her through the large house, past William's study, and into a grand room with vaulted windows and books stacked to the ceiling. Amelia gasped in delight.

"Take your pick," Nathaniel said.

Amelia walked into the room, taking in the tall shelves and the colorful books. Dark green, maroon and beige spines with some titles etched in gold. "Remarkable!" A dream come true. She actually lived in a house with an impressive library. Who knew? She couldn't wait to lose herself within the pages of one of these marvelous titles. As she scanned the shelves for something she might enjoy, she spun around to Nathaniel. "Where are your Yellow Backs?"

Nathaniel straightened. "Yellow Backs?" He motioned to the impressive shelves surrounding them. "When you have all these to choose from?"

Amelia bit her lip. Did he look down on her for wanting a dime novel? After all, those were her favorite to teach from. The books were short enough to hold the attention of children, and especially anyone who was learning to read. Slogging through a thick novel when someone didn't even know their letters would take far too much time, and might not even be worth the read. She feared even the dime novel would be too long.

"Well, I'm afraid we're all out of those."

"You used to have them?"

Nathaniel shrugged sheepishly. "I used to read them."

"Really?" Amelia stepped closer to her benefactor. "Then you know just how exciting they can be."

Nathaniel studied her with a smirk on his lips.

"Is there any way we can find some?" She folded her hands, hoping beyond hope he'd take her to town. Perhaps they'd get to ride one of the trolleys?

Still watching her with those handsome eyes, he nodded. "I'll call for the carriage."

She stepped toward him. "May we ride in one of those electric carriages?"

Nathaniel chuckled and walked toward the door, and then he turned to face her. "Hmm. Only one night here and already making demands."

"I'm sorry." Amelia's face went hot. "I never …"

"No." Nathaniel strode toward her. "It's a joke. I'm only making fun." He captured her by the hand. "Come. Let's race."

With that, he led her to the door, and he ran with her through corridor after corridor. She struggled to keep up as he rounded a corner, still holding on to her hand. Suddenly, he released her and disappeared down a dark passageway. Breathless, she stumbled to a stop.

"Mr. Ward?" she called, her trembling voice echoing off the bare walls.

"It's Nathaniel." His hot breath came against her ear, sending shivers of pleasure down her cheek. "Come." He turned her around on wobbly legs, and led her deeper into the cavern.

"Where are we going?" she whispered, barely picking up shadows of light streaking across the walls and floor.

"Follow me."

"Do I have a choice?"

He chuckled, a low deep rumble in his chest, sending shivers tumbling down her back. He then pushed open a door. "Careful. Let me help you." He guided her down a narrow flight of stairs as she gripped his arm for support in the dark. Finally, they reached the bottom, and he opened a door. The light blinded her as he escorted her outside. "Be right back."

Amelia's vision adjusted to the light as Nathaniel strode toward the carriage house, his gait confident in the warm air.

Who was this man?

Chapter Seventeen

Nothing but noise surrounded them as they zipped through the streets of Chicago on one of the city's trolleys. Amelia laughed as people walked along the sidewalks, and carriages trotted by when the trolley slowed down enough for folks to hop off. "It's like one vast construction site!" she shouted above the voices of the passengers and the bell of the streetcar.

Nathaniel pointed to one tall building. "They're called skyscrapers. A new story goes up every day."

"Good heavens!" She arched her head out the window to see all the way to the top.

The crack, crack of a gun went off from the sidewalk. Amelia ducked back into the trolley and took cover against Nathaniel's chest.

"Rivet guns," Nathaniel said, his arm closing

around her. "They're the new rage."

Amelia pulled away, self-conscious of the intimacy they displayed in public.

"We'll get off here." Nathaniel strode to the door, and stepped down to the bottom step, but the trolley hadn't stopped. He reached up for her as she neared the opening.

"But it's still moving." She shook her head, remembering how others leaped off without falling, but she didn't trust her flexibility in the confining dress and corset. Having a maid help her get dressed was fine and dandy, but not when it meant tying a corset so tight that she could barely breathe. "It's too fast."

"I've got you." He held his hands out to her.

She took them and stepped down.

"On three, jump." He took her by the waist. "One, two, three."

Together, they stepped off the streetcar, and with Nathaniel's strong hold, she kept her balance. They rushed to the sidewalk, and breathless, Amelia turned to watch the trolley continue on without them.

Nathaniel laughed and ran his hand through his hair. Looking down on his new bride, he swelled with pride at her willingness to trust him. Her cheeks flushed pink as her gaze darted up at him in wide-eyed wonder and at the city surrounding them. Her neck arched, and she held her hat in place as she looked up and up to the top of the ten-story Pullman building.

"Mr. Pullman's office is all the way at the top."

"Unbelievable," she said just loud enough for him to hear. "I've never seen the like."

Some people walked by and a man shouted at the group, pointing at the building. "Mr. Pullman brags about it being fireproof!" They continued on, leaving Nathaniel and Amelia in their wake.

"Can a building really be fireproof?" Amelia asked.

"Who can tell?" Nathaniel said, shrugging.

"Why would that be such a concern?"

Nathaniel stopped. "You don't know?"

"Know what?"

"About the Great Chicago Fire in 1871?" How could she not know?

She wrinkled her brows, shaking her head. "If it was in '71, I was only seven." Then her eyes widened to saucers. "That's the fire Mr. Goldman lost his daughters in, and you lost your parents." She put her hand on her chest. "Heavens. I didn't realize. You were here during that time? I remember it now, learning bits and pieces here and there, but I don't recall much about it. Only that it burned a great deal of the city." She looked around, clearly seeing the city through new eyes. "I had no idea." She shook her head. "Oh, Nathaniel. Please forgive me. I didn't ... I didn't realize."

She called him Nathaniel. He liked the sound of it on her lips. It also brought back memories of his mother. That's what she used to call him. It wasn't far from where they stood right now that he'd escaped the fire. He cringed at the memory.

They had been running, trying to escape when his

mother fell and became trapped under a wooden beam. As she lay unconscious, crowds pushed around them, threatening to carry them in their massive wave down the burning street. His father set Rachel, his little sister, down, the ends of her blonde hair singed. She and Michael, his brother, clung to each other against a building to keep from being swept away by the people.

Nathaniel and his father pulled with all their might to lift the wooden plank off his mother's legs. Explosions cracked across the sky, and a billow of orange burst above them, making the ground and buildings appear as if it were daylight. Choking on the smoke and his eyes burning, they tugged again, but the plank wouldn't move. They tried again. Michael joined in, and together they heaved.

No movement. Nothing.

Father grabbed Rachel and shoved her into Nathaniel's arms. "Go! Get them to the water!"

"But you need help!" Nathaniel couldn't leave.

His father grabbed him by his nightshirt and shoved him against the brick building. "Save your brother and sister," he said between clenched teeth. "Save them now!"

Rachel clung to him, her legs and arms wrapped securely around him, and Michael clung to his shirt so as not to lose him as they ran for their lives. The falling embers, the sweltering heat, the fiery wind, all drove Nathaniel and his brother and sister to the pier.

Flames ate up the landing, and hundreds of people crammed to the end, threatening to fall into the lake below. Jostled by the herd, Nathaniel tightened his arms around Rachel and held Michael against him so he wouldn't get yanked away. Ashes landed on Nathaniel's arms, burning the light hair and flesh. He swiped them away as they landed on his brother and sister's hair and skin.

Ship masts in the distance burned where people had tried to escape. The torrents of wind blew flaming debris over the water, igniting the ships and sending people overboard.

The entire situation was hopeless. How would any of them survive?

Desperate, Nathaniel fell on his knees and prayed. Clinging to his brother and sister, he prayed for his parents, for himself and Rachel and Michael. Prayed that the fire would somehow miss his mother and father, prayed that the flames wouldn't reach the end of the pier. Prayed like he'd never prayed before in his short eleven years.

Through the smoke pouring over them and Nathaniel's burning eyes, he saw shadows of people collecting buckets of water from the lake. Frantically, they tossed the water onto the nibbling flames that threatened to engulf them as they made their way down the pier.

Smoke hissed not far from Nathaniel's knees and the blaze finally died.

Since that day, Nathaniel never felt he could adequately thank God for saving him and his siblings.

Nathaniel told the story to Amelia as tears streamed down her cheeks.

"And you haven't seen your brother and sister since?"

He shook his head.

"What of William?"

"Will was away on business in St. Louis. When he returned, he found that not only was he homeless, he'd lost his entire family."

"How terrible."

"All is well now." He took her by the arm, and led her down the sidewalk, wishing he'd never brought it up.

"How did you and Will meet?" she asked.

That one question opened a barrage of troublesome memories. Like the evening he arrived back in Chicago—the first time since the fire—when he was just seventeen.

Get to the water!

His father's last words would echo in Nathaniel's mind for the rest of his life. He remembered it like it happened yesterday. But he didn't want to remember, so he shoved the memories to the deep corners of his consciousness, the corners full of shadows and pain.

Now, six years since the fire, alone and with his money wrapped in Amelia's calico purse stashed deep in his pocket, he stood on the Government Pier in Chicago, gazing at the stars. It was here Nathaniel, Michael and Rachel had said goodbye to the amazing city so full of promise—and to their parents.

With a new city and future before him, Nathaniel patted his pocket. He finally had the funds to free his brother and sister from the orphan asylum. He'd worked all sorts of jobs: in mines, with cattle and horses, in nearby factories. Anything he could find. During that time, he went without in order to save as much as he possibly could to rescue his siblings and have enough so they could fend for themselves.

Taking a deep breath, he left the pier behind, along with the memories and the pain. Time to begin anew.

Marveling at how the city had grown, how it had rebuilt itself after the fire, he wandered the streets marked with a few unfinished plots and leftover skeletal remains of buildings. He crossed streets and turned corners, noting that most the buildings were now made of brick. The city during the Great Fire had been nothing but timber, like a box of matchsticks, with its wooden houses and raised boardwalks to avoid the swamps below. His family had been there a week when the fire hit. It was a miracle he'd even found the dock.

Nathaniel looked for an inn. But did he really want to stay in one? He knew how to find shelter on the street, and that'd mean he'd save money. He'd taken the Transcontinental Railroad upon his return. This time, he paid for his trip. He felt he owed the railroad at least that much after all his free rides.

"Your wallet, old-timer, or your life!" A young man's voice carried from around the corner.

"Stop!" a man's voice shouted.

Nathaniel jogged to the commotion. Several boys frisked a white-bearded man in an alley, pushing him against a building. Some laughed and one knocked off his top hat. The man swung his cane, trying to fight them off.

"Get out!" Nathaniel charged at the boys, most of them younger and a few his age. He grabbed one of the larger boys by the shirt who was pummeling the man. Nathaniel yanked him off his feet as the old man slid down the brick wall.

"Get him!"

A boy came at Nathaniel and swung, pain sliced his arm.

Nathaniel slugged him. The hoodlum stumbled backward and Nathaniel grabbed the boy's wrist, trying to wrestle the knife out of his hand. Just as he got hold of the blade, someone grabbed him from behind. Nathaniel head-butted him and swung around, brandishing the knife.

"He's got the tickler!"

Several ran. One sped past him, the light of the moon catching his profile.

Michael.

The boy stopped—nothing but a dark shadow—and faced Nathaniel. His heavy breathing echoed through the alley. He then ran and disappeared around the corner.

It couldn't be Michael. He was in the orphan asylum.

The old man groaned.

Nathaniel turned, all the boys gone, and hurried to the man's side.

"Sir? Are you all right?" Nathaniel grabbed his arm and helped him to his feet, the cane clattering to the ground.

Nathaniel kicked it up and snatched it out of the air.

"Thank you." The old man straightened, his hands trembling on his lapels. "That was quite a display of hand-to-hand combat." His voice shook as he spoke, and he took a step and faltered.

Nathaniel caught him. "Where do you live? I'll take you home."

"Oh, that won't be—" He fell against Nathaniel.

"I insist, sir. Where do you live?"

The man pointed, and Nathaniel led the way, holding him up as they walked.

"I could have held my own back there, but it's been a long day."

Nathaniel smiled, as he led him down the empty street. Clearly the man's pride had been wounded.

Eventually, they came to a three-story, brick house in an upper-class neighborhood. Nathaniel helped him up the porch steps, and when they reached the door, the man held out a key. With unsteady hands, he failed to get the key in its hole.

The door swung open, and a maid stood before them. Her eyes widened and her hands flew to her cheeks. "Mr. Goldman!"

"He was attacked." As Nathaniel helped Mr. Goldman into his home, impressions rushed at him: mahogany furnishings, a chandelier hanging in the hall, and a settee in the parlor. Books, vases, and statues lined numerous shelves on both sides of a large hearth. He helped the man off with his coat and handed it to the maid.

"Over there." Mr. Goldman motioned to a high-backed chair not far from the fireplace.

Nathaniel helped him into the leather seat, making sure he was comfortable, and bent in front of him, studying his expression. The paleness beneath his white beard and mustache concerned him. After working in the mines in the Rocky Mountains, Nathaniel observed men who got too close to a blast. For a moment they would seem fine and later go into some form of shock. He motioned to the maid. "Fetch a doctor."

"No, no." Mr. Goldman grabbed Nathaniel's pained arm. "I don't need a doctor. I'll be fine." He cleared his throat. "I'm just shaken up. That's all." His gaze met Nathaniel's. "What's your name, son?"

"Nathaniel Ward, sir."

"You're a good boy." Mr. Goldman nodded and patted his hand. "I thank you for your help."

"I'm just glad I was there." Remembering his manners, he removed his hat.

"Margie, tea please. And for Mr. Ward here."

"Yes, sir." Margie curtsied and hurried to do Mr. Goldman's bidding.

Nathaniel stared down at the plush rug. He'd never been called Mr. Ward before. That was his father. Not him. What a contradicting sensation that evoked. He felt all grown up, but at the same time, he longed to be a child and have his father with him. Sucking in a deep breath, he looked back at the old man.

Seeing that his color had returned, Nathaniel stood. "I trust you're going to be well, sir." The rich house and all its upper-class furnishings made Nathaniel remember how out of place he was, so he put his hat back on. "I'll be on my way."

"No!" Mr. Goldman raised his finger to stop him. "You're staying for tea." His tone was one Nathaniel didn't dare refuse. In fact, it made him smile.

The warmth and comfort of the wealthy house drew him in, so Nathaniel didn't see anything wrong in staying for a while. He turned to take a seat, and out of habit, patted his pocket, feeling for his savings. No bulge met his hand. He patted it again, but his hand came flat against his thigh. He looked down and felt through his other pockets. Empty. His money was gone. Amelia's purse and all his savings. Gone!

"Did those boys get to you too?" Frowning, Mr. Goldman shook his head.

Nathaniel's gaze darted around the room, at the window, out onto the street. He had to get his money back. It was his life, his hope for a future. "Excuse me," Nathaniel said, his voice choking. Trembling, he turned to the door.

"Don't leave, son. I'll reimburse you for your loss."

"It was all I had." Nathaniel's ragged voice exposed his grief. There was no way anyone could reimburse him for that amount. He clenched his fists as the room spun. All these five years the purse had never been stolen. He'd always taken great care to protect it, and the one time it held his future, he had to lose it, to lose everything. He wanted to rage, to shout obscenities, to throw aside all manners and propriety. He bent as if he'd been punched in the gut, resting his trembling hands on his knees. How could he go on? How could he start all over again?

Well, with Mr. Goldman he'd managed to start all over again. He'd shared most of the story with Amelia, but not the part about his money being in her purse.

"It's wonderful that you were able to rescue William."

"God's hand was in it. He put me in the right place at the right time. He did on many occasions," Nathaniel added, thinking of how easily he found her. If only he could find his brother and sister.

They continued on down the sidewalk. He stopped in front of a small bookstore and motioned to the wooden shelf near the entrance. "Yellow Backs, my lady."

Amelia turned, and her contemplative countenance turned to sheer surprise when she saw the dime novels. "There's so many. I've never seen so many at one time." She collected one, then another. "How do I decide?"

"You can have as many as you'd like."

"Oh, I can't. I can't."

"Yes, you can," Nathaniel said, chuckling at her enthusiasm.

Nathaniel had learned that Michael had escaped the orphanage, which made him believe the boy he saw his first night back in Chicago must have been his brother. It ate at Nathaniel that he hadn't chased him down right then. What was his brother doing robbing old men? Robbing him? He shook his head. Swindled by his own flesh and blood. Didn't Michael remember God, where he came from? Had he no shame? All Nathaniel could do was pray that the boy wasn't Michael. That Michael hadn't gone down such a destructive path. But his gut told him different. Nathaniel had been on the streets long enough to know what the real world was like.

As for his sister, she had been moved to another city because of overcrowding, and her paperwork was lost. His heart grieved. He had to find them. Somehow, some way.

As they worked their way deeper into the store, Amelia stopped suddenly, arms full of Yellow Backs, and she looked down at a Bible displayed on a table.

"I left mine at home," she whispered, disappointment reflecting from her face. She then looked up at Nathaniel, mist in her eyes. "May I exchange all these for this?"

"As I said, you may have them all." Nathaniel's chest filled with satisfaction.

"But it's so expensive," she said, her green eyes wide with surprise, and biting her lip, she stared back down at the Bible as if she were seeing gold.

Nathaniel chuckled. "Have you forgotten where you live, my lady?"

As if in a daze, she handed Nathaniel all the Yellow Backs, and he fought to balance them as she turned back to the Bible. With reverence she brushed her fingers along its cover, caressing its brown spine and opening its pages. "Can I really have this?" she whispered.

"Yes, of course," Nathaniel said as he motioned with his chin to the clerk. "We'd like to make a purchase.

On the way home, Nathaniel carried all the Yellow Backs, while Amelia hugged her new Bible, wrapped in soft fabric, to her chest, beaming as if she'd just struck gold. "This is the best day ever," she said.

Nathaniel looked down at his new bride, pleasure consuming him. "Yes. The best day ever."

Chapter Eighteen

After returning home, Nathaniel went to his study to do some work, and Amelia went straight to Nathaniel's room, the only familiar place she felt slightly at home. The only place in the house—other than the dining room—that she knew how to find. It was there she sat on the cushioned chair and read from her new Bible. She happened upon the book of James, the same book she read long ago in the wilderness of Green Pines. This time she read it again. Perhaps she'd discover something new? She came across the passage about how every good and perfect gift is from above, coming down from the Father of lights.

Amelia looked around the elegant room— Nathaniel's room—still feeling like a visitor, and yet,

Nathaniel had called this place her home. It all felt unreal, like she was in a dream. But God declared in His word that all these good things were from Him, her heavenly Father. And not just the material blessings, but the blessing of her new husband. A man who was patient, kind and generous.

She brushed her fingers over the open pages of her new Bible and then glanced over at the Yellow Backs stacked on the small table nearby. As the light shifted against the windowpane, the rays glided into the room. In the short time she'd been here, this room had become her sanctuary. She set her Bible down on the chair, went to the window, and opened one of its latches. The crystal waters in the distance sparkled against the sun, and a light wind whispered blessings to come. Did all this truly come from God above? Did He truly love her that much?

She remembered the dark cabin, the small windows, and sitting in the rocker with her father's rifle on her lap, drenched in fear. And now, here she stood amidst such breathtaking beauty as seagulls soared above in the blue sky calling out to her in freedom. Tears came to her eyes and the scene before her blurred. Dare she believe it? Dare she believe this freedom was hers? This freedom to live, love and breathe?

She looked around the room, at all its fine furnishings. She never longed to be rich. She simply longed to be free. To be free of the abuse. To be free to make her own decisions. Her thoughts fell on Nathaniel. He didn't seem to be angry about their situation. Nor was he angry with her. Even if she wasn't a gift to him, he was a gift to her. The man who set her free, even if not by choice. Who would have thought that the terrible night in Green Pines when she was forced to marry could turn out to be a blessing? Only God could turn something so dreadful into something good.

She prayed she could be a blessing to Nathaniel, that she would be a good wife for him. Wife. What was she thinking? Something dark lurked beneath the surface. Something she couldn't quite put her finger on. Something she feared would keep her from being the "good wife" Nathaniel deserved. A long, slow breath escaped her.

Perhaps she'd take a stroll through the house and become better acquainted with Nathaniel's home ... her home. This amazing gift from her heavenly Father. She made her way to the dining room, since she knew how to find it, and she knew she'd be able to get back to her room from that point. As she passed that familiar chamber, she made her way down another familiar hall. Wasn't this where Mr. Goldman—William's—study was? She came upon an open door and peered inside.

William looked up from his desk. "Well, well. What do we have here?" He stood. "Come in."

Amelia froze, feeling like she'd been caught spying.

"Come in!"

Amelia stepped into the warm, inviting space, despite all its formality. Having been here already when he showed the photos of his family, she recognized the vanilla tobacco scents coming from his pipe and breathed in the pleasing aroma.

"What brings you to this side of the house?"

She shrugged self-consciously, feeling like a waif lost in a mansion. "I thought I'd get to know the surroundings."

"Well, let me show you around!" William came to the front of his desk, gave her his elbow, and Amelia took it as he led her out of his study. He showed her down corridors and secret compartments, hidden stairs and open chambers with vaulted windows.

"So, how was your outing this morning? Did you find what you needed?" William asked.

"Yes, it was wonderful," she said. "I've never seen a city so impressive, so robust. Not even in Denver."

William nodded as he led her into a grand ballroom with vaulted ceilings and high, majestic windows. Stunned, she felt like a princess in an enchanted castle. "Breathtaking." Amelia turned around, taking in the marble floor, painted walls and long, red draperies in their magnificent splendor. "I've never seen anything so majestic." To think this was now her home.

William stood, grinning. "It's all because of Nate." He shook his head. "You know he was once a street Arab. It's amazing how he created all of this."

"A street Arab?" she asked.

"Street rat." He shrugged.

"Oh, yes." Amelia nodded.

"That's what we call 'em." He turned and guided her across the floor. "Tell me about yourself, little lady."

Amelia stiffened. Why would he want to know

about her? "There's really not much to tell," she said, looking at the room around her. "My life was nothing until I came here."

"Well, I know that isn't true." William led her to one of the big windows.

Outside was a view of a park with a small church house in the distance.

"I was very poor." It was difficult for her to admit. Perhaps William would be ashamed of her.

"Well, that doesn't say anything about you and who you are." He harrumphed and motioned her to follow as he led her through another door to the large dining hall. "You know this room," he said, waving around them. "Come. Let's ring for lunch, shall we?" He went to a wall and opened a small cupboard. Within he pulled on a few strings and then shut the door. "Someone will be here shortly." He motioned for her to sit, and he settled down near her at the head of the table.

"Tell me about your family." Smiling warmly, William folded his wrinkled hands, a gold band on one finger shining in the light, and leaned toward her over the table.

Amelia cocked her head, studying his gaze. By the look in his eyes, she could tell he was sincere. "Well … I … lived in a small house with my father in Green Pines."

William nodded. "And your mother? Any siblings?"

"My mother died when I was young. She died giving birth to my brother who was stillborn." With the dream being so recent, she began to believe her father actually killed the baby within her mother. How could she not have seen it before?

"Oh, I see." He pinched his lips together. "It must have been difficult without a mother."

Amelia nodded, realizing she'd been in denial of the truth all this time. The truth that her father was a murderer.

"And now you're here with us." He spread his hands over the table, smoothing out the cream-colored cloth. "And we are so happy to have you."

She forced a smile and looked down at the tablecloth. "I'm glad," she said, unable to say more. It did her good, really, to know how happy William was to have her in his home, but the reality of her past caused her to feel weak. How grateful she was to be in the place. This safe haven. Perhaps she couldn't accept the truth before because she had nowhere to run? She was trapped with her father.

William leaned back, studying her.

She shifted in her chair.

A servant entered, carrying breads, cheese and small cakes on a platter.

"Will Nathaniel be joining us?"

"Oh, yes. He'll be here shortly." William straightened in his seat. "Forgive me. I'm simply reminded of my own girls, trying to imagine how they would look now." He cleared his throat. "You remind me of them."

"I'm sorry."

"Oh! No need to apologize." He gestured with his hand as if shooing her apology away. "No. No. Don't apologize, dear one." He leaned forward again, opening his mouth, then pinching his lips and shaking his head.

Amelia moved in closer too. What did he wish to say? Was something wrong?

He straightened, shaking his head. "Let's pray." With that, he gave a sharp nod, closed his eyes and began thanking God for the food. As he continued, he added, "And Lord, please be with our Amelia. She's going through some big changes, coming from so far away. Please help her to know that she's loved here, that she doesn't have to be afraid, and that she's under our protection, but more importantly, that she's under Your protection."

Amelia couldn't help but peek, seeing his bushy eyebrows drawn together in earnest as he prayed.

"I thank You for the blessing you've brought into this house through this precious new bride of Nate's, and I pray we can be a light to her as she is to us." With that he closed the prayer and said, "Let's dig in!"

Amelia simply watched William grab the bread as he tore off a piece and then helped himself to some cheese.

He motioned to the tray of food. "Help yourself. It's good food!"

She swallowed. This time she found herself opening her mouth to speak and then closing it. "I … I am very … thank you for that prayer." Unable to eat, she folded her hands in her lap and looked down at her empty plate. How could William feel she was a blessing? What had she done? Nothing at all. She didn't deserve such praise or honor. Really, she didn't belong in such a beautiful place with such kind, loving people. Tears welled in her eyes.

"So you started without me?" Nathaniel's voice carried from the doorway.

"I was hungry." William said as he took a bite. Chewing, he motioned for Nathaniel to sit down.

Nathaniel sat, said a silent prayer, and then took his own helping from the tray. "Aren't you going to eat?" he asked, his hand stopped in mid-air as he looked from Amelia's empty plate to her face.

Quickly, she nodded, and with a trembling hand took a small portion of the bread. But with both Nathaniel and William studying her, she could no longer control her tears and several slid down her cheeks.

"What's the matter?" Nathaniel leaned on the table. "What happened?" He straightened and faced William. "What did you say to the poor girl? What did you do?"

William looked from Amelia to Nathaniel in mock defense. "I didn't do anything. Nothing at all! I simply gave her a tour of the house and now we're eating." He took a bite as if to prove his point. "I think she's happy," he said with his mouth full. "That's what it is. She's happy." He pointed at Nathaniel with his bread. "Women do that, you know. My wife and girls would do that." He shook his head. "Oh, it was bothersome. I never knew which way was up or down, where I was going, or what to do. Constantly walking on eggshells." He winked at Amelia. "You're happy, right?"

As if her mouth had a will of its own, Amelia's

lips tugged into a smile, and then she broke into giggles. Yes, it was so good to be here, to be amongst people who cared. A relief, actually.

"You see!" William waved his hands in the air, one fist with bread, the other with cheese. "What'd I tell ya? She's happy! The Lord be praised, our Amelia is happy!"

Watching the spectacle William displayed only made Amelia laugh harder, and finally, Nathaniel — after looking back and forth between the two as if they'd lost their minds — joined in and chuckled.

Really, she was more confused, but William could put a smile on anyone's face.

Perhaps she was ... happy ... after all?

Later that evening, the tailor arrived in feigned humbleness with two garments. "Now, here we have a costume of the finest French silk." His assistant, Tom, grinning from behind the dress, held up a beautiful light blue garment with an intricately plaited skirt.

Claire giggled, watching the man.

The tailor turned sharply toward her, but immediately looked away, clearing his throat and forcing his attention back on his task. "And a handsome Queen Coronet Bonnet to match." He motioned to the bonnet, clearly trying to impress her with his goods. "The French lace trimmings, along with these elegant strings and ribbon, are a perfect complement to—"

"It's beautiful." The elaborate dress with its grand sash sweeping over the front took Amelia's breath away. Could this beauty truly belong to her?

"E-hem!" The tailor motioned for Tom to pick up the next garment.

Tom jumped at the command, turning away from Claire, and reached for the next costume.

Claire blushed and lowered her gaze to the floor.

As Tom held up the next garment, he hid his face behind the dress as if he were hiding from the tailor and Amelia, but when Amelia noticed Claire cover her smile behind her hand, she knew the tailor's assistant must have been flirting with her from behind the dress.

"I want to make sure each costume fits properly before I continued with the rest of the wardrobe," the tailor said, reclaiming Amelia's attention. "I'd like to have a fitted pattern to use for all the finery I'm going to create."

"Thank you." Amelia smiled, excited about the new clothes, but also curious to know if the tailor was aware of his assistant's shenanigans.

"I brought a variety of fabric colors for you to choose. I'd hate to make a garment, only for you to detest it."

"I could never detest anything." How could she dislike anything that was about to be made for her, especially when all she ever owned were those two dresses that hadn't fit?

He turned to his satchel and pulled out different colors of cloth. "What do you think of these?" He held up swatches of fabric over his arm, displaying them with finesse.

Amelia stepped closer, looking through the many

hues. She pointed to the ones she liked. Really, there were so many, but her hand paused when she spotted the brilliant color she'd seen so often since her marriage ... royal blue. "Oh." Her hand touched the pristine cloth. "This is lovely."

"I already have plans for that one." He looked down at her through his spectacles and cleared his throat. "Something has already been ordered in that color by your husband."

She pulled her hand back. What could that mean? "Yes, of course." She shouldn't be surprised that Nathaniel would have picked something out for her, and especially in that color. It seemed his favorite blue was becoming her own.

The next day was Sunday morning, and with Claire's help, Amelia was dressed and ready in her light-blue frock with the hat and all its finery.

Together, William and Nathaniel escorted them toward the small church house Amelia had seen through one of the large windows of the estate. Other servants either followed behind or arrived before them.

It was a fine crisp morning, and Amelia secretly enjoyed being on Nathaniel's arm. He looked straight ahead, his dimpled chin lifted, as the birds soared above their heads.

"This will be an introduction to your brothers and sisters in Christ, here in Chicago." He grinned down at her.

Amelia hugged her new Bible. She prayed she wouldn't find another Miss Bruster amongst the fold.

As if sensing her fears, he added, "You don't need

to worry. They are going to love you."

Love her? Who would do that? She swallowed and nodded.

As they came to the front and walked up the few steps to the doors, a preacher in a black vest and black silk necktie greeted them.

"Brother Thomas, I'd like for you to meet my wife," Nathaniel said, introducing her to him.

How strange to hear the title wife spill from his lips. Thankfully, he spoke the word with pride, rather than disdain.

Preacher Thomas's eyes lit up and he took her hand in both his, bending over her. "Welcome, welcome, sister Amelia. We're so glad you could join us on this fine Sunday morn."

Did she detect a subtle Irish brogue?

"It's nice to meet you," Amelia said.

"Come in, come in," Preacher Thomas said as he ushered them through the wooden doors.

The services were touching, the singing was amazing, and again, Amelia recalled the verse about every good gift coming from God. No one shunned her, no one looked down their noses at her. Instead, they embraced her and called her sister. She'd never experienced such a welcome to the body of Christ in all her days, except with Lillian. How wonderful to meet so many people like her precious Mrs. Forester.

Chapter Nineteen

A week past and Amelia had already started teaching Claire her letters. "Remember, each one makes a sound." As she helped Claire sound out the letters, a knock came to the door. Amelia stood from the comfort of the bay window, the light flooding the room as she headed for the door.

"Ach no, miss! That's me duty!" Claire dropped the book and darted in front of her. Before Amelia could reach it, she swung open the wooden frame.

Nathaniel stood with a sparkle in his eyes and a grin on his lips. "Would you like to join me for a walk around the grounds? It's beautiful weather, and I'm almost caught up with work. Have a lot to do after being gone for so long." He winked.

"That would be lovely," Amelia said, glancing at

Claire, her gaze darting to the book left on the bay window, then back to her.

Claire nodded, her expression telling her she'd work on her letter sounds while she was gone.

Amelia and Nathaniel walked side by side through the large garden behind the house, Nathaniel with his hands behind his back. Hard to believe this same elegantly clad man was the one who rescued her from Jeb. Despite enjoying the full view of his cleft chin, she missed the unshaven man from Green Pines. He seemed different then … less formal, less intimidating.

"We're going to have a ball." He looked straight ahead as they strolled between the sassafras and lilac trees.

"Really? What for?" She kept up with his stride, attempting to sound as nonchalant as he did as they entered the mini forest, birds chirping happily in the lilac-scented air. A ball? She'd never been to such a thing. How was one to behave?

"To introduce you to society." He stopped and faced her, that wonderful chin so close she fought the urge to place her forefinger right into its dent. "This was William's idea, and I think he's right. People need to meet you, to meet my new wife." His frown told her he wasn't happy about the event.

"What will be expected of me?" Was he embarrassed to be seen with her in public?

"I don't want it." His jaw ticked. "It's like throwing you to the wolves. The pompous gossips will eat you alive."

So he wished to protect her? Or was it his own

pride he wished to protect? She looked down at the ground. "I don't want to shame you."

He grabbed her by the arms and he forced her to look at him. "You could never do that," he said with earnest. "Those snobs don't hold a candle to you." He spoke between clenched teeth. He also didn't loosen his grip on her, so she couldn't look away to hide, to hide the admiration she felt for this intelligent man.

"I have nothing to offer. No talents, nothing that could make you and Mr. Goldman—"

"Stop." He gently shook her.

Was he angry? Would he actually harm her when she had been so convinced he never would?

He released her. He must have seen the fear in her eyes.

"Forgive me." He raked his hand through his hair and paced. "I just … I just—" He stood over her.

Her breath caught in her throat from his searing gaze. Not of anger, but of … another kind of … passion.

He stepped closer, backing her against a tree, the branches dangling next to them with its scent swirling around them, making her feel almost dizzy and like a fairy princess from one of her dime novels.

Nathaniel brushed her cheek with the backs of his fingers, gently sweeping against her skin, sending sensations all the way down her neck to her toes, bringing to mind that one helpless moment in the dark hall of his enormous house. Only this time, he bent closer, slowly closing in the slight distance between them. His breath of mint tea mingled with her own, and gently, his lips caressed hers, one time, then two. Cupping the back of her head with his large hand, he pulled her closer, stroking her with his mouth, compelling her mind and body to lose itself in sensations she never knew existed, igniting within her a desire so deep, so dizzyingly unfathomable, she clung to him.

His kiss became swift, increasingly intense, and then with such fierceness she could taste his hunger, his desire. He held her so tight, she came off the ground, and it was then she realized his strength. The power in his arms she never recognized the first time he carried her through those muddy woods. The power he kept in check beneath this unrestrained passion. Heat poured over her, melted into her, causing her to gasp for breath.

"When I introduce you as my wife, I expect us to be wed in the true sense of the word," he whispered savagely against her ear.

Helpless against his overpowering grasp, she turned her face away, still clinging to his strength. "I'm afraid," she whispered into his neck, her words escaping against her will, revealing her deepest, most terrifying fear. The darkness she'd kept so well hidden.

"I'll be gentle." He loosened his hold and searched her face, his hand cupping her cheek.

Heat flooded her neck. Had she ever wanted anything, or anyone more? She looked away from his intense stare, attempting to hide her face. What did this man bring out of her? How could she keep these terrifying sensations away? If she wasn't careful, she would end up carrying his child. She had to protect herself. She had to battle this enticement. Her mother's last screams ripped through her mind.

"I don't want to die!" Amelia tore herself from his grip, and she ran, hit with the emptiness of his warmth.

He caught her and swung her around to face him, holding her captive in his arms. "What do you mean?" He held her so close, she could feel the galloping of his heartbeat against her palm. "Talk to me." He bent and held her face in his hands, keeping her from avoiding his probing stare. "What happened? What did he do to you?"

"My mother ..." Amelia couldn't fight back the tears. Saying the words out loud made it all the more real, made the pain that had been dead for so long come back to life, as if it were climbing out of the grave where she had desperately kept it buried. The pain was too great. The anguish barely tolerable.

"What'd he do to her?" Fire came to his eyes, but she knew the anger wasn't aimed at her.

"She died giving birth ... because he ... he beat her." Amelia cried, tears hot on her cheeks. "He killed ... the baby. While it was still inside her." The words came out on a ragged breath, and she could barely get them past the knot in her throat, but they came out as if they had a will of their own, and they sounded like death. As if they were a part of some demon that she kept hidden deep within her soul. The words. The hateful words.

The truth.

Amelia fell against him. She couldn't bear it any longer. The deep dark secret she had buried for so long. The agonizing fear that ate away at her like a dog gnawing at her heels, ready to rip away her heart at the threat of every marriage proposal.

"I'm here." Nathaniel pressed her to him. "I'm here," he said tenderly and held her there. Holding her against his strong chest, he wrapped her in his sturdy arms, and kept her there as she wept. The agony of the truth lay bare before them, but the calm quiet of the trees, the soft fluttering of the birds, and the overwhelming scents of lilacs—her beloved flower—made her sink further into Nathaniel's arms, soaking in his strength, his resolve, and that's when she suddenly realized, she didn't have to bear it alone. She no longer had to face the demon by herself.

Nathaniel held Amelia more firmly in his arms as she wept. The news of her father outraged him. He knew the man was stupid and foolish. But this? He thought about going back to Green Pines, hunting him down, thrashing him for the murderer he was, and hanging him by his throat from the nearest tree. Every inch of him ached to do that. To pummel him. To make him pay.

"'Vengeance is mine,'" says the Lord.

Of course, that scripture would come to his mind. Certainly, not by accident.

"Then promise me, Lord," he whispered between clenched teeth. "Promise me you'll avenge all he's done."

Amelia sniffed, her head coming off his chest.

"Let's walk." He led her further into the trees, lilac blossoms crowning over them in the sunlight, contrasting with the dark nightmares Amelia just revealed. No wonder she never wanted to marry. Thank you God for leading me to her. For rescuing her from that monster, that demon, called her father.

"I'm sorry," she whispered.

He stopped. "For what?"

She waved about, and then wiped the tears from her face. "For this. For the miserable mess I've created."

Nathaniel bent closer to her, the lilac scent still wreaking havoc on his senses from the trees he deliberately planted because they reminded him of her. "Amelia. Listen to me."

Her emerald eyes met his.

"This is not your fault. None of it is." He gritted his teeth. "I'm amazed you survived. Not just physically, but … spiritually." He took a lock of her hair between his fingers, the soft texture tantalizing him. "Very few would have done as well as you under such circumstances."

"What if he comes back? What if he finds me? What if he finds us? If he discovers how wealthy you are, he might—"

"He won't." He'd make sure of that. How? He didn't know. But he'd ask the Almighty to take care of it. His gaze drifted to the trees. Please, Father. Please don't ever let her have to see him again.

She giggled.

He stopped and looked at her, puzzled.

"I know I must sound crazy," she said, her eyes swollen and red from crying. "But … I," she shrugged, "believe you." She cast him a half-smile, a smile that said she trusted him.

He encased her small hands in his own. "You're safe here."

"Yes. I know." She nodded. "Perhaps you'll despise me for saying this, but our forced wedding has turned out to be a huge blessing for me."

"Of course, of course." He took her under his arm and started walking. "And for me."

"Really?" Her surprised voice revealed tones of disbelief. "Now, I don't believe you."

"It's true." He chuckled. "You have no idea how difficult it is to find a wife who's not after your money."

Before he could continue, she giggled again.

Was he about to reveal all? To tell her how he sought her? How he was the one she met on the streets so long ago? Dare he?

"How do you know I'm not after your money?" Hands on her hips, she shook her shoulders at him, and it made him want to snatch her up into his arms again, but he forced his thumbs into his belt loops. "After all, you would have been shot had you not married me."

He grinned, his lips pulling into a gradual smile. Seeing the pleasant beam on her beautiful face, he didn't dare break the spell.

The following day, Amelia managed to find the library. As she entered, she imagined all the characters from each book, floating around the grand room: pirates, princes, sailors, ships—all an escape from the realities of life. However, the need for adventure, the need for escape, wasn't as necessary anymore. Her new life had provided all that. It had become what she found between the pages. Still, she scanned through title after title, mesmerized at the amount of choices available to her, all just a fingertip away. She spotted a connecting wooden ladder, making it possible to reach the books on the upper shelves. What might it be like to climb such a unique ladder? She gripped the wood and carefully managed each step until she made it to the very top. Not even looking at the titles, she turned to look around the room just to experience the height. A figure stood in the doorway, and she gasped.

"Mr. Goldman." She quickly climbed back down, her freedom short lived.

William chuckled. "Did you find what you were looking for?" he asked.

She smiled, looking down at the wooden floor. "Not yet."

"The choices can be overwhelming, I know." He put his thumbs through his belt loops. "Tell me. Do you know how to dance?"

Why did he want to know that? Then she remembered the ball. "Well, a little. I was taught as a child, but it's been so long, I'm not sure how much I remember."

"Would you allow me to be your instructor?"

"Of course," she said, curious how well she'd do.

He took her down to the ballroom, and as he guided her though a number of steps, she felt more at ease, and the movements became familiar again.

"Miss Amelia, I must say, you're a natural."

263

"Thank you," she said, self-conscious as she stared at his neck.

"I must say something else." William grinned down at her. "You bring life into this big empty house. You are a blessing to us. To me. You remind me so much of my daughters."

She smiled, filled with warmth from his fatherly tone. What were his daughters like? Were they as kind and compassionate as William?

He bent down so he could look her in the eye. "They're with the good Lord now, waiting for me to join them." Then he straightened and guided her across the floor. "How does it feel to be sought after?"

What an odd question. "Well, I'm not sure …" what you mean, then she realized he must be talking about God. How He sent his son to die for everyone, seeking mankind for Himself. "Sometimes it's hard to believe He would die for me. I can more easily believe He would be willing to die for everyone else, but I can't imagine the Lord wanting to sacrifice so much for me."

"Oh … oh, yes. Yes." He cleared his throat and studied her. "He most certainly did die for you, Miss Amelia. You are His precious child. And I can attest to that. I would have given my life for my girls, given everything I had to save them from that wretched fire." He sighed. "It makes me better understand the sacrifice of our Lord. I most certainly never would have been willing to sacrifice any of them for anyone, not even someone good, not even someone deserving of life. If it meant sacrificing one of my daughters to save another person, it wouldn't happen. No one would have been worth their death."

"I've never thought of it that way."

"You'll understand it even more once you have children."

She nodded, her cheeks warming. At this rate, the likelihood of that ever happening was slim.

"You should know," he said with a serious tone. "You are a daughter to me, and I would never let anything happen to you. While this ball is necessary to introduce you to society — and a part of me feels like I'm sacrificing you to them — please know that you are far more valuable to me than any of those high-society snobs. No matter how nasty they get — and they can be nasty — you remember that you are now my daughter, and none of them can shine as bright as you with your humble spirit. Not one."

Amelia stopped, unable to take another step. Her own father never expressed such love, such passion toward her.

"The way I felt — still feel — toward my own girls is how I feel about you." A tear ran down William's face, and tears welled into Amelia's eyes.

She hugged him.

"You're my girl." William's arms wrapped around her with a fatherly embrace. "My precious girl."

Amelia rested her cheek on his chest, barely able to comprehend such devotion.

"You were sought, Amelia. And thank the good Lord, you were found."

"She doesn't know?" William stormed into Nathaniel's study. "Why haven't you told her she's the one?"

"What are you talking about?" Nathaniel looked up from his work, trying to remove his mind from numbers to William's complaints.

"I was just giving her dance lessons in preparation for the ball—she's a fast learner, by the way—and she has no idea you're the one she helped on the streets." He lifted his hands. "Why? Why haven't you told her?"

"She'll think I'm a stalker."

"Well, you are." Will shrugged. "Who cares?"

"I don't want to frighten her. She's had enough to deal with." He hadn't shared the details he discovered from Amelia yesterday.

Will slumped onto one of the wing-backed chairs and crossed his heel over his knee. "Did it ever occur to you," he said quietly, motioning out the door, "it might actually make her feel loved? Wanted?"

Nathaniel pushed away from his work, stood and stared out the window as dust floated on the air in the sunlight and hovered over the nearby armchair. "She knows she's wanted." She did now, anyway.

Will harrumphed and shifted in his seat. "Sure. Now that she's been forced on someone. Maybe she thinks you've just given in to the circumstances?" He leaned forward and pointed at Nathaniel. "Look. I know women. I had four living with me for several years. They want to know, they need to know, that they're loved. Even the Good Book says so." He got up and marched over to the desk and grabbed Nathaniel's Bible. He flipped through the pages. "Here. 'Husbands, love your wives, just as Christ also loved the church and gave Himself up for her.'"

"But I am loving her." Nathaniel faced him. "What if I tell her and it terrifies her? What if it makes her mistrust me?" He raked a hand through his hair. "She'll want to know why I didn't tell her to begin with."

"And why didn't you?"

"Would you allow a man to court you who said he was the boy from her past who lived on the streets and now hunted her down years later? She'd think I was crazy!"

"Of course, I wouldn't. I'm a man after all. Not a woman." He patted his belly. "In case you haven't noticed."

Nathaniel shook his head. "I'm beginning to think you're the crazy one."

Will laughed and moved toward him, hands behind his back. "I can see your point. Maybe after you've been married for twenty-some-odd years, you can tell her. By then, she'll have had enough time to deduce the fact that you are, indeed, cracked." He turned and sauntered out of the room.

Sandi Rog

Chapter Twenty

About a month after her arrival and two weeks before the ball, Amelia's clothes were finally delivered. Taffeta, crinoline, and silk fabrics arrived, many of which Claire and other servants ogled over as they showed them off to Amelia and put them away in the new, large armoire recently purchased for her. Since arriving and giving Claire reading lessons, more of the servants joined them. In fact, Amelia had a small class going on in Nathaniel's room. Thankfully, he hadn't tried to join her in his room at night, but with two weeks before the ball, and his declaration beneath the lilac trees, Amelia closely watched the door at night.

But now, she kept her eyes open for the blue costume that Nathaniel had picked out for her. What could it be?

With great flare, the tailor removed a royal blue gown that made all the beautiful dresses look like pauper's clothing. The majestic color glowed, outshining everything in the room with the sun lancing its rays through the bay window onto the stunning fabric.

"It's ..."

"Gorgeous!" Claire interrupted. "I've never seen the like! Never seen anything more beautiful, more striking!"

Claire expressed everything Amelia wished to say, but the words had lodged in her throat. The bodice was so fine, made with such delicate lace. It swooped low in the back, connecting to dainty shoulder straps. It came together at the waist where the bustle cascaded in folds to the ground, leaving a train in its wake. Could such an amazing dress truly belong to her?

"It's exquisite," she finally whispered.

A week later, Nathaniel strode down the windy street in the middle of Chicago, having just concluded some business with Mr. Pullman. As he headed up the walkway to meet with another banker, something familiar and waving in the wind from a woman's arm, caught his eye. A calico reticule with blue and yellow flowers. Amelia's reticule. He'd recognize that anywhere.

He jogged toward the woman, a woman of modest means. What was she doing with Amelia's purse? As he came up beside her, he could see without a doubt it was Amelia's bag.

"Excuse me, ma'am." Nathaniel removed his hat as he addressed the woman, not old, but not young, either. "Would you be kind enough tell me where you got your bag?"

The woman looked up at Nathaniel, her brows furrowed. "What business is it of yours?" she asked.

"I know the owner."

She straightened and clutched Amelia's purse in her fist. "It belongs to me," the woman said.

"I'm not accusing you of anything."

"Then what do you want?" she asked, the wind blowing loose strands from her knotted hair into her face. She shoved it out of the way, glaring at Nathaniel.

"Is there a name on the inside?"

The woman paused, furrowing her brows.

"Does it read, 'Amelia E. Taylor?'"

The woman's mouth gaped open and she clutched the purse to her chest.

Nathaniel stepped closer to her, hovering over her. "How much do you want for it?"

"Want?"

"Yes. I'll buy it from you. I just happen to know the owner." He stepped closer to her.

She looked at the reticule, then back up at Nathaniel. "How much are you willing to pay?"

Nathaniel held out a handful of money and the woman gasped. She looked around as if she feared someone might be watching. She moved into a nearby alley and he followed her. Away from peering eyes, she snatched the money from his outstretched hand, then turned to run.

Nathaniel caught her and swung toward him. "Where'd you get the bag?" He knew it had to be his brother. Did this woman know where to find him?

"A friend. He gave it to me." The woman looked away from Nathaniel, clearly afraid he might strike her.

"His name?" He practically shook her. "What's his name?"

"Michael."

Nathaniel felt as though she punched him in the gut. "Michael Ward?"

Her eyes lifted in surprise and slowly she nodded.

"Where is he?"

"I don't know." She shook her head. "I honestly don't know. He left town. I don't know where he went."

"Are you sure?"

The woman nodded, tears filling her eyes.

Nathaniel grabbed the reticule and forcefully emptied it into her hands, and then he released her. The woman ran, and Nathaniel watched her go.

With desperate, fumbling fingers, he opened up the purse and saw Amelia's name embroidered inside.

So ... it was Michael who robbed him that night.

Amelia and Claire leaped off the trolley onto the windy Chicago street. She grabbed Claire's arm as they jogged to the sidewalk, Claire giggling all the way. Was this how Amelia had reacted with Nathaniel? It was quite an adventure, and when she heard that Nathaniel had gone to town—and the daily monotony at the house began to take its toll—she decided to pay downtown Chicago a visit. It wasn't like the city was terribly far from her house, anyway. In fact, she could walk there just fine, but she needed an excuse to take the streetcar, and visiting Claire's family was just that.

Being with Claire also brought on memories of Violet. Amelia missed her friend so much that she sent a letter off to Widow Forester to see if she could find out how she fared, assuming Lillian could tell her anything.

Claire led Amelia to DeKoven Street on the city's southwest side. Before long, they arrived at a small dwelling, and Claire burst through the wooden door, slamming it against the wall.

"What? Who ... Oh, my!" an older woman shouted, her hand on her ample bosom. "Is that me darlin' girl?" Claire flung herself into the woman's arms, and they held each other tight for a long time. "Ach, child, how I've missed you."

It made Amelia long for her own mother. What must it be like to be hugged in such a way?

The woman then held Claire away from her. "Let me be having a gander at you." Tears streamed down the woman's cheeks. Then she spotted Amelia who stood near the door, taking in the small room with its small table, worn cupboards, and scratched wooden floor. It brought back memories of her own little house in the woods, and for the first time ever, in her pristine new clothes, Amelia felt overdressed as she looked at Claire's mother's dingy blouse and faded skirt.

The woman straightened and brushed her hands off on her threadbare apron. "And who might this be?" She looked to Claire for information as her gaze flickered self-consciously from Amelia to her daughter.

"Ma, this is me mistress." Straightening with a flash of pride, she motioned to Amelia, stepping nearby to introduce her. "We're having a day out on the town." Claire smiled, her cheeks rosy pink.

The woman lifted her skirt and, to Amelia's surprise, curtsied. "Tis an honor to be meeting you."

Such respect, such formal behavior. Amelia had never experienced such treatment. Uncomfortable with the attention, Amelia took the woman's hands into her own. "It's wonderful to meet you. Claire has been so good to me, I can't tell you how much I love having her around."

The woman's eyes widened in disbelief.

"Sure, Ma, wasn't I telling you she's a kind soul?"

"Well, goodness me!" The woman's head nodded furiously as she motioned to the small table and chairs. "Please, will you be sitting for a while? Can I pour you a cup of buttermilk?"

Amelia enjoyed getting to know Claire's mother and discovered her brother wasn't home because he delivered milk for the neighbors across the street. Apparently, these particular neighbors, Patrick and Catherine O'Leary, were accused of causing the Great Chicago Fire.

"Ach, they hadn't a thing to do with it," Claire's mama said. "Who would be burning down their own barn? They said a cow kicked a lantern. I'm having none of it. Mrs. O'Leary was never out there at that time of night milking. Nothing but lies that man wrote in that newspaper of his. Nothing but lies, and now this poor woman's life is ruined."

"I can't believe they put the blame on her," Amelia said, dumbfounded by the accusation. Could it be true, though? Could the woman have been guilty? After all, if it was put in the local paper? Would a reporter write such a terrible falsehood?

Soon their visit had come to an end, and it was time to head back home. It was still strange referring to Nathaniel Ward's mansion as "home."

"I want to give Claire the day off." Amelia stood and slipped into her coat.

Claire got up to help her. Amelia had yet to get used to help with such basic needs.

Amelia looked pointedly at Claire's mother who peered over her teacup, brows raised. "She works very hard, and I think it'll be nice for her to have some time with her family."

"Ach, Miss Amelia. I cannot." Claire lifted her hands.

"Yes, you can. I'm giving you permission to do so. I will tell Mr. Goldman and Mr. Ward that I insisted. And you shall be paid. Every person deserves a break every now and then."

"Saints be praised." Claire's mother put her hand to her mouth. "Thank you, miss, and may God and His angels keep you close to hand. I've been missing my wee daughter that much!"

"I can see that." Amelia giggled and turned to

Claire. "You can have the week. That way you'll be back in time for the ball. I'll definitely need your help preparing for that." Amelia chuckled, knowing she was clueless as to how to prepare for such a thing. It was a wonder Claire knew anything about it. Perhaps they'd both have to fumble through the preparations.

"Oh, thank you, Miss Amelia! I thank you from the bottom of my heart. And I'll be praying the Lord enfold you close while we're apart." Claire hugged her and Amelia held her tight.

How she missed Violet.

After exploring shop after shop on her way home, Amelia stood in front of Goldman's Department Store. He was right. Windows lined the sidewalk so that passersby could look in, and several young children had their noses glued to the window admiring the toys on display, while their mothers chatted with one another, pointing at dresses and other household goods. It was in essence a giant dry-goods store. Did it also sell Yellow Backs? Sure enough, as she strolled along the walkway, books were on display in another window, and dime novels were arranged behind a set of larger volumes. Why didn't Mr. Ward bring her here, to his own store, to buy them? Then she recalled how Mr. Ward refused to have visitors to meet her and his words of not wanting to put her on display.

Despite the temptation, she didn't go in, and turned toward the trolley station and headed in that direction. As she strolled along, she noticed a familiar figure in the distance ahead.

Nathaniel.

She stopped in her tracks. Could that really be him? As she studied the man, she knew.

It was Nathaniel Ward with another woman. Why was he hovering over her? Let alone moving with her between the buildings where no one could see them?

Amelia made an about-face and headed back home. The carriage had dropped her off at the trolley station as she'd requested, but this time, she didn't care to get on the car. She'd just walk home, rather than ride it around town. The time alone would do her good.

What was he doing with that woman? From what she could tell, the woman was young enough that she could be someone he'd be interested in. But why would he meet up with another woman when he recently had been so kind, so loving? How could he do this to her? Then she mentally knocked herself upside the head. He didn't do anything to her. Instead, marriage was done to him. Tears filled her eyes. She had begun to believe he might actually love her. He had been so good, so gentle, so compassionate.

Numb and tuning out the sounds of rivet guns and shouts, crossing over bridges, not caring when a young man whistled her way, Amelia ignored it all as she made her way back to North Astor Street. Soon, she came to the lilac trees lining the drive. The pleasant aroma reminded her of the time she spent under the lilac trees in the back with Nathaniel ... and the passionate kiss they'd shared. Her favorite scent would from now on be a reminder of that one, precious moment in time. The lash of pain that came from that special memory made her sadly realize one enormous truth.

Amelia loved Nathaniel Ward.

Chapter Twenty-One

Amelia managed to avoid Nathaniel for the rest of the week. Instead of watching for the doorknob to move at night, she simply locked it. Too bad she hadn't had the nerve to do that sooner. It meant Claire had to knock to get in, and Amelia was fine with that. She simply couldn't bring herself to have any intimate contact with Mr. Ward, even if it was his right. Nor did she care that the ball had arrived.

"You look absolutely stunning." Claire stood in front of Amelia, making one last touch to her hair. "Breathtaking."

Claire's admiration managed to bring a feeble grin to Amelia's lips.

"Miss, if you don't mind me saying, you should smile. Sure, you're that lovely when you smile."

Amelia looked down at her elegant dress and smoothed out the royal blue gown that made her feel like Cinderella, a new character she discovered from a book she recently found in Nathaniel's library. "Thank you for this, Claire. I never imagined you could turn this old cinder-girl into a princess."

A knock sounded on the door. "They're waiting." William's voice carried through the thick wood. "May I have a look-see?"

"Of course, come in," Amelia called, always warmed by William's presence.

Claire opened the door and stepped away so William could see her. The lamplight lit up the room in the fading sun, dancing off the shimmering blue of Amelia's dress.

Tears came to William's eyes. "Just like my own daughters," he said, taking small steps toward her. He held out his arms.

Amelia moved forward and stepped into his embrace. He squeezed her tight as her cheek brushed against his snowy beard and rested against his lapel.

"That's my girl." He patted her shoulder. "That's my girl." He held her away and kissed her forehead.

Tears sprang to Amelia's eyes. Her father had never touched her in such a way, never held her close and made any sort of fatherly gesture of love as William did just now. "Thank you." The words barely made it past her lips.

"No." He gently patted her cheek with his hand. "Thank you."

With that, he turned to leave, quietly closing the door behind him.

Claire stood, watching him leave, staring at the door, long after it closed. Then she turned to Amelia who did the same.

Did that really happen? Did William just come in here? She continued to stare at the wooden frame, breathing in the faint fragrance of his cologne. Proof that William truly had just been there, in this very room, leaving the love, the admiration, in his wake.

Before long, Amelia found herself standing at the top of the familiar marble stairs, gazing down at elegantly clad strangers in the grand ballroom that burst with lights sparkling from the chandeliers. Crinoline fabrics in all sorts of colors swayed around the room in high-class fashion, gentlemen making their way about the space, and others dancing in time to the music from the band of musicians who were tucked away in the far corner. The scents of cologne and perfume wafted up the stairs and floated up the vaulted ceilings to the tall windows.

Nathaniel in his royal blue vest and waistcoat came to the bottom of the wide stairs, his clean-shaven face lifted, emphasizing his perfectly cut hair and the cleft in his chin that Amelia so longed to touch. The music came to a majestic crescendo then suddenly lowered into a gradual suspension. William came to Amelia's side, gently placed her hand on the crook of his arm, and puffed up his chest.

"Introducing, the lovely Mrs. Amelia Elizabeth Ward!" His voice carried above the multitude of onlookers.

The crowd gasped and clapped as the music ascended again, and Amelia felt heat climb from her chest to the ends of her ringlets as William escorted her down the grand marble steps.

At the bottom of the staircase, William handed Amelia over to Nathaniel, and he engulfed her fingers into his own and lifted them to his lips, placing a kiss on her knuckles and sending a weakness through her wrist that soared all the way to her shoulder. As he pulled her close and led her into the crowd, people gathered, introducing themselves and spilling compliments, admirations and congratulations over her and Nathaniel. Amelia shook so many hands, kissed so many cheeks, and accepted so many flatteries, there was no way she could remember each and every one.

Swept into a sea of dancers and led by Nathaniel's deft moves, she recalled the steps William taught her as they dazzled the crowed with the Mazurka, one of the most skillful couples' dances in America.

"He taught you well," Nathaniel said to her above the music and noise, his admiring gaze seizing hers.

"Thank you," Amelia said, glad to know he was so pleased.

After several other dances such as the Polka, and a Cotillion where they exchanged partners and were directed by William in a playful banter of games, they finally broke into a Waltz.

Breathless, Amelia again found herself turning about the floor in Nathaniel's strong arms. "You're beautiful, my love."

His tender words took her aback, and she looked away to the open doors where food was set out on long tables and trays.

"What's wrong?" Nathaniel leaned toward her, his breath, hot against her ear.

She took a deep, shuddering breath. Dare she tell him what she saw? Surely, now was not the time to bare such revelations. Keeping her gaze away from his for fear he might read the truth in her eyes, she focused on his chest.

"Why don't we get some food?" Keeping her in his firm grasp, he twirled them away from the dance floor and escorted her to the double French doors that opened to the back garden. Lamps and candlelight lit up decorated tables and chairs, which spread out in glory across the lawn.

Nathaniel stopped at one of the large serving tables and picked up a plate. "What would you like to eat?"

"My, my," a female voice said from behind them. "It's so very nice that we finally get to meet."

Amelia turned, and immediately she sensed Nathaniel stiffen next to her, as she was faced with a beautiful woman who belonged to the pretentious voice. Surely, this wasn't the woman she saw with Nathaniel. No, it couldn't be. The other woman wasn't nearly as refined.

"My name is Charlotte," the woman said, shooting a sidelong bat of her eyelashes to Nathaniel and not even looking at Amelia.

Amelia took the woman's outstretched hand, and Charlotte's grasp was so tight on her fingers, she couldn't let go.

"Nathan and I go way back," she said, still not releasing Amelia's hand and casting a smug grin at her.

"Not really," Nathaniel said, his cleft chin lifted in condescension, "and the name's Mr. Ward."

Charlotte released Amelia's hand, and in the lamplight she could see the woman's cheeks burn bright red.

"Very well then." The woman straightened, looking around them as if to see if anyone else had heard the exchange. "Umm …" she said as if trying to find the right words. "Welcome to Chicago."

"Thank—"

Charlotte pivoted and walked away.

All Amelia's doubts and fears rushed forth. Desperate to get away from Nathaniel, she rushed across the grass toward the lilac trees. She didn't dare go back inside, or even stay out on the lawn. She had to get as far away from peering eyes as she could. Perhaps she could hide her face behind the low-hanging branches and blossoms. Glancing over her shoulder, she saw that Nathaniel followed her, trailing behind her into the sweet-smelling trees lit up with darting lights.

"Please." She pivoted and faced him. "Go away," she whispered, swiping the tears from her eyes.

Nathaniel's jaw ticked. "I knew we shouldn't have done this," he said, motioning vehemently toward the house.

"It's not that," Amelia said, moving deeper into the trees for fear someone might hear and discover them.

"That woman … Charlotte," he said her name as if he wanted to spit. "She's nothing to me."

Amelia straightened, finally drawing in the courage to speak. "I saw you," she said, her voice breaking. "I saw you with another woman on the streets. I was there. You were standing … inappropriately close, and then …"

Nathaniel's eyes widened. "You were there?"

Amelia nodded, tears streaming down her cheeks. What a fool she was. Why bother even telling the man? He had no reason to love a woman forced on him.

Nathaniel bent close to her, his face desperate. "I have a confession to make."

"No." Amelia shook her head, pushing him away but to no avail. "I don't want to hear it." She wrenched from his grasp and scurried further into the trees, strange lightning bugs dancing on the air. She couldn't bear to hear how much he loved this other woman.

Nathaniel caught her by the arm and swung her around. "Listen to me," he said, his voice urgent. "I need you to listen."

Panting, Amelia stopped, staring up at the man she'd come to love. His frown, not that of anger, but of resolve, revealing to her mind that he was about to come clean. She hugged herself, barely able to remain standing as she prepared for the onslaught of heartache he was about to unleash.

Sandi Rog

Chapter Twenty-Two

Slowly, Nathaniel pulled something out from inside his vest. "Something special was stolen from me, and that woman on the street had it. I bought it back from her. She meant nothing to me. But this … this meant everything to me." As he let the small item fall over his large trembling hand, she recognized the fabric colors, the pattern, the faded and thinned drawstrings.

"You dropped this," he said, his voice tender and quivering. "After you emptied all your money into my hands, you ran back to the sidewalk on the other side. I found it in the street, not long after … after you …."

Amelia took the reticule into her hands, the beloved purse her mother had made, and she looked up at Nathaniel, stunned. The dark hair, the eyes, the … cleft chin.

The memories of the day she lost it tumbled through her mind.

"I work for food." The street boy reached for a bag of flour and hefted it onto the wooden

sidewalk, sending a wave of dust over the hem of Amelia's dress — and his bare feet.

No shoes? Amelia studied the boy. It didn't seem to bother him that he was barefoot. He hefted another bag to the sidewalk. Dirt smudged his forearms beneath his rolled up sleeves. Obviously, he was used to labor.

"I don't need help." Amelia's father, wearing his frock coat and shiny top hat, waved the boy away. "Get on outta here." He then motioned with his cane for the driver of the wagon to take the rest of the bags into his restaurant.

The boy's shoulders slumped. Blowing out a breath, his gaze fell on Amelia. Dark hair in need of a trim tumbled beneath his worn hat, and his blue eyes narrowed in disgust as they swept over her.

Tightening her grip on her parasol and reticule, she straightened in her crinoline dress, suddenly wishing she wasn't so clean and full of ruffles.

The boy turned to go.

In all her nine years, Amelia had never witnessed Father pick up a bag of grain, and he wasn't about to change now as he dictated to the driver where he wanted the goods. Why couldn't he let the boy do it? At least then Father would get his work done and the boy could benefit.

The boy ambled down the sidewalk, his feet leaving imprints in the dirt on the boards. His trousers came high above his ankles, and his holey shirt fell loose on one side over his waist. What would her father call him? A street rat. It was the first time she'd ever seen one up close.

She had plans to spend her savings on a new parasol and gloves, but the thought of replacing the ones that were unsoiled and in good condition, no longer interested her.

Seeing that Father paid her no mind, she followed the boy as he rounded the corner and made his way down the busy street, his stride sure and confident despite her father's scorn. Dare she approach him? He was older, and normally she wouldn't go near such a boy. Still, like a fly drawn to food, she continued down the wooden sidewalk, her dainty steps picking up their pace to catch him.

"Wa … wait," Amelia called in hesitation since she'd never spoken to a street rat before.

The boy didn't stop, disappearing into a crowd of men in cowboy hats and jingling spurs as they headed into a saloon. The scent of alcohol and the noise of piano music overwhelmed her. Father would tan her hide if he knew she'd come this close to such a place. Squeezing between them, she spotted the boy striding down the sidewalk. Thankfully, he hadn't gone in with the cowhands. But now he was farther along, so she picked up her skirt and ran to catch him.

He slapped his hat on his leg, and dust flew up from his britches as he shoved it back onto his head.

Breathless, she reached his side. "Wait."

The boy looked down at her, surprise reflecting in his captivating gaze, and he stopped. Then, recognition spread over his features and his blue eyes narrowed. "What do you want?"

She lifted her trembling reticule. "I have money." Her voice was small, even to her own ears. "You can get yourself some new clothes."

"I don't need clothes." He lifted his chin and furrowed his brows. "And I don't take handouts."

Amelia stepped back, a spark of anger igniting helpful embers of courage. "I wasn't going to give it to you." Now how would she get herself out of that lie? "Umm … I want to hire you." She puffed up her chest, feeling mighty smart for concocting such a grand idea on such short notice.

"What do you want me to do?" He cocked his head.

Taking a deep breath, she looked around. "Maybe you could …." Cowboys strode by and ladies swished past with colorful dresses and makeup. A sharp contrast with the dusty buildings. That's when she realized, she was on the wrong side of town. Why was her father's restaurant near such horrid establishments? Winnie would be furious. Her nanny would never have allowed her to come here, let alone to chase down a boy. Good thing she had the day off.

"Look." Bending toward her with his hands stuffed in his pockets, the boy glared at her as if he could see right through her charade. "I don't got time for distractions when there's work to be done and food to be earned." He turned to leave.

"Don't go!" She dared catch his arm, but quickly

released it, as if he might bite her for taking such liberties. "I need you ... I need for you to ... hold this for me." Amelia opened her parasol and held it out to him.

He raised an eyebrow, looking at her as if she'd lost her mind.

"Here." She brandished the umbrella at him. "Take it."

Rolling his eyes, he took it.

She motioned to the nearest shop across the street. "I need to go over there, thank you," she said, as if speaking to one of the house servants. She lifted her chin and walked toward the shop.

He kept up with her, and an uncontrollable grin tugged on her lips. When they reached the other side of the street, she took a deep breath and faced him. "Thank you very much, kind sir." She opened her calico purse. "Here are your wages."

Still holding the parasol, he stuffed his free hand in his pocket.

She shook the reticule at him.

He didn't take it.

She glanced toward her father, unseen around the corner. Hopefully, he was still busy. If Father caught her ... she hated to think what he might do if he caught her.

Stomping her foot, she faced the boy. She grabbed his hand and emptied her purse into it as coins fell onto his palm and onto the ground. "Take it," she said, closing his dirt-covered fingers around the money. "You've earned it." With that, she grabbed her parasol, turned and ran across the street, dodging horses and carriages.

"What's your name?" the boy called.

As she approached the sidewalk, she looked at him.

Thank goodness he didn't come after her. He stood there with his legs braced apart, his cleft chin lifted toward her, and her coins locked in his fist.

She'd never see him again, so it might be safe to—

Instead of giving him her name, she kissed her hand. With careful aim, she blew her kiss to him, imagining it soar all the way across the street.

To her delight, the boy's mouth lifted into a half-smile.

She'd hit her mark.

Amelia gaped at Nathaniel, lightning bugs dancing on the air and lilac blossoms with their sweet scent hanging all around them.

He looked down on her with that same half grin she remembered.

"You," she whispered. "You were the boy." It was meant to be a question, but the realization came as she spoke the words.

He nodded.

She studied him, soaking in every texture, every angle and contour of his face. Slowly, she reached up to touch him, the tips of her fingers quivering against his smooth firm skin, gradually sliding over his cheek onto his jaw and down to his chin. As his breath grazed against her palm, she placed her fingertip against his dimple, pressing gently into its cleft.

"How did this happen?" she whispered as realization dawned. He had her purse. Her name was in it. He searched for her and found her.

He sought her out.

"You found me," she said. "But the wedding ..."

He grasped her hand and kissed it.

"You wanted me?" She almost choked as she said the words, almost afraid to believe it could be true. Could it be he actually sought her out? After all these years? After that one encounter? That single moment in time?

He nodded and kissed the tips of her fingers, grazing over knuckles, sending heat coursing down her arm. This time she allowed it. She didn't stop him. He'd actually wanted her. She was loved.

"I ... I love you," she said, the whispered words echoing off the dense forest of lilacs.

He bent, cupping her face in his hands, and kissed her gently, pulling away after one brush, and then another. "I love you too," he said, his voice ragged and hot against her mouth. "From that very first day we met." He pulled her closer, kissing her so thoroughly she lost her senses. "I didn't want to frighten you." He brushed his lips to hers again. "I'm sorry for

deceiving you." Again, a touch, a peck. "Forgive me."

"I forgive you." She arched her head back, giving him better access, and he grazed his lips against her neck. Without warning, he swung her into his arms and carried her through the trees, the bugs with their lights flying into his hair.

"What are those creatures?" she asked, breathless.

"Fireflies," he said, continuing through the trees

until they came to the opening.

"Nathaniel, what are you doing?" She pushed against his chest. "Put me down. People will see."

"I don't care," he said, his voice gruff. He marched with her across the lawn as heads turned and voices murmured. Some chuckled, others whistled.

Amelia buried her face in his shoulder. "Nathaniel."

"Keep saying my name, love. It only makes me more determined." He carried her through the doors and the music rushed over them as he pushed through the people. The crowd parted as he carried her to the grand staircase, up the steps and around the balcony amidst cheers from the men and gasps from the women.

Amelia peeked down into the atrium and saw smiling faces, and one distorted frown on an angry Charlotte. Funny how she spotted her in the mass of people when she wasn't searching for her. It made her remember what started the conversation in the garden. The woman on the street. But that no longer mattered. Amelia knew the truth. He sought her out. She was loved.

Nathaniel carried her to his room, kicking open the door, and startling Claire. "Leave."

Wide eyed, Claire jumped from her chair and scurried out of the room, closing the door behind her.

Nathaniel dropped Amelia onto the bed, onto his bed, the blankets and cushions pillowing around, and he hovered over her.

"Are you afraid?" he asked, breathless.

"Not anymore," she whispered, lifting her fingers

to touch his chin. "Your love took it all away."

Sandi Rog

Epilogue

Amelia sat next to Nathaniel on the blanket spread out over the grass not far from the little white church house near their home. Birds twittered above their heads as William chased after the ducks with little Rachel on his arm. Their blonde two-year-old, named after Nathaniel's sister, giggled with glee.

Amelia rubbed her fat belly, feeling the thumps of another little one ready to join the outside world. "He's kicking," she said, placing Nathaniel's hand over the foot or hand causing the pressure.

Nathaniel cocked a half grin. "He?"

Amelia shrugged. "Only the good Lord knows." Smiling, she snagged up a strawberry and popped it into his mouth, deliberately brushing her forefinger over the whiskered cleft in his chin. She leaned over and kissed it.

It was so good to be married. Amelia never thought she'd feel this way. And now she could also be happy for her friend. She'd finally heard from Violet. Her friend had a little girl named Grace. Violet said she named her that because the Lord had shown her grace. She never returned to Green Pines though, and stayed on in Denver, helping at the home for unwed mothers, the same home that had helped her. Amelia received letters from her often, and recently she learned that Violet and the doctor who came to the home on regular visits, and loved Grace as if she were his own, were engaged to be married. Amelia was so happy for her dear, sweet friend.

Apparently, Jeb and Sam got what they deserved. After Amelia's father found them tied to his porch, with the help of Preacher Forbs, he carted them off to Denver and had them arrested. Decked in stripes, they were taken up north to work on the railroad tracks. No one had heard from them since.

According to the letters from Lillian Forester, Amelia's father kept to himself in the cabin they once shared. He'd hardly ever paid rent, she overheard Nathaniel say to William one day, but Nathaniel was willing to let it go for Amelia's sake. She was the reason he bought the land anyway. Her father had slowed down on his many trips attempting to get rich. Occasionally, he'd step foot in the church house, and Lillian believed when he heard all the gossip about Nathaniel and Amelia from Miss Bruster, he'd discovered that Nathaniel had wealth, which was the true reason he forced Amelia and Nathaniel's hand.

To her relief, her father never attempted to contact her.

It was good to be surrounded by people who loved her. And no one criticized her delight in Yellow Backs anymore. William even opened a room to use as a classroom so she could teach the servants how to read.

Little Rachel ran across the blanket, nearly running into the fruit bowl. Nathaniel scooped her up just in time, lifting her into the blue sky above his head, bringing out a rush of giggles and laughter.

"Yes," Amelia whispered, "all good things are a gift from God."

The End

Sandi Rog

Upcoming and Past Releases

Watch for the next book in
The Great Chicago Fire Series:

INTO THE FIRE

Due to release in 2017.

~*~

Other books by Sandi Rog:
The Master's Wall
Yahshua's Bridge
&
Walks Alone

CPSIA information can be obtained
at www.ICGtesting.com
Printed in the USA
FSOW02n2054160916
25123FS

9 780996 274616